...a man who vowed
to betray her.

## "A GIFT FOR PRINCE HENRY," THE EARL SAID.

The girl and the tower guard were right over Simon, the girl kicking and screaming. He got to his feet. Before the guard could hit her again, he thrust his arm in between.

"Stop," he ordered. He knew it was useless to beat anything in that wild-eyed state, particularly a horse, or a woman.

The girl was dressed in a green silk gown trimmed with gold, her face ravishing, thick with paint, with a full, sensuous underlip and wild blue eyes. Her gold hair hung loose to her waist. Magnificent was the word that came to his mind; every man's lustful dream.

Simon stared at her, stunned by her beauty. But he immediately hardened his heart.

He wanted no part of it, he decided. Taking the prince's would-be whore to London was no task for an honorable knight. He was only human.

At that moment the girl, with a piercing cry, lunged forward and sank her teeth into his hand. . . .

## Books by Maggie Davis

### Writing as Maggie Davis:

EAGLES

ROMMEL'S GOLD

THE SHEIK

THE FAR SIDE OF HOME

THE WINTER SERPENT

FORBIDDEN OBJECTS

SATIN DOLL

SATIN DREAMS

WILD MIDNIGHT

MIAMI MIDNIGHT

HUSTLE, SWEET LOVE

DIAMONDS AND PEARLS

TROPIC OF LOVE

DREAMBOAT

### Writing as Katherine Deauxville:

BLOOD RED ROSES

DAGGERS OF GOLD

### Writing as Maggie Daniels:

A CHRISTMAS ROMANCE

# DAGGERS OF GOLD

## KATHERINE DEAUXVILLE

ST. MARTIN'S PAPERBACKS

DAGGERS OF GOLD

Copyright © 1993 by Maggie Davis.
Excerpt from *Heat of A Savage Moon* copyright © 1993 by Jane Bonander.

Cover photography by Don Banks.

ISBN: 0-312-92857-2

Printed in the United States of America

St. Martin's Paperbacks edition/January 1993

10 9 8 7 6 5 4 3 2 1

*For Sally Richardson*

*and with many thanks to Jenny Reddaway,
information officer,
Borough of Tamworth, England.*

*W*OMAN IS THE GATE OF THE DEVIL, THE PATH OF WICKEDNESS, THE STING OF THE SERPENT—IN A WORD, A PERILOUS OBJECT.

SAINT JEROME

# Prologue

*T*he bawd mistress came riding into the clearing, one of her girls on a fine Spanish jennet
following her. In spite of the August heat both
women were dressed in undertunics of samite, satin
tabards, silk scarves, and the madam had on a blue
velvet cloak. One could see that it was true that
London whores prided themselves on great style.
They dressed better, they boasted, than the court's
Norman ladies.

"You there, demoiselle," the bawd mistress
called, "don't run away. Be still a moment. Let me
talk to you."

The whole of the forest knew, Ingrith told herself,
walking faster. Including the doxies. But the last
thing she wanted was to go to London to be a whore.
She'd had enough of that.

A young knight with a Crusader's cockleshell
badge stepped out of the crowd, grinning, one arm
outstretched to stop her. Ingrith quickly ducked under it, not wanting to hear what he had to say. It
was all the same, anyway; she wished they would

leave her alone. Out of the corner of her eye she saw the madam still followed. The woman cantered her horse through a pack of houndsmen, then around the sutlers, who were breaking camp and loading their stock of meat pies and sweets onto the wains.

The hamlet of Brockenhurst swarmed with those who followed the king's hunt. Even though the rumor had been abroad since early morning that this would be the hunt's last day in the forest. King William Rufus had waked hungover from a hard night's drinking and a sleep, the gossip went, interrupted by a dream of his coming death. Because of the nightmare, he had not gone to hunt at dawn, but had called his friends together and gotten drunk again before breakfast. Now it was well past noon, and although it was red-deer stag season, *grease time,* the hunt was just starting.

Behind Ingrith the young whore reined in her jennet to wait. But the bawd mistress cantered on, and pulled her horse alongside her.

"Now, you see, girl," she said. "Like yon young Crusader buck back there, you can have your pick." Under rouge and white powder the London madam's face showed its wrinkles, but her body was still shapely. "I wouldn't ask you to do regular trade, not with your looks," she wheedled. "No, what I'd get for you is some nice arrangement with a noble gentleman, an earl, mayhap a baron, even a young one. There's plenty what have noticed you here, with the prince. You have my word I won't pair you with none what's evil or strange in their habits." Her eyes narrowed, taking in Ingrith's copper velvet and silk dress with its jewels. "You're no longer a virgin, now, are you?"

Ingrith walked faster. She was not quite lost but since she'd come to New Forest she, who'd been born to the woods, could scarce find her way. It was said New Forest was cursed. That the old Conqueror had torn down a village and a church and driven out the poor farmers to make it, and had been punished when one of his young sons, Richard, died there while hunting.

In spite of the heat, she shivered. She was Saxon enough to know when a place was cursed, it was cursed. God and the saints knew New Forest had not proved a good place for her, either.

"Fifty percent of what you make," the whore mistress was insisting. "And you don't have to give me a yea or a nay this moment. But if I was you I wouldn't wait too long." She turned to look at the crowds streaming past. "Be warned, though, there's them here what can take what they want. You don't want to have them get by force what you'd be better off selling, now do you?"

Ahead, Ingrith saw the lane with the carters and wagons. She broke into a trot, her heart pounding. She wished the whoremistress and her offers would go away. She had to leave this place before something more happened. Under the trees were the wagons and drovers the sheriff of Hampshire provided to bring the deer carcasses out of the woods. The English stood in silent groups, waiting on the Norman beaters. Their faces showed nothing of what they thought of this royal way of hunting, with hundreds of men on foot herding the deer past so that the Norman lords, at their stands, could slaughter them.

The whore mistress reined in her horse, impatient. "Listen, I'm talking to you, girl. Don't you care what's to become of you?"

Ingrith touched the purse on its strings deep in her skirts, to make sure it was still there. Some of the wagons for hauling the killed deer were never used and were sent back. If she could find one, she was going to pay a drover to take her out of this accursed place.

The woman on the horse leaned down. "What's the matter with you, can't you hear? Listen, that young knight they call the Leopard is not for you. He don't want you, he's evil-marked, that one, like those they say are his people." She put out her hand, but Ingrith dodged it. "Be reasonable. If anything's to happen they'll blame him. And blame *them*, too!"

Ingrith stopped short. She turned to look up at her, not sure. "What do you mean, 'if anything's to happen'?"

The other woman smiled. "Ah, you harkened that time, didn't you? Now, what will it be? You come to London and I'll set you up, and you'n me can make a dear lot. Stay here, and you'll be tumbled by a pack of bootlickers what won't be quick to get you back on your feet, neither."

She grabbed the palfrey's bridle. "You must tell me!" If this woman knew something about Simon de Bocage, she wanted to hear it. "What did you mean, they'll blame the Leopard?"

But the other woman drew back. "Bah, girl, would I tell, if I knew?" She wheeled the palfrey around, giving up. "Well, if you must throw yourself away, there's naught I can do.

"If you got ears," she flung over her shoulder as she rode off, "you've heard what's been said. They made sport of it, why you were sent here, didn't they? You'll be a fool if you stay."

Ingrith stood in the crowded road, watching the two women trot off. The madam's words were a puzzle. But one thing was sure: rumor always knew when something was going to happen.

She touched her hand to her lips. Simon de Bocage was sending her away, not wanting her. But he had kissed her. It seemed as though she could still feel his lips, warm and burning, against her mouth.

Mother of God, she thought suddenly, what a fool she'd been. She should have known what that kiss meant!

She looked around. Lackeys, traders, villeins, soldiers, whores, flowed through the village and northward. She needed to go back the other way.

She turned and began to push against them. Immediately two knights seized her, offering her money. She kicked out at them, fighting them off, her velvet skirts dragging.

She knew now that Simon had said farewell with that kiss. Go to Wroxeter, he'd told her. Not to put her aside, but because he'd wanted her safe. Dear God in heaven, what did he expect to happen? Her mind told her all sorts of terrible things. This place, New Forest, was full of treachery; even King William had known it.

Whatever it was, she had to go to him.

She hiked up the gown's copper skirts with both

hands and threaded her way through the crowd, heading back toward the camp.

To find Simon de Bocage—perhaps to save him—she had to do the thing she feared most.

# Morlaix

# Chapter One

A thunderstorm came rolling off the Welsh mountains, blue-black with rain. The Benedictine lay brother lifted a fold of his habit over his breviary and continued reading. Behind, the wagons pulled to a stop and the drovers jumped out to cover the wine barrels with pieces of hide.

Simon de Bocage drew the hood of his cloak up against the downpour. Feeling the movement, the Saracen mare tossed her head and pulled at the bit. She was a desert horse, and hated rain. Which they'd had, steadily enough, since they'd left the coast at Folkestone.

Good English weather, Simon told himself as water ran down between his neck and his mail. And still better than burning in some Outremer desert. There had been times these past two years when even a spoonful of water would have been a sweet miracle.

The wine merchant pushed his palfrey up beside him. Water poured from his wide-brimmed hat like a veil. "Thank God and the holy saints," he shouted, "there is the river. We should see Morlaix Castle at the bridge."

Simon leaned forward in his saddle to see the gray shape rising against the Welsh mountains. A sudden, familiar pain attacked him somewhere over his breastbone. It was stupid to feel a thing so keenly, so hopelessly, he told himself; he had only to deliver the bishops' letter and leave. One would be a fool to linger, anyway, when she was already married.

On the far side of the river the meadow was crowded with tents of wedding guests and their knights, foot soldiery, baggage and dogs. There were ditches dug to empty the chamberpots, strings of tethered horses and guard fires. In places where the grass had been trampled the ground was fast turning to mud.

Simon kept his eyes on Morlaix, fighting the old, foolish dreams that leaped up in him. Once again he was a green boy, a beardless squire, helplessly besotted with his cousin, Alys de Bocage.

He'd never thought to come back again to Morlaix. Not still yearning for a shy, sweet maid he could never have. If they'd told him his destination in Rouen weeks ago, he knew he would have refused.

Under the bridge a group of naked men were bathing, the water around them dimpled with rain. The wine merchant sucked in his breath. "Sir knight, see, there are a score of them. And we are but three."

They seemed harmless enough to Simon. Probably the household knights of some wedding guest.

As they approached, one of the bathers lifted his hand in greeting. He acknowledged it with a nod.

The wine merchant shouldered his horse close. "King William should find a way to keep this riffraff in the Holy Land," he complained. "I say with Jerusalem conquered, they should stay to protect what was gained by the sword, and so many blessed martyred lives."

Simon said nothing. Given his choice, he would have traveled alone, but in Chirk the monk had approached to beg protection in the name of the church, and the wine merchant had offered a quarter barrel of his best dry yellow from Sancerre in France. Which, the merchant had reminded Simon, since he was going to the wedding at the castle, would make a fine gift.

The horses slowed at the bridge. Behind them the wagons pulled to a stop.

When he'd been a page at Castle Morlaix there had been a small woods here, and a pen for cattle. He'd often swum in the river with Gilbert and the twins in the summer, just as the knights below now were doing. But not Alys, he remembered. No girl of good birth could swim naked, not even with her brothers.

He laid the reins against his mare's neck and let out the destrier's lead. His arm ached from the war horse's pulling against it, as steady and resisting as a towed boat.

"You do not know England, now," the merchant was saying, "if you have been long gone in the Holy Land. The country is filled with those who call themselves Christian knights, yet roam like thieves, or worse."

Simon made a noncommittal noise, kicking the mare into a trot. The merchant had talked all the way from Chirk of renegades who murdered and plundered the unwary, and the country's lawlessness under King William Rufus. It was strange to hear such things here in the Welsh marches, where Fulk de Jobourg had so long stood for justice and order. In the past his cousin had resisted even his own treacherous leige lord, the Earl of Chester. And once, years ago, old King William the Conqueror's scheming brothers.

The wine merchant kicked his palfrey up to keep pace with the mare. "Yet even these outlaw knights and brigands are nothing compared to those unholy companions with whom the king surrounds himself. They claim they are knights, but we know them as robbers and worse. Have you not heard of Robert FitzHaimo, beautiful as a woman, on whom the king lavishes his favors?" He looked around, although there was no one to hear. "A court of 'fornicators and catamites vilely stained.' That is what our own archbishop, the blessed Anselm, has called them."

The corners of Simon's mouth twitched. *Fornicators and catamites vilely stained.* Since leaving France he'd found merchants were the most condemning of William Rufus, a rough and extravagant knight with a taste for boys. But it was difficult for most to understand barracks life, where one seldom dealt with women. At Tamworth, a band of knights had chased Simon off the road and into some covering woods with, apparently, robbery not their main intent. From his exile in France, Anselm,

England's Archbishop of Canterbury, denounced this sort of thing almost daily.

Rain beat like a drum on the boards of the bridge. Head down, the Saracen mare crabwalked. Simon touched her with his spurs. Startled, the horse stretched her neck and charged, trying to drag his leg against the rails. Behind them the wine merchant's two drovers shouted and whipped up their mules.

He brought the heaving, sweating mare to a halt on the bridge's far side. The men in the river whistled between their teeth.

The lay brother jogged past on his donkey. "They are offering for your horse," he said, not looking up.

Simon had heard them. And what they were offering. He held the mare in as she high-stepped onto the road. She'd withstood the voyage across the channel from France well enough; he was baffled that now that they were at last in England, she refused to settle down.

Castle Morlaix's walls were hung with red and white cloth. The banners of high-ranking guests drooped, rain-soaked, from the portal gate.

There was a blast of horns from the keep. The stallion lifted his head, yanking at the tether. The other horses broke into a trot. They splashed up the incline, the wagons falling behind.

On either side were bright gonfalons: the Baron of Malmsbury's tent; then a cluster marking the Earl of Chester's vassals, their lord absent in Normandy; the standards of the Earl of Hatford; and a lesser Montgomery. An orange sun on a yellow field, the device of the all-powerful Clares, Prince

Henry's friends, hung from the tallest pole. It was said of the Clares that if they were reconnoitering hell they would send a flag to the devil to let him know they were there.

The lay brother put away his breviary and kicked his donkey into a trot. A group of young pages with food in their hands burst out of the castle archway and ran past them down the road.

The portal sentry stepped onto the drawbridge, and waved the Benedictine brother past. "Here now, looking for food and drink?" He seized the mare's bridle, his eyes on Simon's mail and the state of his boots. "Nobody's to be let in, you know."

The other knight stepped out into the rain. "Now that's a horse." He ran his hand down the Saracen mare's neck. She bared her teeth, and he laughed. "A bit dish-faced, isn't she?"

Simon pulled on the reins. The mare crouched on her haunches, backing away. He said, "It's a sign of the breed."

The first knight stepped to one side to let the wine merchant pass. Simon looked beyond the gate. The ward was filled with people. On the open fires turned spits of starlings and grouse, and under them simmered stew kettles. A leafy bower had been put up over some kegs of ale. There was a mob around it. The great hall, big as a manor house, backed against the rear curtain wall. They could hear music and the din of voices.

"If you want wedding food and drink," the first guard was saying, "it's back down there in the camp. They will give you what you need in plenty."

The wine merchant was riding away. "My wine," Simon called. The merchant did not look back.

He swung the destrier into the path of the second wagon. The portal knight jumped back as he turned both horses in the narrow archway.

Simon kneed the mare forward, the destrier jerking at his lead. He was beginning to feel tired. The rain didn't help. He trotted the horses back to the wine wagon.

The drover sat hunched on the wagon seat. Simon leaned from the saddle. "A caskette of the yellow Sancerre," he told him, "as I was promised."

The man lifted sullen eyes. Simon said nothing, merely looked at him. After a moment the drover scrambled over the wagon seat, back among the barrels. He found a small rundlet of wine. Simon leaned down to take it. The drover looked away, crossing himself.

He turned the horses back under the arch. The castle chamberlain had come up, iron keys dangling. Simon barely recognized Ivor the reeve, he'd changed into an old man while he was gone, stooped, his hair white. The woman with him held the edge of her red cloak above her head. She stepped under the arch and threw it back.

He hadn't expected the lady of Morlaix. She was still beautiful, he saw, with her white skin and dark hair. Gilbert, her oldest, was his own age. As a child she'd seemed a goddess to him.

She peered up at him. "Sir knight, we are filled to the walls here—" Abruptly, she gave a girlish squeal and stepped forward, hands out.

He threw the reins over the mare's neck and dismounted, the rundlet in his arms. The Lady Alwyn threw herself against him. He towered over her, balancing the wine.

"Ah, Simon, is it really you?" A shadow crossed her face. "Holy Mother, you are too late! No, I don't mean that; God will give them happiness. But they are married, they've gone now to the bridal chamber." Her hands grabbed his cloak. "My poor heart, don't look like that."

She thought he had come to stop the marriage. For a moment he didn't know what to tell her. To cover it he dropped to one knee on the cobblestones and bent his head.

"Lady," he said formally, "the wedding is not my reason for coming, it is another task which sends me here. But accept my prayers for God's blessing on your daughter on this happy event." Silently he cursed himself for being there; he only wanted now to get away. "And His holy and generous blessing on your liege lord, my cousin Fulk de Jobourg, joyous blessings on all your family and those in Castle Morlaix on this most favored occasion."

She bit her lip. "Get up, you're kneeling in a puddle." She tugged at his hand. "For the love you bear me," the Lady Alwyn said as he got to his feet, "accept God's holy will. It will be a love match, I promise you; she looks on him with favor. We cannot always have the one we desire." Her eyes searched his face. "Are you listening?"

"My lady, I always listen to you." Simon lifted her hand to his lips. "I did even as a child."

She looked thoughtful. "You are like your mother. She was beautiful, do you remember? Everyone said it."

He remembered how his mother looked. "Milady, I am not beautiful. Even those who love me will grant that."

"You know you are." She looked annoyed. "I saw you last with your first beard, and your voice still cracking."

He almost smiled. The last visit to Morlaix he'd been a half-grown boy dragged on yet another one of his father's harebrained ventures, that time, service to some rustic lordling in Aquitaine. No money. Miserable horses. They'd not even been able to afford him decent mail, or a sword.

He gave the rundlet of wine to the chamberlain. "Ivor, the years have been good to you." He could not meet his eyes. It seemed everyone had grown old since he left.

The chamberlain embraced him, muttering something about that fine knight, his father, and went off with the wine cask.

The Lady Alwyn took his arm. Inside Morlaix, Simon needed no guide, for castle pages learned every nook and cranny to hide from work, or share food and talk. The kitchen, hayricks by the stables, under the beds in the knights' barracks; behind the armorer's shed, he knew them all.

Beyond the new hall were the storerooms where he and Gilbert had played king of the mountain on wool sacks. And the stables where the twins, Hugh and Alain, fought over their ponies. The bread ovens where Alys jumped down one time, breaking her arm.

Sweet Jesu, every time he looked at her mother he thought of her. It was like a dagger turning in his heart.

They crossed the ward. The storm was passing. The sun somewhere above made the air steamy. By the dog pens, the abbot of St. Botolph's knights had

resumed their dice game, using one wall as a back-
board. The hunting dogs inside barked fiercely.

"Milady," Simon said, "I have come to see your
lord, Fulk de Jobourg. I bring a message for the—"
He searched for a good word. "The council."

She looked at him out of the corner of her eye. "I
have nothing to do with that."

He shrugged. "Milady, I am but the messenger."
He followed her across the wet grass, past a group
of musicians waiting their turn in the hall.

They reached the door of the old tower. She motioned to the guards and they stepped back. "Use
the stairs to my old room. You will remember it,
the old bedchamber for the lord and lady." She put
out her hand and touched his arm. "Simon, there
is a girl. She has been here for some days."

She looked up, and his eyes followed. Midway on
the wall of the tower there was a window with an
iron grille. He didn't remember it being there before. He thought he saw some movement behind
the bars, as though someone looked down.

"The old tower is no longer used as the knights'
barracks, it holds prisoners. And hostages, when we
have any." She hesitated, frowning. "You must
know my husband does not willingly meet with the
likes of Malmsbury. And Hatford."

"My lady," he assured her, "I know little of this,
and seek to learn less. I only carry a letter."

"About this girl." Her fingers pressed his arm.
"Promise me you will not lend yourself to anything
that is—that is lacking in honor."

He did not know what she expected him to say.
"Milady, do not fear for my honor, or yours. I will
defend both to death."

He took her hand and lifted her fingers to his lips. For the first time, looking up at him, she smiled.

He left her standing there and passed between the guards. Then up the tower stairs, narrow and unlit. Coming down, a man in a knight's velvet short coat squeezed past him.

He turned. "Simon de Bocage!" He pounded him with his fists. "We have heard tales of you from the east."

Guy de Yerville, he remembered. A vassal of Fulk de Jobourg's. Everyone looked so much older.

The other's face fell. "Ah, cursed luck, man! They are just married. You—"

Simon pounded him back, just as fervently. They all thought he had come to do foul murder. "Nay, de Yerville," he told him, "I am here from the bishops at Rouen, with a letter."

De Yerville looked relieved. "I must go make a speech at the feast for our Fleming guests. But Hatford is above, drunk and holding the floor. According to him we are all too timid to follow where he would lead us."

He turned and rushed down the stairs. Simon climbed to the top. The sentry there jumped ahead to open the wooden door.

The room inside was noisy. He stood for a second, seeing how it had changed. The big bed with its heavy hangings was gone, its place filled with chairs and a trestle table spread with platters of meat and pastries, tankards of ale, dirty dishes. Someone had lighted a fire, and there was a blaze of candles bright enough to say a mass. The light picked out faces, hands, clothing, gems.

"Sweet Christ, Lucifer fallen!" It was the voice

of one of the Clares. His cousin, Fulk de Jobourg came around the table. "Nay, FitzGilbert, the devil was never so comely. This is my kinsman, Simon de Bocage." He put his arm around Simon's shoulder. "You see a knight's flowing curls such as Hatford was just denouncing." In Simon's ear he growled, "They are married. There is nothing you can do about it."

Fulk let him go and went back to his chair. Simon stared after him. He supposed they had their reasons, but every mention of the cursed marriage stabbed him like a knife. Deliver the letter, he told himself. You need never come back.

He looked around for a place for his cloak and, finding none, dropped it on a bench. He looked for Fulk's son, Gilbert, but he was not there.

At the hearth the Earl of Hatford was saying, "I tell you we cannot long endure this mockery of the king's filthy life."

Someone said, "Other kings have had filthy lives, Rotrou."

The earl turned to glare at him. "The king's father, William the Conqueror, did not."

"Peace, peace," the abbot of St. Botolph's said, mildly.

The earl propped his arm on the mantel. The cup he was holding tilted, spilling wine into his sleeve. "And the more that ass of an archbishop, Anselm, rails from France," he went on, "the more the king robs and punishes the church. William Rufus well makes use of that accursed demon he's made Bishop of Durham with all his baggage of mistresses and bastards, Ranulph Flambard."

FitzGilbert's son moved some dishes aside and motioned for Simon to sit down. He shook his head.

He knew that Baron Malmsbury hated England's king for the theft of his Norman lands that the king had given to one of his favorites. Beyond the baron were two cousins of the Clares: Walter, nephew of the sheriff of Devon, and Godfrey, kinsman to Robert of Meules. In France it was said the Clares wished to put Prince Henry upon the English throne. Next to the Clares he saw the abbot of St. Botolph's priory, full-jowled, handsome in his purple robes. The holy church in England hated the king, a blasphemous soldier who stole its revenues. At the rear stood landed knights, a mailed marcher constable, some minor Welsh chiefs.

Simon took the letter out of his shortcoat. Courtesy demanded he hand it to Fulk de Jobourg, Baron of Morlaix, but then his cousin promptly handed it to the Clares, who could read it. The abbot motioned to a knight who went to the door and called to the guards on the stairs.

FitzGilbert of Devon passed the letter to the abbot, who read it at length and said only, "Our holy brothers the bishops send their support. But no money."

"In Italy," Godfrey of Meules put in, "they say Duke Robert speaks of seeing Normandy within a month."

"August," Hatford told him. "My spies tell me August."

The other Clare began to talk of strategy. Duke Robert had put his duchy in pawn to his brother the king for thirty thousand silver marks so that he could make the Crusade to free Jerusalem. Now, with the war over, Robert had stopped in Italy long enough to acquire a rich wife—something his brother, the king of England, had not expected. If Duke Robert demanded his duchy back, FitzGilbert wanted to know, would the king give it back to him? Or would there be war?

Simon felt tiredness dragging at him. He had ridden for two days, pushing his horses, and the heat of the fire made him dull. He felt himself far removed from intriguing. In France they believed England's king would seize Normandy before his brother could return. In Rouen the bishops had talked of imprisonment, exile. Even the possibility of England's throne seized for the youngest brother, Prince Henry.

Malmsbury was saying, "We are being driven to beggar ourselves to support that loutish devil in London."

"And the Jews." Hatford downed the last of his wine. "The king holds England by the throat with the damned Jewish moneylenders."

Simon looked around the room. Such talk made him uneasy. The penalties for treason were so harsh one did not care to think about them. His stomach hurt; he wished now he had accepted FitzGilbert's offer of something to eat.

Malmsbury put his arm along the back of his chair. "How come you here, de Bocage?" he asked. "Are you but the bishops' courier?" His eyes observed Simon's worn boots, his Crusader's long hair. "Or something more?"

Simon picked up a cup from the table and poured himself some wine. His unease was growing. He was not landed, not noble like his de Jobourg cousins, only a fighting man such as they were accustomed to hiring. "I am but the messenger, milord. I have this year come from Jerusalem with the Count of Flanders, having been the count's sworn man. As was my father, Geoffrey de Bocage."

He had to mention his father. They all knew of him, anyway.

"I was in Rouen with a letter my lord the Count of Flanders sent to the bishops. It was in my mind after that to go on to England and visit an estate my mother's father held, in Wroxeter." The wool business. Simon knew how that would sound to them. "Knowing this, the bishops persuaded me to carry the message that my lord, the abbot of St. Botolph's priory, now holds."

There was the sound of footsteps on the stairs. Those who had been below at the wedding feast came into the room, noisily. A big man shouldered his way through the crowd.

"Holy mother Mary, are my eyes seeing at last the famed scourge of the Turks?" Gilbert de Jobourg was huge and ruddy like his father. He seized Simon and held him at arm's length. "Are you still monkish? What are you reading now?"

"Some Aristotle." He loved Gilbert but he could have throttled him. A young knight looked Simon over, awed. From his chair Fulk shouted for more wine.

The abbot got up and walked to the fire and spoke in a low voice to the Earl of Hatford. The other nodded.

Hand at his back, Gilbert pushed Simon toward the wine table. "Everyone knows you are lovelorn now that my sister is wed to the Frenchman, but give me a few days and nights now that you have returned and my friends and I will remedy that." He thrust a cup of wine at him. Under his breath he said, "I pray you, do what my father wants."

Behind Fulk, the abbot was going around the room speaking to each man. Simon sipped the wine, his eyes following them. They were hatching something, that much was plain. He did not think the de Jobourgs would plot against him. His nerves were tight as wires. Damn them, here in this northwest corner of England, what did they think they could do?

The Earl of Hatford raised his voice. "De Bocage, you are well known, a parfit knight, far-famed since Antioch and Jerusalem. What say you to that?"

He saw Gilbert had left his side to go to Fulk.

"I know naught of it, milord." He was thinking there was no way he could depart the room now without seeming to bolt.

Baron Malmsbury came to stand in front of him. The room was warm, there were dark stains of sweat across his satin coat. "Now that we have seen you, de Bocage," he said, "what would you say if I told you that you well fit a plan of ours that needs must be done?"

His face felt like wood. *Alys.* It was a wild thought. He told himself they could not punish him for having loved her.

Footsteps came up the tower stairs. A woman's voice said something, high and plaintive. Then the tower door was thrown open. Two knights pushed a girl inside.

She was dressed in a green silk gown trimmed with gold, her face ravishing, thick with paint, with a full, sensuous underlip, and wild blue eyes. Her gold hair hung loose to her waist, but her skin was sun-darkened as a serf's. She was obviously English. "Magnificent" was the word that came to mind; every man's lustful wet dream.

Seeing only men, the girl turned to run. The knights hauled her back. She fought them, squealing and kicking.

"This is old Leofwine's granddaughter." Malmsbury lifted his voice over the sounds of the scuffling. "The thane was killed long ago, but he was one of Harold Godwineson's magnates. The daughters of one of his sons, Edmund, have been living with the mother in a hut by the river on my land. One could hardly tell them from villeins, until one of my knights got a child on one of them." He studied the girl. "This is the pick of the litter."

"A gift for Prince Henry," Hatford put in. "Knowing Henry's taste."

Simon looked around the room. The prince boasted he'd sired more bastards in England than any man, a strange vice for one so lawyerlike, and canny.

The Saxon girl wrenched her arm out of the knight's grip and fell against the wine table, knocking it over. Malmsbury jumped up, exclaiming, wine dripping from his clothes. The guard knights lunged for her. One grabbed the front of her gown. The other hit her at the side of her head with his fist.

They were right over Simon, the girl screaming and flailing. He got to his feet. Before they could hit her again he thrust his arm in between.

"Here." The girl's face turned to him with a

glazed look. "Stop," Simon said. It was useless to beat anything in that state, even a horse; he supposed women were no different.

Quick as a snake the girl's head struck. He jerked his arm away, but not before she'd snagged his thumb between white teeth.

"God's wounds!" For a moment, considering the strength of her jaws, Simon wondered if he were about to lose it. With his free hand he gripped her chin. Her panicked eyes stared at him, unseeing.

He managed to get his thumb back. It spurted blood, a strip of flesh hanging. The room broke into encouraging cheers.

"She's likely one of my poachers," Malmsbury was shouting. "They say she can draw a hunting bow as well as any man."

Someone in the back called, "Send Prince Henry a sword and shield, so he can properly woo her!"

There was loud laughter. The abbot's expression was severe. Wild-eyed, the girl was trying to push the knights out of the way.

"Yes," the abbot of St. Botolph's said, frowning. "But first we must do something about that."

# Chapter Two

Someone got a cloth from the overturned wine table and Simon bound up his thumb. The tower room had been cleared after the guards took the Saxon girl away. There remained only the abbot of St. Botolph's, the Earl of Hatford, the two Clares, Fulk de Jobourg, and Gilbert. Simon tried to catch Gilbert's eye, but Gilbert was studying the far wall.

"Come, de Bocage," Malmsbury said, "is it taking the girl to Prince Henry that galls you? Then be assured the Welsh prince sent his daughter, Nest, to Henry, and they pleased each other well. So much so she is in her home in Glamorgan, now, to have Prince Henry's second child."

The abbot said, "Bertrand, please."

Simon swung a leg over a bench, sat down at the table, and reached for an empty plate. As he shoved some boiled mutton onto it he told himself he could not believe such madness of his own kin. They spoke as if they had not even thought of the danger. Although there was that in marvelous plenty.

The fire in his belly was raging and his bitten

hand throbbed. He tried to remember when he had last taken food. In Chirk, with the wine merchant. It was a dispiriting thought.

The abbot leaned forward. "Now then, de Bocage, I fear you did not—"

"Milord abbot," Simon said shortly, "I am no Jew." He tore a piece of mutton apart, careful of his thumb, and put some of it in his mouth. "Bring me any holy relic that you may have and I will swear on it that I am not a Jew, and never could be."

The mutton was tough, and he was finding that he was not all that hungry; it was only that his stomach hurt. He knew he could not be a part of their intriguing, he'd had enough of that in the Holy Land. And as for taking the prince's would-be whore to London, that was no task for an honorable knight. It would make him the butt of jokes for the rest of his days.

He stared down at his plate for a moment before he said, "Milords, my mother was but half-Jewish in her blood, raised for most of her life, as was I, in a good Christian household."

Fulk said, "Now consider—"

He lifted his head to stare at him. The last thing he wanted at that moment was to have the de Jobourgs try to persuade him. The abbot of St. Botolph's said quickly, "Now, good knight, listen to Morlaix."

Simon shook his head. "Nay, milord abbot, you have the wrong man. My mother's mother was lost on the road in Flanders when she was no more than a babe, one of a family of goldsmiths from Falaise who had been robbed, then murdered by outlaws."

He lifted the wine cup and saw that it was empty. Before he could get up, Malmsbury took it to the sideboard and brought it back filled.

"This babe, my grandmother," Simon went on, "was found by the wool merchant Belefroun, who brought her in Christian charity to his own house and raised her as his own. When she was of an age Belefroun then married her to his son, my grandfather, for whom I am named."

Looking down, Simon saw his hand was not all that steady. He was not surprised; he'd just been betrayed into explaining his infernal bloodlines. "Their daughter, my mother, Sophia Belefroun, was pleased to marry here in England a young knight, Geoffrey de Bocage, kinsman to the Baron of Morlaix. Who, as you know, is my cousin, Fulk de Jobourg."

At that precise moment Simon lost track of what he was saying. He sat staring into the air, suddenly struck by the thought that none of this had been by accident. Since France, he thought. Since he'd gone to the Rouen bishops with the count's letter. Nor was it happenstance that the bishops' message to Prince Henry's supporters had been waiting for him.

It was all suddenly clear. Who else, he told himself, for their plot but Simon de Bocage, Sophia the Jewess's son? When all these years he'd thought the thing hidden. If not actually forgotten.

He lifted his wine cup and stared into it. Damn the heathen Jews, he thought. He knew it was not fair nor seemly to curse one's relations, but the taint of his Jewish blood had dogged him, relentlessly, in an unforgiving Christian world. As a child in this very castle he'd been beaten for it by the page master; then in squires' training at Chester he'd been hauled from his bed by older boys wanting to test him, to fight with him to prove that Jewish blood was more cowardly. It had been no wonder he had become the fiercest, most devout squire in Christendom, always at matins in the middle of any night praying with the monks. He'd even thought of holy orders before his father had put a stop to it.

Now, he saw, he would have to prove it again. He looked around the room, seeing their faces turned to him. Abbot Nigel of St. Botolph's; all churchmen detested the king. Across from the abbot, the Earl of Hatford, who hated William Rufus for his stolen lands. Then the two Clares. Who behaved as though their candidate, Prince Henry, was already upon the throne.

It had been Simon's dream, after two years of war, to study in the university schools in Paris. It was not too late, he was not yet thirty, and he'd had two years of murderous intrigue among the magnates of the Crusades; there was nothing here, in this room, they could tell him that would make him want more. He suddenly thought of his shadowy mother, who had lived for only a few years with Geoffrey de Bocage.

"You see in me," Simon said, "one born of a Christian father, baptised in the true church. In manhood I swore a Crusader's oath which still binds me." He made himself smile. "For that, I know of no Jew in England who would claim me!"

The abbot said, impatient, "Come, de Bocage, not only are you a famed knight but they say you are *beauclerc* like the prince, that you can cipher, and know Latin. Was it not you who negotiated with the Turks in the long parley at Antioch?"

He kept his rueful smile. "Milord abbot, were I as clever as all that I would not find myself here."

He knew by their faces he had not convinced them. Inwardly he cursed. Someone had told these marcher lords that since the descent of the Hebrew race was reckoned by the female line, he was considered, through his mother and grandmother, to be fully a Jew. He could not believe they had faith in this, but they had. Still, he could see how it fitted their schemes. Even Prince Henry's wealthy supporters like the Clares could not provide for England's treasury. There was only one power that could do that, the clannish, devious Jews whom William Rufus had imported to finance his extravagant rule. Without the moneylenders, even Henry could not succeed as king.

Now, under cover of one task, delivering the girl to Prince Henry, they would have him do yet another. For who better, according to their way of thinking, for an envoy to guarantee the Jews their safety and commerce than some Norman knight? Who, it was said, had a claim to be part Jew?

Or all Jew, if one understood the abbot's argument.

Simon pushed back his chair, picking up his cloak from the bench. Fulk de Jobourg got quickly to his feet. "Stay." His cousin stepped in front of him. "It is not finished."

"By the Cross, it is for me." He scowled at Fulk, remembering another matter. "Morlaix, I was not thought good enough to marry your daughter. But now you tell me I am good enough for"—he could not bring himself to put a name to it—"*this*."

Fulk opened his eyes wide. "God is my judge, I did not forbid you to marry her, boy. Seven degrees of kinship did that."

They were suddenly nose to nose. "Close kinship changes," Simon shouted, "with how much is paid to the church. My Alys's fate was that of all heiresses sold to the highest bidder!"

"*Your* Alys?"

Fulk made a lunge for him. They would have been at each other's throats but the abbot quickly stepped in between. "Now, now," he said, "this does not concern kinship. De Bocage, your honor is safe. Is it the Saxon girl that concerns you?" He took Simon by the arm and turned him away. "Consider, there can be nothing but great fortune in it for such as she. It is well known Prince Henry provides well for his women."

Walter of Devon called, "Yes, when the prince has money."

"We must have you, de Bocage," Hatford bellowed. He paced the hearth, hands behind his back. "How can any of us do it? God help us, we are not Jews!"

Malmsbury said, "Christ in heaven, Rotrou, sit down."

The abbot persisted. "Nay, this is a task for a proven knight returned from God's holy war in Jerusalem." They all got out of their seats to gather around him. "A knight sworn to uphold God's justice."

Simon fastened his cloak. "Are you appealing to me now as a Christian or as a Jew?"

FitzGilbert said quickly, "We have pressing use for you, de Bocage, and you are free of any lord's service. We will reward you well."

God's wounds, they thought they were doing him a favor. "FitzGilbert, if I am so devoted to God's holy justice, then surely I am too pious to deliver any whore, willing or not, to Prince Henry."

Hatford came around the table and thrust his face into his. "Look you," he shouted, "we are not wanting some nithing knight back from the Holy Land with much fame and an empty belly. We have looked you over, lad, and Jew or no Jew we must have you." He stopped. "You needn't tell the Jews of your reputation," he said in a different voice. "Don't want to scare them to death."

The abbot said, "Rotrou, in God's name, sit down."

Walter of Devon said, "There must be some way for us to gain our own English king."

There was a silence. Simon knew they regarded this as a thing of great importance. Only Henry, of all the Conqueror's sons, had been born an Englishman.

The abbot of St. Botolph's looked resigned. "We will write a message to the Jews in London to ask if they will pledge their loyalty to a new king as they do to the present one."

"Can we be subtle," Malmsbury asked, "so that the Jews will have the bowels to respond? They are not famous for it."

Hatford stamped across the hearth. "By the tripes of Saint David, everything now rests on the damned Jews!"

The door to the stairwell had opened. Someone whispered. Walter of Devon got up and went to it.

"We must not frighten the moneylenders," the other Clare was saying. "By all means, let us seek to prevent the flight of England's credit."

The door to the stair was thrown open. The Saxon girl stood there with her guards. She had discarded the gold-trimmed mantle and now wore a plain gown of linen that clung to her body. Her hair was pulled back, the rouge and paint rubbed away. Subdued, she looked even younger.

She stepped into the room, shrugging the knights' hands away.

The abbot pointed to Simon. "Now, girl, behave yourself, and look why you have been brought here. We have a far-famed knight who wishes to be assured that you know what is offered you, and will consent."

Simon looked up, surprised. He'd wished no such thing.

The girl turned her head. The intense blue of her eyes regarded him warily. Cautious, he put his wrapped hand behind him.

Walter FitzGilbert said, "Girl, we are asking this knight to take you to London, to see you to the one who awaits your safe arrival with much pleasure and longing."

The Saxon girl continued to stare. Simon wondered what they'd done to her. There was a red mark at her temple where the guard knight had struck her.

"FitzGilbert," he reminded them, "I have refused."

"Nay, de Bocage, take a good look." The other

Clare stood up and went to the girl. He touched her bright hair with his hand. "She is the granddaughter of Harold Godwineson's thane, Leofwine. Her once-noble family has been scattered, the women left to provide for themselves by stealing firewood from Malmsbury's woods and poaching his game. Turn around," he told her.

She gave him a defiant look. But after a moment's hesitation she turned.

Simon watched her, thinking she was too beautiful to beg one's pity, and there was a waywardness there that grated; he preferred women gentle and refined. Still, they were showing her like a side of meat. She did not deserve that.

The girl said something so low they had to strain to hear.

"Speak up," FitzGilbert told her.

Those remarkable eyes found Simon's again. "Yes," she said softly, "I will go with him."

A murmur ran around the room.

Under his breath, Simon groaned. Somehow, in the minutes since he'd last seen her they'd persuaded the Saxon girl to say she wished him for her pimp-protector to London. In this way they hoped to make him accept what they wished him to do. Including the part with the Jews.

He was not taken in. He said, "Tell the girl you will find someone else."

Her stare was still fixed on him. "Yes," she said more loudly, "I will go with him."

Simon felt a sudden rush of temper. The damned girl was hopeless, except as a beautiful animal; he was certain the prince would instantly bed her. He wanted no part of it.

He turned away, ramming his helmet on his head, although he did not need to be helmed within the castle gates. "You do me much honor, milords." He no longer cared what they thought. "But I must still refuse."

There was no way they could force him. And the devil with it. He thought of Alys, married to some French lord's son from Artois. She would haunt him forever. His stomach was like a furnace.

He could not wait to get out of Morlaix.

He went to the door, pushing past the girl standing there. She said something, held out her hand, palm up.

Simon did not stop to hear what it was.

# Chapter Three

The July sun rode high and hot in the sky. A group of sweating villeins trotted down the Wroxeter road, carrying hay rakes on their shoulders. They looked longingly at Ingrith sitting in the shade under the oak tree.

"Saxon," she heard one of them say.

Ingrith broke off a piece of bread, put it in her mouth and chewed it, watching them. She was used to being looked at. And most villeins did not love the old Saxons, in spite of their hate for the Normans. They had a saying, *New lords no worse'n the old ones*.

These, she thought, watching them, were going to some lord's fields to work. The summer had been good and the haying plentiful. There were well-dressed freemen among them with leather boots, carrying knives in their belts. Next to them the villeins were like serfs, barefoot, clad only in long shirts the color of earth.

One of them, staring at Ingrith, ran into the man in front. The gangmaster promptly ran up to hit him across the shoulders with a short whip. Ingrith tried not to laugh.

The knights who had brought her from Morlaix had tethered their horses on the other side of the oak trees and were playing a game of dice. It was hot even in the shade, but they had not shed their heavy mail or their swords. Beyond them lay a stone wall, beyond that a field of green pasture with flocks of sheep.

Since morning there had been few travelers on the Wroxeter road. All that had passed were a wine merchant and his wagons, a troop of household knights under the banner of Hugh de Yerville, a vassal of the Baron of Morlaix, and the villeins going to work some lord's crop of hay. The Morlaix knights told Ingrith that travelers would be scarce until the wedding feast was over and the guests departed. And that would not be until the Lady Alys, daughter of the baron, and her new husband left for France.

Ingrith picked up the last piece of cheese from her lap, broke it into small pieces, and ate each one slowly. When she was through she licked the salty-tasting grease from her fingers. It was wonderful to have so much to eat. Normans, both at the Baron of Malsmbury's desmesne and at Castle Morlaix, took regular meals. They broke fast at morning, ate at noon, always at the end of the day. And she'd made the most of it.

She looked down, searching for a spot on the green silk to wipe her fingers. She'd been given only fine gowns, nothing for ordinary wear, and the green was fast showing dirt. She leaned back against the seat of the wagon, thinking that before the bread and cheese they'd had yellow plums. At dawn, before they'd left Castle Morlaix, they'd been given cold meat and very good beer. At least they weren't going to let her go hungry.

The hay workers were nearly out of sight, at the bend by the trees. While Ingrith watched a wind rose, shaking the villeins' long shirts and lifting them, showing breechless white rumps, pumping thighs. Between their legs, a glimpse of jouncing privates.

All the villeins Ingrith had ever known were cruel and thieving. When her father had lain sick, wounded by drunken knights that had come looking for Saxons to harry, villeins had stolen their cow and much of the winter grain. And then set fire to the oat field for spite.

She shifted on the wagon seat. Perhaps it was true, as the villeins said, that there was no difference in lords, whether they be Saxon or Norman. She could not see, though, how anyone could mistrust her father, brave Edmund Leofwineson, more than the Norman Bertrand de Crecy, Baron of Malmsbury. Who now had all of their land.

The wind moved through the oak tree, spattering light. The paint the women at Morlaix had put on her face made it itch. So did the false hair. She lifted the end of one plait, took the ribbons out, and began to unravel it.

Almost at once a knight rose from the dice game and came over to the wagon. He was older than the others, the one they called Drogo. He'd doffed his helmet. Under it the heat had flattened his sandy hair against his head.

"Put your feet down," he told her. His eyes passed

the length of her bare legs. "That is the way a harlot sits, like that. No wonder the villeins see all."

The false braid came loose in her hand. Drogo stared at it. "God is my judge," he said under his breath. He turned away.

Ingrith watched him go back to the others. She heard them discussing her. Drogo imitated her Saxon accent. The rest laughed. The young, brown-eyed knight who had given her the cheese looked at her over his shoulder. She raked her fingers through her loose hair. When combed, it fell to her elbows.

The women at Morlaix had said it was fashionable in France to add false hair until the braids hung to one's knees. One had been tiring woman to the Baron of Malmsbury's wife, the other the mistress of a bawds' house in Chester, brought in to teach her the other things as well. They had pared her fingernails, filed the calluses on her feet, soaked her face in buttermilk, taught her to walk slowly and to sit and stand in a decorous fashion, not with her elbows propped against the wall or mantelpiece like some layabout squire. They were also the first to tell her the truth—that she was to be sent to a great lord in the south to be his leman.

She poked at the heel of one shoe with her toe, hoping that her mother and sisters had been told what had become of her. She didn't know how her mother would feel to learn that she was still alive. And for what.

*You must be willing*, was what she'd been told by the lords at Morlaix. In return for what they called her willingness, her mother and sisters would be given a house and a piece of land on Malmsbury's holdings. Marauding knights would not molest them, and monks from the priory of St. David's would see to it that they were cared for. That meant that her mother, her sisters, and Gudrun's baby would not starve this winter.

Afterward it had occurred to Ingrith that the monks would not like the baby because Gudrun had been raped and could not name the father. She told herself it would make no difference; the monks had to feed them. She was sure of it.

She kicked off the fancy red leather shoe. Sweat had left lines like paint across her toes. In winter the daughters of Edmund Leofwineson wore rags around their feet stuffed with hay. In this manner, and bundled in skins, they went into the baron's forest to steal firewood. It had been like this, hindered by their rag-wrapped feet and packs of wood, that a troop of young knights had ridden them down. Only this last time it was Ingrith, not Gudrun, they wanted.

Ingrith bent over on the wagon seat, her arms wrapped around her knees, remembering the day knights had ravished Gudrun in the oat field. *Lie down and hide and do not move*, Gudrun had told her. Pressed flat against the earth she could not see Gudrun being raped but she could hear it, the Normans shouting encouragement to each other. Gudrun's shrieks that died to hoarse rasping as the last one took her.

The memory of it made her tighten her arms about her knees and press her face into them as sudden misery overcame her. So far from home, a voice inside reminded. She kept her head down, not

wanting these Normans to see Ingrith Edmundsdaughter weeping even a few small tears.

The knights yelled out over someone's win. Ingrith quickly wiped her eyes with the back of her
hand and sat up. She got down and went around
to the back of the little painted wagon and pulled
down the tailgate. The wain held two chests of her
clothes. In the biggest there was a cloak made of
marten skins, although she was still not sure where
one would wear such an elegant thing in midsummer.

She pushed back the top of the largest chest and
pulled out a scarf sewed with red pieces that glittered. She threw the scarf over her head.

The misery faded a little as she turned slowly,
holding the thin silk over her face, looking through
it at the road and the grove of oaks, the sheep in
their field, all suddenly turned the color of sunsets.

She'd heard many times that her grandfather,
thane Leofwine, had once had great riches. Before
her wits had left her, her mother had told stories
of how the Saxon King Edward, called the Confessor, had come to visit Leofwine's manor at Edgerton
with his court one St. Bartholomew's Feast. The
court had stayed so long they'd eaten all of the
manor's harvest and Leofwine had had to borrow
from the old Bishop of Durham for food for the rest
of the year. When her mother had come to Leofwine's manor as a young bride, she'd brought no
fewer than four pack mules to carry her jewels and
clothes.

Someone was coming down the road. Ingrith
closed the chest, went to the front of the wagon and
climbed up on the seat. The Morlaix knights were

passing around a leather bottle of wine. Two were stretched out, asleep on the grass.

Quickly she pulled the scarf down to cover her face. A piece of glitter fell into her hand. When she looked at it she saw it was only a sliver of mica. Against the silk it had sparkled like a real gem.

"Drogo," one of the knights called.

The approaching horsemen went under overhanging trees and into the sunlight again. Drogo kicked one of the sleeping knights awake. He lifted himself on his elbow, yawning.

One rider was ruddy and big, his helmet slung from his saddle horn. There were red lights in his close-cropped hair. Ingrith recognized the other knight on a long-legged mare, leading a gray warhorse. His black hair was long and curling to his shoulders. When he turned to say something to the other knight, his profile showed clearcut as a hawk's.

So he has given in, she thought. She wondered what they had threatened him with.

Norman knights all looked alike with their long noses, big jaws. Her father and brothers had been fair-haired, strong men with bright blue eyes, fierce, steadfast, like the *fyrdmen* who had fought with Harold Godwineson at Senlac and proudly fallen where they stood.

The dark knight reined in under the oaks. The Morlaix knights scrambled to their feet. One kicked the wine bottle into the weeds.

He lifted his eyes to Ingrith standing on the wagon seat. "Gilbert, is this the way you keep your knights? In Palestine they'd be ripe for ambush."

The other knight cantered up. He looked up at

Ingrith, smiling. "Peace, Simon, I'm told there are few Saracen in Chestershire."

Now he was staring at the wagon. "What the devil is this?"

Drogo came forward, putting on his helmet. He saluted the red knight. "Sir Gilbert, we were told you would be here at noontide."

"Yes, well, we are late." Gilbert swung down from the saddle. "So late my sister's infernal wedding is not far behind."

The other knight dismounted, throwing the reins over the mare's neck. "God's face, we are traveling fast, we can't do it with that." He walked to the wagon and looked up at Ingrith. "Get down," he said.

Ingrith held the scarf over her face and looked down at him. This was the knight who had kept the castle guard from beating her. She saw he still had his hand bound in a strip of white cloth.

He was more handsome, she decided, with his sun-darkened skin and long curling black hair, than the lord of Morlaix's son. His mouth curved down, then up at the corners like a cat's. And his eyes were not black, but the color of winter leaves with gold specks in them. He was the sort women would sigh for, but his manner was cold.

Drogo was saying, "The stablemaster provided the wagon, Sir Gilbert. The little cart was for the procession of the Lady Alys, your sister, and her new husband. It was to carry musicians playing special tunes for their wedded happiness when they began their journey."

Gilbert struck his forehead. "Simon, did you hear this? We have taken my sister's damned musicians' wain! By the tripes of Saint Joseph, she will roast us alive."

Drogo said, "There was no other way. We were told the Saxon demoiselle cannot ride a horse."

"Everyone knows how to ride a horse. Simon," Gilbert said, turning, "they brought the wagon because the girl cannot ride."

The dark knight still stared at her. "I said, get down," he repeated.

Ingrith drew back, pressing the red veil to her face. They were not going to make her ride a horse. She would fight them first. They would have to hurt her, perhaps mark her, and she had heard Baron Malmsbury caution the dark one against that.

"She's lived no better than a serf, Sir Gilbert," Drogo said. "You should see how she eats. And she fights with her fists, like a man."

The other knight made a disbelieving noise under his breath. "God's wounds, they're afraid of her. Get down," he told Ingrith again.

Gilbert stroked his chin. "Malmsbury says the grandfather was a kinsman of Harold Godwineson's. Surely they would have had some sort of horse."

Ingrith stood stock-still. Thane Leofwine's sons had horses, many of them, until the Normans seized them. From behind the veil she said, "I will walk."

"The devil you will." The one called Simon turned to Morlaix's son. "Curse this whole venture, Gilbert. I would gladly give it to you, with my blessing."

The other smiled. "Hah, you resisted my father no better than I. But you are the anointed one." He stepped up to the side of the wagon. "Come down, girl." He held up his arms. "We will unhitch the mule from the wagon and you can ride that."

Ingrith did not move.

Gilbert frowned up at her. "She needs taming. This is what comes of letting good-looking women live wild, like beasts."

He reached for her again.

Ingrith looked down, her heart pounding, and balled her hands into fists. Although if she fought them now and they killed her, she was not sure if the bargain to look after her sisters and her mother would be honored.

The other knight said, "Dammit, girl, we will be riding hard, we can't follow you at a snail's pace in this thing."

It was not Ingrith's fault that she did not know horses, or how to ride. But she was Edmund Leofwineson's daughter, and they did not know it now but she did not intend to go south to become some Norman lord's whore.

She abruptly sat down on the wagon seat and pulled the veil away from her face. In all her life she could not remember that people had ever said that she was clever. But she had a scheme that was far better than the fate they had in store for her.

She shook out her hair with one hand. The wind picked it up and lifted it about her arms and shoulders, bright as sunlight. The lord of Morlaix's son stared.

"By the cross," Gilbert murmured, "I had forgotten."

"Yes, and a virgin." The corners of the other knight's mouth deepened. "With all that is glorious, Gilbert, including the dirt."

Ingrith braced her feet against the footboard of the wagon seat. "I will ride in the wagon," she said. She folded her arms across her breasts and regarded them steadily.

Simon de Bocage stared at her for a long moment. "Gilbert," he said, "get me a rope."

Gilbert de Jobourg threw back his red head and laughed.

# Chapter Four

*T*he friar's fingers snaked out to pick up the scraps of rabbit left on the spit, then tucked them into some hidden place in his habit. He was young and good-looking, but plainly ill-fed. Begging friars were forbidden by the laws of their order to ask for food or shelter, but since Gilbert de Jobourg had invited this one to share their dinner he was now rather furtively collecting his meat for the morrow.

"So the Truce of God was not working," the friar said. He licked his fingers, staring at the empty spit, plainly wishing for more. "The holy church had protested much that with their constant warring the magnates were tearing France—yea, all of Europe—apart."

Ingrith watched from the shadows by the wagon. She too had saved some rabbit from the meal. She chewed on a bone as she listened to the friar, who, now that the eating was over, was preaching about peace, and caring for the poor and oppressed. Most of the knights were talking among themselves and not listening, but she hiked herself closer. She had never heard of the Truce of God before.

People said more and more friars were coming to England from the south part of France, where there were many heretics. She had seen them preaching on country roadsides against such things as monks with fat cheeks and big bellies, and the riches of priories. And saying that Christ himself came of poor folk, and that even the Pope was a naked servant of God. Sometimes, because people misunderstood, the friars were stoned.

"Countrysides were made barren," the young friar went on in his ringing voice, "villeins were starving, the people of the towns ruined. In Normandy Duke Robert himself, before he went on Crusade, led his knights, neighbor against neighbor."

One of the Morlaix knights looked up. "As God is my judge, Duke Robert is a valorous man."

"Then I say to you," the friar shot at him, "what is valor at the destruction of one's own demesne? The barons were impoverishing themselves, destroying those hapless souls, their vassals. The Truce of God was not honored, it was then the church saw some way to call valorous knights, their squires and foot soldiers, in a just cause far from their suffering lands. And so this is how it came about." He looked around the circle. "That the Pope preached the Crusade to free the Holy Land."

Ingrith looked across the fire to where Gilbert of Morlaix sat with his cousin, the knight de Bocage. *That one*, she thought, watching him. If it had not been for Gilbert he would have bound her hand and foot and tossed her on the accursed mule. But, no need to damage the cargo, Gilbert had said, which would undoubtedly happen if they used force to make her do something she did not want to do. So in the end the other knight had walked away and not made her ride the beast.

He had cruel eyes, she decided as she licked the last of the juice from the bone and tossed it into the weeds. He had kept the guard from beating her in the tower room at Morlaix, it was true. But then he had showed how pitiless he could be about the horse.

Someone said, "Friar, you cannot say that the Pope preached a holy war because of the nobles. That makes a mockery of that brave and noble cause to free Christ's sepulcher!"

Ingrith put down her meat and bread in her lap and leaned forward to look at the speaker. Morlaix's company had been joined at sundown by some knights going north to serve the Earl of Chester's bailiff. The newcomers still looked and sounded like squires with their newly forged ring mail and loud, uncertain voices. A few had their hunting dogs with them, long-headed alaunts.

The new Chester knights had brought fresh bread from Chirk and the Morlaix party still had a good share of wedding wine, so they'd joined in the meal with the drink flowing freely. When the friar began to speak some of the Morlaix men drifted away, but the bailiff's young recruits had stayed, not wanting to turn in.

All knew of the great Crusade to free Jerusalem from the infidels, but no one there had heard of the Truce of God. Ingrith was not sure, even, where France was. From her place in the shadows she watched, thinking she'd never heard talk like this before.

A Morlaix knight leaned over the shoulder of a bailiff's knight. "Watch yourselves, children," he told them, "or yon friar will preach all night. They live for disputation. It is their meat and drink."

Gilbert de Jobourg grimaced. "Not this one. Not the way he has eaten and drunk here tonight."

There was loud laughter. The young brother only smiled. While they were taking their meal he had offered to recite poetry translating, he told them, to Norman French as he went from the Latin of ancient Romans.

Ingrith had not been able to follow his poems, the French was too different. They were not about love, nor even about ancient battles, but something on nature and the fields and the trees of the countryside.

The friar raised a pointing finger to the sky. "It is God's truth that the barons burn and sack each other's villages when they make these wars, and turn out the poor. Knights win in battle mostly unscathed, but the common soldiers, less well armed, are slaughtered in great numbers. And the suffering of the peasants, the burning of the fields and the carrying off of the beasts, is great."

Hooting, the young Chester knights threw bits of bread at him. "One lives for valor, you man in skirts," one of them shouted. "Would you take our livelihood?"

Undaunted, the friar cried, "God looks down and sees that the villein's home is destroyed and his family starves while his victorious lord rides away! Even then, alas, it is not over. This same lord will come back to his vassal to claim that which he has lost. And punish him brutally if he cannot pay it."

Drogo came to the fire. "Look you, preacher, it is man's nature to war."

A young Chester knight shouted, "Do you dare denounce well-earned plunder?"

"Wait." A young knight got up and crossed to the other side. "Here is one who can speak for us. A knight who has fought for God among the heathen. A sworn Crusader from the Holy Land."

Simon de Bocage said, without looking up, "All war is stealing."

There was an outburst from the younger knights. A voice cried, "Sir, surely there is more to it than that!"

"Plunder, then." He looked around at them. "We left a wasteland behind us to the Danube, not a piece of bread, not a donkey in its stall. And this was called forage, not plunder, supposed only to feed us until we reached Palestine."

There was a silence. Then another voice said, "Truly, sir, you were there?"

Gilbert looked at his cousin. "Aye, the Leopard was there. Antioch and Jerusalem, too."

There was a babble of voices. "Antioch," a Chester knight said, awed. "And the finding of the Holy Lance in the Crusade's darkest hour. We have heard such wondrous tales."

"Were you there, sir," another wanted to know, "at the finding of the Holy Lance that pierced our Lord Christ's side?"

Simon looked across the fire, frowning. "Yes, and Peter Bartholomew tried to pass himself off as a monk. But the truth of it was, he was but a servant to a Flemish pilgrim. And before that, a rope dancer and traveling show trickster."

Ingrith took out a piece of bread where she'd hidden it in her bodice and broke off a piece. She'd heard only a little herself, and that from priests, how the Holy Lance that had pierced Christ's side at the crucifixion had saved God's armies besieged by the heathen Saracen. But now what Simon de Bocage was saying sounded quite different.

Slowly, he answered their questions. But instead of fine holy wars with blazing heroes and kings, he told of armies under their Christian princes not faring well, of verminous men wracked by fever, brutalized, bewildered and starving by the time they reached the great city of Antioch.

The Christian forces had encircled Antioch and besieged it. When victory was gained the Crusaders rushed inside the walls to loot and plunder and murder. But the Turks and Saracens craftily encircled them, and made the Christian armies the besieged.

In the silence the friar said, "I have heard it was to the chaplain to the Count of Toulouse to whom Peter Bartholomew first spoke about his dream that Saint Andrew and Christ himself had come to him outside Antioch's walls with a message for our Holy army."

The dark knight shrugged. "Antioch teemed with visionaries. Starving men saw angels, Christ and the Virgin Mary, the throne of God—it was a nightly occurrence."

Ingrith watched him across the leaping flames. He was not saying what the young knights wanted to hear. He was not like the rest of them, not even like his cousin, Gilbert. But from the moment she had seen him she had known, somehow, that he would help her escape. Since that first meeting in the tower at Morlaix a wonderful plan had come to her. That if this knight, picked to take her to London, were to break his oath and deliver her as something less than a virgin, then the lords and barons would punish him more than they would her.

It was so simple Ingrith had worried for days there was something wrong with it. Yet, she reasoned, if he delivered spoiled goods, it was plain they would no longer want her.

"But the Pope himself has vouched for the miracle," a young knight was arguing.

"Miracle?" He raised a skeptical brow. "The papal legate was the most doubtful of all, even though he gave permission to excavate under the Church of St. Peter."

Ingrith was sure her plan would work. She had considered that she could not run away; if she did the Normans would only catch and punish her. But if the Norman knight would be blamed, the marcher lords would not turn her mother and sisters out of their house for something that was not her fault. That is, that she, a maid of almost seventeen years had been seduced and despoiled by their sworn knight while on her way to London to be some great man's leman.

Simon de Bocage was describing the church in the besieged city, and the search for what had been seen in Peter Bartholomew's vision. A hole was dug that looked as though it would undermine St. Peter's, altar and all, but it was empty. Then, when the crowd was drifting away, Peter Bartholomew himself leaped into the pit and found something which he held up and proclaimed as the Holy Lance of Christ. A thing small enough to fit into the palm of his hand.

A young knight cried from across the fire, "The miracle!"

Ingrith turned to look at him. It was possible she had not thought of everything, she told herself. But even if they whipped and branded her afterward and sold her to a bawdyhouse, she could think of another plan. If she could think of the first scheme, she was sure she could think of another. And she wanted to be free, she was desperate.

Ah, God in heaven, she had seen enough of the world now, and the Normans and their women, to know one did not have to live in starving and misery! Or to be taken, like a beast, to serve some man in a far distant place.

"Yes, the miracle," Simon was telling them. His dark face was sardonic. "The Count of Toulouse's chaplain snatched the thing up and began kissing it. It would have taken a brave man at that moment to say that the lance had been shaken out of Bartholomew's sleeve and dropped into the hole. But I have always thought that would be no large feat for a traveling-show trickster."

Several young Chester knights got to their feet. One shouted, "You lie! Who could declare false this miracle that so many witnessed?"

A redheaded knight angrily strode up. "Deny, sir, that the Holy Lance became our talisman, unwrapped from its fine silk and brocade swaddlings to show and inspire Christian men when they went into battle. And from that time on that it guided them to God's holy victories!"

He looked up at him. "You are Norman, are you not? Well, know that Normans were skeptical to a man, it was only the cloud-headed Provençals that believed in it. So many doubted, even in all the ecstasy and fainting, that Peter Bartholomew pleaded to take the ordeal by fire, carrying the lance in his hands, to prove that it was true."

"And was vindicated," someone yelled.

"Yes, Bartholomew walked through the fire holding it, saying that if it was the true lance of Christ he would emerge unburned. But if false, he would be consumed by fire. Afterward the crowd carried him on their shoulders, his skin hanging in shreds, shouting and singing in triumph. One week later he died." He stood up. "I have seen men take that long to die of burns."

Simon walked away from the fire. The other bailiff's knights stayed where they were, arguing. Some Morlaix knights went off to the meadow to lie down in their cloaks to sleep. A heavy dew was falling. One came back to the fire for a wineskin and then went off again, calling to the others.

Ingrith hugged her knees. She didn't see why Simon de Bocage was called a hero when he did not believe in the holy miracle of which even the far reaches of the Welsh marches had heard. From what he said, the Holy Lance was a sham. The great holy war in the east did not sound at all the way other people told of it.

She heard someone come up in the dark. She jumped when a voice said, "You do not need to hide.

I told Chester's men you were a rich merchant's young wife and we were your escorts."

She got to her feet and brushed the remains of the food out of her skirt. In the meadow, the bailiff's knights were drunkenly singing. She said, "Did they believe you?"

"No." He pushed her ahead of him. "They think I am taking you to Shrewsbury, to Robert of Belleme."

She twisted to look back at him. "Who is that?"

"Satan himself." He was serious. "Get into the wagon. I will sleep beside you in there, Gilbert on the other side."

He helped Gilbert haul the chests out of the wagon bed. When they were through Ingrith crawled over the tailgate. "Keep on your mail," she heard him say to Gilbert. "And your sword."

The two men climbed into the wagon and lay down. After a few minutes they sat up to unbuckle their greatswords and put them within reach. The floorboards were full of splinters that caught on their mail. Gilbert muttered, settling himself. He sat up again to pull off his helmet and place it by his hip.

"Our knights are between us and the meadow," he said, lying down again and closing his eyes. "Drogo stands guard."

Simon de Bocage removed his helmet and lay down with a thump, making the wagon shake. Lying on their backs they crossed themselves, then put their palms together and muttered their prayers.

Ingrith did not join them. Her family had done little praying since England's defeat. She crossed her hands over her breast and drew her body into a small space. The wagon bed was narrow, it would be hard to sleep.

In a few moments they were snoring. She lay awake, staring at the stars.

She was lying between two Norman knights, their bodies hemming her in. Her breath suddenly began to come in gasps. Ingrith tried not to give in to it, afraid they would hear and waken, but she could not put her panic aside. There had been eight of them that day she and her sisters came out of the woods carrying the firewood on their backs. They had looked like serfs with their heads covered, in their muddy clothes. Gudrun started for the river, the baby on her hip bouncing and screaming. She had been raped before; her baby Edith was some Norman knight's child.

Ingrith had taken a stick of wood from her pack, hoping to kill one of them before they took her. "Ah, here's the meat," one of them had shouted. She remembered fighting them, kicking and biting, but a knight dragged her up before him. The last she had seen of her sisters they were standing in the muddy field weeping as she bounced across a Norman knight's saddle.

Next to her the ruddy knight, Gilbert, stirred and turned on his side. The other Norman made a snoring noise through his nose. She thought about the story of the Holy Lance, and wondered why he didn't believe in it, when the Pope and all of Christendom knew that the Lance was real.

Slowly, the terrible gasping went away. After a while she turned her face to him. The light from the fire had died down but she could make out the shadows of his eyes, the set, carved jaw.

No one needed to explain to her what men did to women; she had been there in the oat field when it happened to Gudrun. Even at best, in marriage, the thing was hardly pleasurable. She'd never heard even the villeins' wives boast of it. What farm animals did was clumsy and base. What men did to women was the same.

She studied his face. Black lashes lay against his smooth-shaven cheek. Asleep, his mouth was sensuous.

Normans like this one had harried Edmund Leofwineson and his sons to their deaths. In her dreams she could still hear them pounding on the door in the middle of the night. The last of Leofwine's line, her young brother Wulfstan, was fallen upon by three knights from the Chester garrison. Three men against one lone thirteen-year-old boy, giving no quarter, because they wanted the sport of killing a Saxon.

Perhaps once long ago she would have thought it unworthy to trick this Norman. To let him take the blame. But not now.

Not even when it was likely that they would kill him for what they would see as his treachery.

She closed her eyes, willing herself to sleep.

She could not say that she cared.

# Chapter Five

*T*he wain broke down at St. Dunstan's cross. The knight driving it leaped clear but Ingrith, taken by surprise, went over backwards into the wagon bed.

Simon cantered up quickly. He reached down and hauled her upright. "Christ in heaven, do you never wear shoes?"

Shoes? She'd been flat on her back, her skirt around her ears. When he lifted her, she'd pressed against him, thinking of her plan, but he let go of her so quickly she dropped down in the wagon and almost went over again.

The mule, its ears laid back, would not pull the wain out of the crossroads. The rear axle had broken and it dragged in the dirt like an anchor. After several heaves the knights fell back, rubbing their shoulders.

Gilbert climbed down from his horse, pulled his hauberk over his head, and flung it into the wagon. The sun was warm. He peeled off his padded undershirt and flexed his muscles. He was a big man;

the skin of his arms and shoulders were covered with gold freckles. Sitting on the bank, Ingrith watched him.

Simon de Bocage saw it. "Gilbert, the power of the mind, not brute strength, is what's wanted," he called to him.

In answer Gilbert reached up with both hands and dragged Simon from his horse. "I knew we were lacking something," he said, grinning.

Sitting in the dirt, Simon unbuckled his sword, then peeled off his mail and shirt. Stripped to the waist he was taller than Gilbert, sleek-muscled where the other was massive. A line of fine black hair ran from his breastbone into the waist of his hose.

They looked each other over. Then, with the knights watching, they grunted and pulled until they had turned the wagon over on its side. Only a small part of the wood had burst and frayed. The rest had been sawn nearly in two.

"Christ crucified, we are lucky it brought us beyond Chirk." Gilbert squatted on his haunches. "How did this happen?"

Simon rubbed his dirty hands together. "If this was the musicians' wagon, perhaps what we are seeing is their revenge."

Gilbert cursed, feelingly. "Miserable offal. I agree with my father, music is inflicted on mankind by the Devil. Ballad singers and harpists are the worst."

"With some rope from the wagon," Drogo offered, "we can lash the axle with a sapling."

A small oak was uprooted and a young knight

with big hands trimmed it with his sword. It was bound to the axle with a length of rope.

When they were through, Simon took Ingrith by the arm. "You are not getting back in the wagon." With his hand in the small of her back he pushed her to his horse.

When she saw what he wanted her to do she dug in her heels. He dragged her, resisting. She managed to twist out of his grip and tried to scramble away. He grabbed her by the skirt of her dress. Frightened by the scuffle, the Saracen mare shied and kicked out at them.

"God's wounds!" Simon kneed the mare hard in the belly, then grabbed the reins and yanked her head around. He looped the reins under his elbow and hauled Ingrith to him hand over hand by her long skirt. Frantic, she tried to bite him.

The knights moved their horses up to watch. "They are two against you, Simon," Gilbert called, "the horse and the girl. I'll wager a firkin of wine you lose."

Simon grabbed the girl by the elbow. She was proving to be a large measure of trouble. First she'd tried to sever his thumb, and now she would not ride a horse.

Quickly, while the mare danced around them, he shoved her off balance, then bent to lift her. She was not light, but before she could struggle he had boosted her over his shield and onto the mare's crupper. He kicked the mare again, hard, as she curled her neck and tried to bite the girl's leg. The girl shrieked.

From his saddle, Gilbert roared with laughter. The knights cheered. Grim-faced, Simon mounted and dragged the girl upright behind him. She sat with both legs hanging over one side. He seized her leg behind the knee and forced it over the horse's back. The mare walked in a circle, stiff-legged, neck arched, spewing foam from her bit. Cursing, Simon hit her between the ears with his fist, knowing full well it would do no good. The mare hardly felt it.

Gilbert wiped the tears from his eyes.

"Shut up," Simon said.

He turned the mare in the direction of the road. Behind him, Gilbert led the destrier. In the rear, someone took the mule's reins. The sun went under a cloud and a wind blew over the ripening grain fields. The girl stopped sobbing and clutched his shoulders. After a few minutes she put her arms around his waist. Through his mail he could feel the warmth of her body pressed against him.

In the morning, Simon told himself, he would see to it they left the wain by the roadside and made her ride the mule. It didn't matter how much she shrieked, they had a long way to go. Too long to put up with Saxon foolishness. His bitten hand throbbed, even now.

The Morlaix knights formed a double column, horses at a walk. The friar they'd picked up at evening meal had fallen behind and had not caught up, and no one mentioned him.

They traveled under a cloudy sky as far as the Stafford byway. The road there curled over a line of small hills. On it, a troop of twenty or more knights were coming from the east.

Gilbert ordered his knights to take up their shields and put on their helmets. Aimeric broke out the Morlaix colors and rode up to take a place beside him.

The two columns dressed their lines. A man in plum-colored velvet rode with the Earl of Shrewsbury's standard above, a provost's banner below. A number of prisoners chained together, on foot, brought up the rear.

Gilbert said, his lips not moving, "That is not a mountain on horseback in front of us but the Frankish butcher, Heinrich of Máinz, captain of Shrewsbury's garrison. Belleme's lands are near." He cut his eyes. "A sweet lot, are they not?"

Simon grunted. The Earl of Shrewsbury's knights wore ring mail so bright it shot sparks of light. Fine burnished steel helmets with nasals and cheekpieces covered their heads and faces. Robert of Belleme of Normandy, the Earl of Shrewsbury, whom the holy church denounced as Satan incarnate, was one of the richest men in western Christendom.

Under his breath Simon said, "A fine turnout."

"Oh, deadly." Gilbert rose in his stirrups. The shackled men, heads bent, shuffled in the rear. "Sweet Jesu, I know that prisoner." He sat down again. "Ernaut Cadurcis, I fought with him in Glamorgan under Chester."

The German in the barrel helmet with a bronze eagle crest rode past the provost. "De Jobourg," he called.

The Earl of Shrewsbury's captain saluted Gilbert. He stared, curious, at Simon, then slowed his mount to a walk to look at the girl. The provost did not stop. The Shrewsbury knights passed two by two, eyes gleaming. The prisoners hobbled slowly, a man-at-arms followed at their back with a pike.

Gilbert swore again. He turned in the saddle, watching a man in a bloodstained jacket. "By all that's holy, that is Cadurcis."

Simon slowed the Saracen mare. "Gilbert, they outnumber us two to one."

"Ah no, not that. Cadurcis is no better than those that have him. It's Belleme's taste for knights that turns my stomach."

The mare broke into a trot to keep up with the destrier. The girl's grip on Simon tightened as she bounced behind him.

"He's Satan," Gilbert shouted, "that filth Belleme. The church denounces him, but does nothing. The whole tribe of Montgomerys are the devil's own spawn. The mother, Mabel Talvas, was hell's own demon, murdered naked in her bed after her bath. And after an unspeakable life."

Simon stared after the prisoners. "They are all knights?"

"Yes, he does not ransom them, God rot his soul, like an honorable man. This German gathers them in his net when Belleme is in England. Then he delivers them to his castle in Shrewsbury so that Belleme may vilely abuse brave knights for his mealtime amusement." Gilbert's voice grated. "Goddamn them, while Belleme is eating his dinner they torture them for a show, like juggling or wrestling! And his high-born women are just as avid."

There was a moment's silence. "I have seen Saracen torture," Simon said. "It breaks strong men."

"You have seen nothing." Gilbert spat into the dirt. "They tell me knights weep like babes when one arm and then the other is cut off and laid before them. The wounds are sealed with a hot iron so they will not bleed to death too quickly. Then they begin on the legs."

Simon turned and looked back. "The German liked the girl."

He snorted. "Yes, well, you cannot say she looks like a rich merchant's wife, riding like that. If his German wits are working, he may think to come back for her."

Under his breath, Simon swore. "I would as lief be traveling with an open sack of gold tied to my saddle as this girl. There must be some way to make her decent. Give her a cloak to wear, a bag to cover her head. Or dress her as a boy."

Gilbert stared. "A boy? Simon, you would never get that form into male clothes. Or if you did, we would be fighting off both—"

"Gilbert," he said shortly, "let it rest."

The road turned south at a stand of hawthorne trees. Here they passed between swampy meadows dotted with ponds. Locusts droned in the weeds, and the warm air was full of stinging gnats. The knights swatted at them, cursing.

After a while Simon said, "This mad journey is no task for an honorable knight, Gilbert. If it were not for you and your father, I would be on the road to Paris and a quiet life in the colleges."

His cousin turned to him. "You? In the colleges? When any of my knights would gladly give both balls to fight as you do? You are famous even in Wales. Even in benighted Scotland."

"Gilbert."

"God's wounds, Simon, do not sulk because we've met Belleme's butchers. Prince Henry has pledged to rid England of him, I have heard with my own ears. Belleme and the rest of King William's friends have starved and burned us out since the last rebellion. We will not be forgetting the year of ninety-five, and how noble families were destroyed. In all truth, I do not know how Morlaix was spared."

"Your father is the boldest of barons."

Gilbert looked gloomy. "England is in disgrace, the Pope would excommunicate the king if it were not for the archbishop, who is himself in exile. Now the barons are squeezed, down to villeins and sokemen, even the towns, so that one cannot make a good trade nor bring in a decent crop. Ask my father. It is damnable persecution and robbery, day and night."

Simon looked away. "I have no love for the English, they will always give you the worst of it. More than the French."

"God's face, what does that mean?"

"You know what I'm saying. If they think you have the curse of Jewish blood."

"Oh, that." Gilbert looked uncomfortable. "By the cross, Simon, believe me when I say my sister loved you as a brother. I swear to you this had nothing to do with her marriage."

"Gilbert."

"She always knew she would marry, you know how it is with girls like Alys," the other man said rapidly. "A few months, and if the Frenchman treats her well, she will love him dearly."

"Christ in heaven, Gilbert, will you shut up?"

He shrugged. "Well, it's risky to speak of any Jew, although I hear that they are a goodly race. Good to their own, is what I mean. At least their women are pretty."

"Gilbert, being part Jew has dogged me sorely all my life, as well you know." He stopped for a moment, frowning. "It is hard to understand, when in the east the Saracens grant the Hebrew as much as any other good citizen."

"Perhaps it is because the Jews killed Christ," Gilbert said earnestly. "Or so the priests tell us."

Simon turned in the saddle. "Why do you believe that? One has only to read the Scripture to know it is untrue."

"Cousin, first one has to be able to read. And since I cannot, I must believe what I'm told." He said, persuasive, "Come, you and I are Englishmen, like Prince Henry himself we were born here, and we are much different from our Norman fathers. And Simon, for what you are doing the prince will love you much."

"Hah."

"Ah, but you agreed to it."

Simon said, harshly, "I was mad." He settled in his saddle and closed his eyes. "Not for threats nor for money. Help us to save England, your father said."

Gilbert laughed.

The wagon's axle gave way again in a place where the Wrexham road crossed over a marsh. There was nowhere to fix it as the shoulders were too narrow, so with the knights pushing, Gilbert hauling the mule by its reins, they dragged the wain a torturous mile to higher ground. There they found a parklike grove of oak trees with deep grass for the horses. The knights raced for a small stream and waded into it, throwing the cool water on their gnat-bitten faces and heads.

Simon pulled the Saxon girl down from the back of the mare and set her on her feet. Gilbert went off, shouting to Drogo.

"Come, it is not all that bad," he told her. He could not imagine anyone so terrified of riding a horse. A pillion, at that. "You will get used to it. Tomorrow you can ride the mule."

She threw him a vicious look before she stumbled away.

The Morlaix knights watered their horses and began gathering wood for the cook fires. After some while they heard music, as with a traveling show, and a few knights left to climb the bank to the road. The Saxon girl sat down on the ground and put her head in her hands.

It was still warm, though the afternoon light was fading. Simon walked the Saracen mare and the stallion and watered them. The mare pretended unknown terrors when he curried her but the war horse stood still, only turning its big head to look back as Simon picked out his feet. In battle the stallion was fierce, ramming other horses, biting, lashing out with his huge hooves. All other times he was mild and steady.

Music and voices crossed the marsh on the wind. A shepherd came into sight on the road, hurrying a flock of sheep ahead of mailed outriders. Musicians appeared behind the sheep, playing viols and drums. Then came a wagonload of mummers singing to the musicians' tunes.

Gilbert had been soaking his feet in the stream. "Sweet Jesu, it's my sister." He hobbled across the grass, pulling on his boots. "Where's the accursed wagon? Hide it! Get it out of sight!"

Horns blatted a fanfare. Clouds of blackbirds lifted from the oak trees. A troop of knights carrying pennants rode past. The groom's party rode heavy-boned Flemish horses with bridles of silver-chased leather, cheekpieces decorated with tassels. The men wore velvet and silk without mail, their long hair, oiled and curled, reaching to their shoulders. The women were in glittering samite, silk veils, with pins and bracelets of enamelwork and jewels. A dwarf bounded along under the horses' hooves, beating a drum and bawling jokes and dirty songs.

The Morlaix knights lined the road to watch. The dwarf ran back and picked up a drumstick he had dropped. Men-at-arms came down each side of the road, pikes on their shoulders. Between them rode a dark-haired girl in a heavily embroidered gold dress. She looked tired but she bent, smiling, to speak to the man riding next to her. Both horses had gold-embroidered red hoods, the color of weddings. Red velvet panels hung from the groom's saddle in the French style and dragged in the dust.

Gilbert reached the road just as his sister passed by. She didn't see him, she had eyes only for her calf of a husband, Helias d'Aubigny.

Gilbert wanted to buy meat and wine from the sutlers. Somewhere, he told himself, was Lucie of Dapisoun. He remembered her as sleek and red-headed. Not ravishingly pretty. But still.

Then he remembered his cousin. He thought: Saint George save us, *Simon*. And Alys.

He had never been able to fathom his cousin's passion for his twit of a sister, who was no great beauty. But he could not deny the passion was there.

He had reflected many times that some men were certain—in the case of his cousin Simon, from childhood—that there was only one woman in this world to love. His own experience had shown him the problem was not that, but rather how to narrow down the delectable choices from eleven or twelve to four or five. Christ in heaven, Gilbert told himself, just deciding on one woman was enough to keep a man a bachelor for life!

He approached some servants unhitching the teams from the baggage wains and asked for the lady Lucie. They pointed, vague. Gilbert went off, seeing there were half a hundred or so members of the wedding party milling about under the trees, shouting for grooms to come unsaddle the horses. He told himself that was the French for you; they would tell you anything you wanted to hear. He would never find d'Aubigny's tantalizing cousin from Artois.

Simon hobbled the mare and the stallion and put them out for the night. The Saxon girl watched him as he tended his horses. That unwavering stare wearied him. Not for the first time, he cursed himself for agreeing to take such a savage creature southward. He called the young knight, Aimeric, to keep a watch on her. He left him squatting on his heels talking to her.

Simon told himself he only wanted to have a moment to see Alys. It was stupid, it was foolish, God knows he did not want to face her, or speak to her, yet his heart was slamming against the bones of his chest just thinking about it. Worse, he could not help a rush of wild yearning. When he gained the road he stopped short, partly hidden in trees.

A double file of men-at-arms trudged along. Then he saw her, riding beside her new husband. Fair Alys with her smiling face. He stood dumbstruck, unable to help himself. She had not changed.

In England this time he'd found everyone older, worn, but here she was, his enduring dream, miraculously the same. The same cloud of soft, dark hair. The fine, winged brows. Her little nose, her sweetly agreeable mouth.

He suddenly wanted to rush up and pull her down from her horse. Hold her tightly to him. His mind reeled with the sense of it. It had been so long since he'd felt tenderness. In the next moment he told himself, *They have been married many days. He's had her more than once by now. She is no longer yours*. Then he thought: *She was never mine*.

The man riding beside her was blond, heavy-eyed, handsome. He could see how some untried maid would find it hard to deny this Frenchman, with her mother and father, her family, urging her on.

The notion made his head pound. God's death, he was mad to think of them together, the Frenchman thrusting himself into her, someone she did not love, and taking her maidenhead.

Simon stepped back, suddenly needing the shadows. The world and time had slipped away while he was in the Holy Land. He wished he'd never come back to England.

He turned from the road and went down the bank, stumbling a little in the dusk.

\* \* \*

Ingrith had seen Simon de Bocage start for the road. Curious, she said to Aimeric, "Let us go up there. I wish to see if it is the wedding from Morlaix."

He looked doubtful. He was a little bit taller than she, broad-shouldered, with silky brown hair. "Demoiselle," he protested, "I do not think it is allowed that you leave our camp."

She stepped to him and put her fingers on the back of his wrist as she had seen Norman women do. His eyes were soft brown. She let her lashes sweep down and up. "We will not go far, only to the road," she murmured. "And you will be with me all the way."

She had never done such a thing before but it worked well enough. At least he followed her. She took long strides, the silk skirts switching around her ankles. She stopped at the top of the bank. It was the Morlaix wedding. She could not help staring openmouthed as it passed. They were enchanted, these French; they sparkled with riches. She did not see the Morlaix bride. She'd had only a glimpse of the Lady Alys once, when she was crossing the ward one rainy day with servants and the lady of the castle, her mother.

Two Frenchwomen slowed their horses to stare at her standing there by the side of the road. One turned in the saddle to say something to a man behind her. All heads turned then to Ingrith.

"Demoiselle," Aimeric said. He took her arm.

She knew she must go. But when she stepped back she saw Simon de Bocage standing under the trees. At that moment a line of men-at-arms came down the road. Riding between them was the bride on a white palfrey. She was small, rather thin, with soft gray eyes and dark hair. Her chin was bony, but her childish mouth was quick to laugh.

She couldn't keep herself from staring at the girl on the pretty white horse. Happiness and good fortune were this little Norman bride's future, and wealth, a long life, many fine children. There were no hardships to speak of in her fine, protected world. It was something she, Ingrith Edmundsdaughter, had never known. Out of the corner of her eye she saw the knight de Bocage, not a stone's throw away. Something in his face stopped her. She'd seen starving serfs stare that way at a loaf of bread.

There was no mistaking that besotted look. Their dour hero was gazing at the little Norman bride like a starveling. Holy Mother, she wondered, could it be he nursed a passion for his liege lord's daughter?

The notion so unsettled her she had to fight down a burst of laughter. If it was true, there was justice in the world, after all! This Norman who had dragged her about, wanting to tie her hand and foot, who had forced her to ride behind him in spite of her terror of horses. Here he was, mooncalfing in the dark where he thought no one could see him!

She must have gurgled out loud. Aimeric turned to look at her. The bride turned, smiling, to the man beside her. From his fine red clothes he could only be the new husband.

Ingrith caught her breath.

Her first thought was that this too could not be. But she heard again the thunder of hooves in the frozen field, the shouts of the knights as they galloped down on her. And then she saw the face of the one who had dragged her up to his saddle.

The new bridegroom bent his head, the late sun striking his face. She saw the shape of his nose, his handsome full mouth.

The maid of Morlaix's new husband was the same man.

# Chapter Six

*A*cross the road the wedding party set up brightly colored tents. The bride and groom retired early. Not so the rest of their guests. Torches were lit, a troop of rope dancers strung their web in the trees, and the traveling mummers put on a loud, bawdy performance. All through the d'Aubigny camp there was a display of candles and torches so extravagant that villeins from nearby villages left the work of the harvest and came to stare at the nobles on their way back to France. After a while the band of musicians put out their coin baskets and struck up a tune in the hope of luring the peasants to dance.

A representation of Morlaix knights, Gilbert with them, went to pay their respects and buy some wine. They didn't return. But Helias d'Aubigny, Gilbert's new brother-in-law, sent back word there was drink and entertainment for all, with his compliments. The Morlaix knights cheered.

They went back and forth in relays, growing merrier after each trip. At midnight, Drogo went over

to call them all back to camp, posting the two sob-
erest knights as guards.

Ingrith lay in the bed of the wagon, wrapped in
the martenskin cloak, listening to the merrymaking
across the road. Simon de Bocage had left early and
alone for the sutlers' wagons; she had seen him
come back much later with a wineskin. Now he was
somewhere in the Morlaix camp drinking.

So he pined for a little chit of a Norman girl he
couldn't have. He'd suffer even more if she told him
the sort of knight his beloved was married to! She
hadn't known the name until she'd seen him. Helias
d'Aubigny. He was the one who had run her down
in the field that day and stolen her, even while he
was in England to be married. If he would do that,
Ingrith told herself, he would hardly be faithful to
his wife, and make her happy.

She shifted to find a more comfortable position
in the wagon bed and put her arm behind her head.
Now more than ever she was certain Simon de Bocage would be her way to escape. She remembered
the first time she had seen him in Morlaix Castle.
She'd known even then that her *wyrd*—her fate—
rested with him, but she could not have said why.

She turned over on her side, pulling the cloak
with her. The broken axle let the wain down so that
she rested on a slope, her feet braced on the tailgate.
But the wagon was the only place, at the moment,
that she wanted to be. Knights still wandered about
under the trees looking for more wine, and talking
about the mummers' show which had charged a
pence to see an entertainment so wicked it was a
good thing the French churchmen had retired for
the night. Some had so much to drink they had

trouble finding their way into the trees to relieve themselves. One staggered up to the wagon, and if Ingrith had not raised up in time, shouting, he would have pissed down the side.

It was at times like these that she wished she could carry a dagger like the Norman ladies. *Now here comes another one,* she thought. She lay still, her fists clenched, listening. She heard him lurching about nearby in the alder bushes.

Falling down in the alder bushes was more like it. There was the sound of branches breaking, a body coming to earth heavily, followed by an oath. The underbrush crackled again as whoever it was got to his feet, cursing.

She suddenly wondered where Drogo was. She had seen the knights' captain earlier, posting the guards, not so sober himself.

Across the road there was a roar of laughter in the mummers' camp, followed by a roll of drums. In the dark the intruder ran into the wagon and rebounded with a grunt. She saw two scarred hands appear and grip the sideboards not far from her face. Alarmed, she sat bolt upright.

A face showed at eye level. She knew it at once even with hooded eyes squinting, the long black hair tangled and wild. He was not wearing his mail. His padded coat was open to his waist, exposing a sun-browned, muscular chest.

Simon de Bocage peered at her hazily. Then as she watched, he sank out of sight. Ingrith leaned over the side and saw him crouched on his knees, shaking his head.

Sweet heaven but he was drunk! Gone was the iron-faced knight, replaced by this stumbling stranger. She watched as he ran his fingers through his hair. She wondered if he had drunk all the wine in the wineskin. If so, he could outdrink a Saxon.

She saw him grasp the wheel and haul himself to his feet. Staggering, he started in the direction of the road.

"No," Ingrith said under her breath. She put one leg over the side of the wagon. He couldn't go back to the wedding party, there was no telling what he would do.

Halfway out of the wagon she stopped. The Baron of Morlaix might be liege lord here, not to mention the wedding so close by with its priests and nobles. On the other hand, there was no better time. She needed him just as he was.

She jumped from the wagon and hurried after him. He had gotten as far as the knights sleeping by the fire. He stopped and looked around, then veered off under the trees and into the alders again. The dark enveloped him. The bushes crashed. She heard a curse.

"De Bocage?" One of the knights raised himself on his elbow. When there was no answer, he lay back down again.

Ingrith had held her breath. Now she had to be quick before he roused the whole camp. With so many knights still about it was not going to be easy to get him alone long enough to have him despoil her.

She groped through the branches. A half-moon had risen but a mist was gathering, making the woods seem mysterious. Somewhere an owl called.

She almost fell over him. He lay on his stomach

in the alders, his feet sticking out. Ingrith bent over him, bracing her hands on her knees.

"Come, you must get up," she whispered. They were still not out of earshot. When he did not move she lifted one heavy arm and rolled him over on his back.

He looked up at her, eyes clouded. "Mmmm," he said.

"Get up," she hissed.

He gazed at her with his long, dark eyes. She grasped both his hands and hauled, glad she was strong, otherwise she would not have been able to move someone of his size. She managed to get him as far as his knees. He wrapped his arms around her waist. They lurched forward and he buried his face in her breasts.

*Mother of heaven.* Breathing hard, she pushed him away. Taking his arm she backed up a few steps, pulling him to his feet. Then she lost her grip on him, and with a groan he pitched forward onto his face. He lay still.

She could have wept. She called him every bad thing she could think of in a whisper. Panting, she rolled him over.

They were now at the top of a knoll. Putting her hands in the small of his back she pushed until she rolled him over again. He was clad only in his boots, belted hose, and the opened jacket. To her horror he kept rolling.

She dove for him and caught a handful of his long hair but it slid out of her grasp. He rolled down the incline for what seemed an eternity and came to a stop at the bottom, his face buried in leaves.

Ingrith plunged down the bank and came to a

stop beside him. She got to her knees and pushed him over on his back and brushed the leaves from his face.

His eyes were closed but he had not hit a stone on his way down nor been damaged in any way, she saw with relief. Except for some dirt in his nostrils he seemed to be unhurt. She brushed it away with shaking fingers.

He hiccoughed, looking at her from under half-closed eyes. "M'drink," he murmured.

"No!" Holy mother, he could wait until the morrow to drown his sorrows. She stared at bare skin over ribbed muscles, the indent of his belly button. A leather sword belt studded with metal was slung at his hips. Under it, she saw, taking a deep breath, was the waistband of his hose.

She reached for the belt buckle. When she tugged at it he stirred and put his hand over hers. "What?" he said.

She knocked his hand away. With a great pull the belt came loose. She dropped it in the grass beside him.

Stretched out, one could see he was sleek, narrow-hipped, long legs covered with cross-gartered hose. The bulge in his crotch, Ingrith thought; that's what she was seeking. She told herself he was a ruthless pillaging Norman robber. Her enemy.

Still, she closed her eyes and said a hurried prayer. She needed all her courage for what she was about to do. She thought of her mothers and sisters.

The waistband of his hose, run through with a cord, would not come undone. She struggled with it. Then, once loosened, the knot still would not give. She could only pull the hose down to his groin.

She pushed her hand under his hips. The hard, warm flesh of his buttocks rested against her wrists as she yanked the hose down from the back. She saw that he wore a cod strap to keep from chafing in the saddle. Her fingers worked at the cloth. At least he was clean. Her probing fingers seemed to tickle him. Eyes closed, he put his hands to his groin, faintly smiling.

She sat back on her heels.

If he was changed when he was drunk, he was even more so when the corners of his mouth turned up in a crooked smile. Without his usual bleak look he was dark and sensuous-looking, a man the maids would sigh for when they sang their spinning songs. Her fingers pulled at the knots in the cod strap and it came away.

She tried not to look, telling herself she really did not want to see. Face turned away, she put her hand around his privates. She found the thing—things— were soft-skinned and dry. Even when she grasped them they moved about alarmingly. Then a substantial part of what she was touching began to swell. Huskily, he groaned.

She had to look down.

He lay on his back with his jacket fallen away showing a hair-sprinkled chest and bare belly. Below that she had pulled his hose down across his thighs.

She sucked in her breath. Oh, sweet Mother Mary, it was truly hideous. A huge, ruddy, ugly thing. Even as she watched, it grew and stuck up farther out of a mat of black hair.

The man before her lifted one knee, then dropped it back. Ingrith took a deep breath. She told herself she'd come this far, that she would disgrace her good Saxon blood if she lacked the will to finish it.

He lifted his head to peer at her. Ingrith pushed him back again. Young girls lost their maidenheads every day, thousands of them if one counted all the virgins in the world.

She reached out to wrap her fingers around his shaft again and stopped. There seemed to be something wrong. She had to bend over him in the darkness to see.

Ah God, it was plain something terrible had happened! She had never seen a man without foreskin to cover his shaft. And she'd seen her share, as men were not overly modest, and most did not move out of sight when they went to make water.

But this?

Even in the dark she could make out a raggedness of skin around the shield-shaped top where the flesh had been before. *I have seen Saracen torture*, he'd said.

Ingrith shuddered. So this was what had been done to him. It was perhaps worse, thinking of his suffering, that they'd not finished the job.

Before she could think more of it she heard voices, footsteps approaching the alders.

She shrank back into the shadows, seeing it was only a pair of Morlaix knights come to relieve themselves. Still shaking, she could hear them talking of the journey on the morrow into Wroxeter. One said something rude about Drogo. Under her Simon de Bocage mumbled again. She clamped her hand over his mouth. Finally the others went away.

*Quick now*, she thought, *before anything more happens*.

With fumbling hands she hiked up her skirts. It was not easy but she straddled him, her thighs settling against his naked flesh. Where their skin touched it filled her with strange feelings.

Reaching down, she grasped his shaft in her hand. She leaned forward and over him, not quite sure where it belonged. Worse, the thing felt as though it were still swelling.

"Alys," he murmured. He suddenly lifted his hands and gripped her shoulders.

Sweet Jesu, she had not counted on tussling with him! She shrugged his hands away. He persisted, pulling at her arms, trying to kiss her. Meanwhile, his private part was getting bigger. She worried it would not go inside her.

Biting her lips, Ingrith pressed down. The silky hard flesh poked inside somewhere. She gasped. She wanted to take it out at once, but now he held her tight; she could not move.

"Alys, love." His eyes were closed. "Kiss me."

She squirmed. God and Saint Mary, the beast was dreaming she was the Norman girl! When he spoke she was surrounded by wine fumes. She was almost weeping with frustration. There was not much time; soon she would be missed and some knight would come looking for her. She crouched over him, skirts held up with one hand, her fingers around him.

She fought back a scream when he suddenly lunged for her. He pulled her to him, kissing the side of her face. She found she could not raise her arms.

"Love, love," he groaned. Holding her tightly, he rolled over. Now he was on top of her, pressing her down. "Ah, Alys, how—"

They sank into the soft summer leaves. Ingrith flailed at him, thinking of the knights not too far away. His mouth was glued to hers. Her hands pummeled his back. They were pressed together, she could feel his body's warm hardness through the silk gown. His hose were down around his knees. Under her skirts she felt his hard shaft slide between her thighs.

"Alys," he was saying hoarsely, "how did this happen? Ah God, how I have waited for this moment!"

This was not what she'd planned, she thought wildly. His lips pressed against hers, opened them, and his tongue stroked into her mouth. She could only gurgle her protest. He was a man on fire, mumbling his love for his Norman Alys. His hands pulled the front of her gown away and closed on her breasts. His knees had pried hers apart, his flesh probing her.

She bit back a howl as his great shaft, like a bludgeon, breached her body's entrance and pushed inside. And kept pushing. There was resistance; it seemed as though her maidenhead would never break. He pulled back, grunting. In the next instant he thrust hard into her again.

She did not faint, she was too strong for that. There was only small pain, anyway, compared to the huge feel of him in her, lunging in a frenzy. *Alys. My love.*

Sobbing, she lifted her hips, trying to throw him off. Strangely, a white core of heat began to grow where he was and the more she thrust her body at him the more it spread. She heard him groan. Then his mouth covered hers. She remembered thinking, bewildered, that the very air about them had become a red furnace, pulsing like his flesh which surged in her body. The world began to rock and tumble. She threw herself against it, impassioned, crying out.

Then without warning he shuddered, groaned, and collapsed on her, his mouth on her mouth. His harsh moan escaping into it.

Ingrith lay under him for a long time. The others would come looking for her, she was sure, and yet she could not move. She was thinking that it was finally over. It was not at all what she'd expected. In all truth, she didn't know what to make of it. But praise the saints, she told herself, when they discovered she was no longer a virgin she would be of no worth to them and they would let her go free.

Lying on her, his face buried in her shoulder, he was snoring through his nose. He had gone to sleep almost immediately, the sot, even while still in her.

She moved, carefully, pushing him out of her way. He rolled onto his side, hand cradling his cheek. She sat up.

Ah, Jesus save her, but she hurt! She held up her skirts and saw her thighs were smeared with the sticky evidence of what he had done to her. There was only one small streak of blood. She stared at it, confused.

She'd surely left blood on him. In the morning he'd see it, and know. In the meantime, her lips were bruised, her body ached, her legs shivered uncontrollably. It had taken forever, it seemed, to lose her virginity.

Ingrith got to her feet, climbed the bank, and limped her way out of the woods. Everyone was asleep. The guard at the fire had his back to her. She crept into the wagon and lay down, pulled the martenskin cloak over her and tried to stop shaking. She pressed her lips tightly together, not knowing why, now, she wanted to weep.

She was no longer a maid, but a woman.

She should be satisfied, she told herself.

When they woke, fog covered the woods. The wedding party across the road was silent. It had kept late hours, with the dancing and mummers' plays.

Ingrith sat up, smelling the aroma of toasting bread. The Morlaix knights were quiet. They went slowly about breaking camp. From the sound of their voices, no one was in a good humor.

Neither was she. Wincing, she climbed down from the wagon. She had not bled, she saw, examining the gown's skirt, but she was surpassing sore. She was more than a little puzzled about the blood because the saints knew it had hurt enough, he was that big and lustful, drunkenly wallowing on her, braying about his skinny Alys when you would not think Normans had that much sentiment in them.

She limped off to the trees to relieve herself. When she came back, Simon de Bocage was at the wagon.

"What ails you?" He didn't wait for her answer but pulled her chests out from under the wain. He began to dump her clothes on the ground.

In the mist's milky light she studied his face. This

was the man who had taken her in the darkness under the alder bushes. She remembered his roaring breath in her ear, his hot kisses on her face and her mouth, the painful feel of him in her body. It was a strange thing, to have been naked with him, lying with him, when he was a Norman. The enemy.

He had balled her dresses up and tied a piece of rope around them. She said, "What are you doing with my clothes?"

He didn't look at her. "You are going to ride the mule. We're leaving the wain here."

Her heart began to pound. She took a gulp of air and said, "I am not going to London."

He looked up, black brows over his nose. He wore his mail hauberk and sword, ready for travel. Behind him, the knights were leading the horses to the stream.

"You're not going to ride a pillion again, it's hard on the mare." He opened the other chest and dumped out her clothes. "You're going to ride the mule."

She brushed back her hair with her hand, aware that it was tangled, and that there were leaves in it. She said, loudly, "I am not going to London because I am no longer a virgin."

He dropped the lid of the trunk and straightened up.

She lifted her chin. "You took my maidenhead last night when you were drunk." She was strangely breathless. "In the—under the alder bushes. There."

He turned slowly to stare at her.

"Therefore," Ingrith said, "the noble Norman who waits for me will not want me."

"Jesu." He stroked his chin, studying her. "I was drunk and took your maidenhead?"

What was the matter with him? Reluctantly, she nodded.

"You were dreaming." His mouth thinned. "Your maidenhead is still intact. And you are going to London."

He bent to pull out the other trunk.

She said, her voice shrill, "There will be signs. Virgin signs. The blood is on your clothes." She was talking to the back of his head. "I will tell your cousin," she said, desperate, "what has happened."

He straightened up. "Leave Gilbert de Jobourg out of this." He pushed his face into hers. "Listen to me, you still have your maidenhead. There was no virginal blood on my clothes when I woke up this morning, I had only a wine demon pounding inside my skull and a foul stomach. Whatever else you try to think of, you are still going to London." He slammed the trunk shut. "If you give me more trouble I will bind you hand and foot as I wanted to do from the beginning, and you will ride the mule that way."

She backed up a step, her mouth an O of disbelief.

Blessed Virgin, was he telling her there was no sign of what he had done to her last night? She remembered the smear of blood on her thigh. She couldn't believe she had bled no more than that.

"I can prove this to you, that you took me! Bring me to a woman, a nurse." She was thinking furiously. None of this made any sense, only that she was going to be robbed of her freedom. "A leech if they have one across the road," she pleaded, "and they will tell you. I swear—"

He pried her fingers away from his arm and thrust the bundle of clothes at her. "Get young Aimeric to tie these on the mule. And get something to eat. You, if no one else, will be hungry before we reach Wroxeter."

Speechless, she stared at him. He claimed nothing had happened. If that meant he remembered nothing of last night in his drunkenness, then she was trapped. If there was no blood she did not know how she was going to convince him.

"And somewhere," he said, bending to push the chests back, "we will find a way to clean you up. You are beginning to stink."

She stared at him, wildly. "God rot you, I am not dirty!"

He shrugged. "All the Saxons I have known slept with their dogs. If not their pigs."

She could not stand it any longer, she wanted to strike him. "Norman murderer, you killed my father," she cried. The knights turned to look at them. "No matter what you say, I will not go to London to be anyone's whore!"

He looked at her. "I did not kill your father, and I did not steal your maidenhead. You may claim that I am the color purple for all I care. But you are riding the mule."

With that he turned on his heel and left her.

Ingrith stared after him, trembling like a madwoman. He couldn't be lying to her, it served no purpose, what would he tell his noble lord when they got to London and they found her no virgin?

It was difficult to think, she was so filled with fear and disappointment. Perhaps she had not bled enough to make a sign. She had never heard of such a thing but she was very strong and sturdy; she supposed it could happen that her maidenhead had surrendered without much pain. And now, if she could believe it, without much blood. Also, he was drunk, thinking he made love to his beloved Alys. Perhaps he truly did not remember.

God in heaven, it was too much! It was all in vain, she thought with a despairing sob. But one thing she knew. When this was over she was going to kill him.

# Chapter Seven

The petitioners stood on the landing outside the king's chambers. They'd been waiting patiently all morning for an audience, and through the open door those who'd had no breakfast had a tantalizing view of tables with plates of partly eaten food and drink, around which a half-dozen hounds scavenged for scraps in the rushes. King William Rufus, bull-shouldered, with pale yellow hair and prominent belly, lounged with his feet up on a stool in front of a roaring fire. The fire was needed: Stafford Castle's six-foot stone walls were always cold, even in midsummer.

A servant pushed through the crowd with a small cask. " 'Way, 'way, for the king's wine," he shouted. A bishop, a sheriff, and several clerks stepped back to let him through.

The king looked out through the open door and saw Raymond of Hesiden. He wagged his cup at him. "Come in, Hesiden, come in." William's bluff, hectoring voice lifted over the noise inside. "Come and join us, don't lallygag about out there in the hall."

Raymond of Hesiden smiled, uneasy. He was only a king's justiciar in the west country, but William Rufus had recently taken a fancy to him, much to the amusement of Hesiden's friends.

"The Bishop of Doncaster won't let me, sir," he called. "He keeps me here on the steps arguing the law of copyhold and halimote until I am weak with it."

The sheriff pressed close and said in his ear, "That's right, Hesiden, don't go in as long as he has these catamites about. Have a care for your good name."

The Bishop of Doncaster nodded in agreement. But a provost from the Welsh marches behind them said, "Nay, go in, Hesiden, and tell the king that his soldiers are taking the harvest from my shire for his bloody taxes. And that the damned shire will rise up and fight this year rather than starve."

There was a murmur from the crowd on the landing. No one wanted to go in while the king's cronies were about for fear of being counted among them. Through the open door they saw the king's drinking companions in shirts cut high above the crotch to show violently colored codpieces, and wearing shoes with pointed toes so long they were worn tied to the ankles to keep the wearer from tripping. Two boys moved into their view. They were dancing a gigue, flicking their long hair up with their hands, darting each other lascivious looks. "Everyone a marvel," Repton's sheriff growled.

All the king's companions were handsome, William Rufus's favorite, Robert FitzHaimo, most of all. The king himself was, like his father the old Conqueror, squat, broad-faced, notably unbeautiful. But a charmer, it was said, when the mood was upon him.

They heard a burst of high-pitched laughter.

"Bah, I'm going," the old provost said. "The king is in his cups. We'll get nothing done here today."

Another chamberlain was coming up the stairs. He pushed his way through them holding a pair of gilt and green leather shoes. The bootlets were intricately made, pierced with openwork to show the hose worn under them, and decorated with tassels and gold bells.

The chamberlain hurried into the king's chamber, leaving the door ajar. They heard the king's voice admiring the shoes.

"How much did they cost?" The husky bellow was William's.

The chamberlain's answer was inaudible.

"Three shillings!" The roar fitted exiled Bishop Anselm's description of the king as a wild bull. "You son of a whore! Since when has a king got to wear shoes as cheap as that?"

On the landing a court clerk muttered, "He wore far cheaper when he was his father's penniless knight."

The chamberlain was protesting the shoes were made especially for the king at a great loss to the Stafford maker. They were practically a gift.

The king threw something across the chamber. They heard a yelp followed by shouts of laughter. The king jumped out of his chair and stamped across the room. "Go and buy me shoes at a price that better befits a king, damn you! Bring me shoes for which you pay no less than a mark of silver!"

The chamberlain backed out onto the landing, rubbing his cheek. Hoots and jeers followed him. Something flew out the door, bells jingling, and landed in the crowd. One of the clerks bent and picked up the other shoe.

The chamberlain pulled the door to with a bang. "Ay, I'll bring him back cheaper." He glared at the closed door. "Believe me, you'll hear him say it. That another pair at the price of a silver mark is more to his royal liking."

The clerk handed him the shoe. "But I'll pay even less for the next pair," he vowed, "and tell him it was more. Hark, such is his fine sensibility"—the chamberlain's lip curled—"he'll never know the difference."

He turned and pushed his way back through the crowd.

The Bishop of Doncaster looked after him, frowning. "Is this how they talk of the king, these lackeys?"

Raymond made a face. "I fear the king encourages it, my lord bishop. It's a thing widely complained of."

Reaching over his shoulder, the sheriff pushed the door open a crack. "By the cross," he whispered, "you should see what they are doing now."

There was a crash inside and squeals, followed by hysterical laughter.

"Have you heard about Peter, one of the chamberlains?" someone said behind them. "He was impregnated by a man, and died of the monstrous growth. They buried him outside the cemetery, like an animal."

The Bishop of Doncaster grimaced in distaste. He took Raymond's arm. "Come, Repton, with Hesiden and me. We are wiser to go below."

People stood aside to let them pass. When they got outside they saw the line stretched across the ward.

"What hope for today?" a king's clerk asked them. He held an armful of writs. The sheriff answered him with a shrug. They walked toward the gate.

The bishop said under his breath, "England cries for a government. And gets nothing."

"Or else must go to Ranulph Flambard," the sheriff said, "and submit to mortification and robbery. It is all the same."

The sky was overcast. A hot summer wind blew across the grass. The bishop grabbed his gown and held it against him. "Does the king plan to hunt again today?"

The sheriff was watching men-at-arms parading by the stables. Raymond Hesiden shook his head.

"I think two more days of this and the king will tire of Stafford and go south. He has said he wishes to hunt in New Forest no later than the feast of Saint James." He added, "It is just as well. The people here are heartily sick of the dicing all night and sleeping all day. And that the lamps are put out after dark, so that all may roam about where they will."

"Ilbert," the sheriff said, "someone wants you."

Two black friars were approaching from the portal gate. The bishop started toward the chapel, motioning them to follow.

They came together at the church porch. The other friar dropped back, hands tucked in his sleeves. The younger one strode forward. His cowl was thrown back, they could see his face with a straight slash of dark brows, curling brown hair.

"God's wounds, Seint-Omer," the sheriff said, "but you look holy. I would ask you to confess me if I didn't know better."

The friar smiled. "I have vows in the first degree, Sheriff, as any crusader. Even those with lady wives." He bowed his head before the bishop. "Milord, I come to report the delay, but not by much. A broken wain on the road to Wroxeter. They did not stay to repair it but went on."

The sheriff scowled at him. "They went on? By the Cross, let us do one thing or the other but not play at breaking wagons!"

The bishop stroked his lower lip. "Our friend Repton favors simple murder." He held out his hand. "Here, be more monkish, Seint-Omer, and kiss my ring."

The friar quickly dropped to one knee and took the bishop's hand. "I have seen the girl Malmsbury gave them. In all truth, she is a Saxon goddess, I have never seen finer." He looked up. "A true English huntress Diana."

The sheriff snorted. "Seint-Omer, remember your vows."

"Only when I am in these clothes," he responded. The bishop made the sign of the cross over Brother Enguerrand's head and he got back to his feet. "My lords, have no fear, it is not ill-done, this scheme. The prince will be amused."

The bishop looked away. "It is this parfit knight

who bothers me. The Count of Flanders's fine berserker."

The sheriff was watching a marvelously dressed figure hurrying toward them. "The one they call the Leopard of Antioch."

"Yes." The bishop assumed a smile. The messenger meant the king would see them now. "But what do they want him for? To escort another girl to the prince? It would seem an excess."

Raymond of Hesiden murmured, "It is rumored the Clares are sending him to the Jews in London on some mysterious mission."

"No, not that." The bishop leaned on the sheriff's arm and motioned to the two friars to follow him. "There is something else." They started across the ward.

"The Leopard of Antioch," the bishop repeated. He shook his head.

The morning fog did not burn off by noon as was usual in midsummer. After partaking of the midday meal, the knights mounted to ride again in a white mist so thick that Gilbert and Simon, together at its head, could not see the last knight, Aimeric, bringing up the rear.

Eventually the road wound into a valley filled with the shadows of tall trees. The singing that the knights had begun in open country died away as the forest and fog closed around them. They began to talk of witches and woods-dwelling wizards, and trolls. Then there were wolves and other wild beasts, both real and enchanted. For once the rear of the column did not straggle.

Talk turned to Robert of Belleme's lands through

which they were passing. They had all heard stories of serf girls kidnapped and raped, then killed, even children taken for vile amusements in Belleme's castle at Shrewsbury. They knew what happened to captive knights.

Their pace slowed even more. Gilbert wanted to put Ingrith on the mule, but Simon was against it. "Well, you will lame your mare carrying double weight." Gilbert looked at Ingrith. "Jesus knows she's no dainty fairy."

Ingrith ducked her head. She didn't want to ride the mule. And, thanks be to God, it didn't want to be ridden; it had showed that in the morning. The end of her spine was still sore where she'd landed on it. As were other places, making the riding uncomfortable.

They went slowly, most times not above a trot. Gilbert complained they would not make Wroxeter before nightfall and would have to camp outside the town, as it was doubtful the watch would let them, an armed escort, in after dark. Beyond Wroxeter they would meet the Roman road, which would take them south to London.

Ingrith's arms were growing cramped. Simon de Bocage was not as massive as his cousin, but he was still a powerful man. When she held him, the links of his mail pressed through the sleeves of the dress and into her arms.

"The mare won't carry more than she's able," he was saying. "She's a desert horse, and they are sturdier than they look."

Careful of her tender seat, Ingrith shifted behind him. Immediately the horse broke her stride and danced sidewise. The man in front of her gave a warning grunt but this time did not turn and shout at her.

She stared at the back of his head. His mail hood, thrown back, showed his tangled black hair. He treated her as though nothing had happened. She could not believe that he remembered nothing of that evening she lay with him, although she knew that men who drank too much sometimes had that trouble. She tried to remember her father and brothers, Saxons, heavy drinkers all, and stories of them nursing their heads after feasts and complaining of fights they could not recall.

She gnawed at her underlip, thinking they were getting farther and farther from the marcher country. From her family. From freedom, if she was ever to have it.

Gilbert was looking the mare over. "That horse is flighty; she has more tricks than a roadside beggar. Now that you have brought her all this way back to England, Simon, will you breed her?"

Ingrith rested her cheek carefully against his mailed back. She could feel the muscles there, his hips shifting as he rode. She was going to have to do something. Before Wroxeter town, if she could.

"I've thought of it, Gilbert. But to mate with something the size of the destrier might kill her."

She had not wasted what she had done, Ingrith told herself, it must only be done again, that was all, so that he would know it. She said a quick prayer for them to stop someplace soon.

"She's still too leggy for my taste." There was a noise and Gilbert turned in the saddle to look. "You will pay heavy for a stud for her."

Something flapped out of the mists over their heads. A diving bird. They ducked.

" 'Ware, 'ware!" a voice shouted.

They heard the pounding hooves of horses, then a horn.

Ingrith clutched the belt in front of her. She felt Simon's body heave as he drew his sword and then dragged up his shield. Ahead, the wall of mist burst apart with horses and men charging down on them.

The Morlaix ranks broke. Drogo and Gilbert shouted to their knights. The shield hit her as Simon dragged it up to cover them. Under them the mare plunged, then reared, squealing. The destrier, its lead dropped, charged off into the woods.

Jarred to her teeth, Ingrith held on as the man she clutched kicked the mare into a charge. His shield caught a clanging blow. He drove the mare into another horse. They struck and her head jerked back with a snap.

All around them were shouts, horses and riders hurtling at them out of the fog. She swallowed a scream as the mare wheeled to dodge an arm wielding a mace. Men ran on foot in between the horses shouting in English. There were blows, grunts, screams of pain.

"God is my judge!" Gilbert appeared in the fog. "Outlaws!"

" 'Ware, 'ware, Shrewsbury!" someone bellowed.

A blow hit his shield. The very air rocked. Simon de Bocage strained forward, dragging her with him, circling the big sword like a scythe. Someone was hit, downed. Horses reared.

Ingrith sobbed with the effort to stay upright. The mare under them stumbled, got up, stumbled again. She clung to him as he lunged from side to side, parrying. He'd forgotten her, they had all forgotten her, she thought wildly. She wondered if she were going to die. There were noises in the mist. *Help me*, a voice cried in English.

Her hands clamped to the sword belt like claws. There was no telling who they were in the fog, crying for help in her own language. A rider bore down on them. The horses struck and the mare went down to her knees. Shouting, de Bocage hauled her up again. Ingrith shut her eyes, unable to cry out. She was unable to do anything but gasp.

Shadowy riders surged around them. Horses clattered up. "Who the devil is this?" a voice shouted in French.

"Morlaix," a half-dozen voices answered.

"*Jesu!* Get out of the way!"

As quick as it had begun the riders galloped off. Horns blew again at a distance. The fog swallowed the sound.

There was a long moment's stillness. A voice in the mist said hoarsely that he thought his arm was broken. Someone cursed.

Gilbert cantered up, shouting to Drogo to get the knights to fall out at the side of the road. Someone took the bridle of the Saracen mare. The fog drifted around them. Simon de Bocage sat unmoving, the shield hanging from his arm.

It was Gilbert who had the mare's reins. "Outlaws, by God, they ran in amongst us with some of Belleme's men pursuing." He brought the mare's head around. "That was not so stupid. In this fog we fought anything, much to their ill luck." He

peered at them. "Sweet Christ, Simon, you are covered with blood. The girl, too. Are you whole?"

"My mare's hurt." His voice sounded distant.

Someone pulled Ingrith down. She staggered,
and her hands found the stirrup. She hung onto it,
leaning against the mare's heaving side.

"Sweet Jesu, Simon, you fight like a madman.
Are you all right?"

There was no answer. "Here, girl." That voice was
Gilbert's, plucking at her dress. "How is our precious cargo?"

She pushed his hands away. She couldn't talk,
her throat was so swollen and dry. Her forehead
throbbed where the shield had hit it. She lifted her
hand to touch it and found a bump, wet with blood.

The knights came up leading their horses. Simon
bent over, examining the mare. The horse stood
shivering, her right foreleg lifted. They gathered
around him.

"They went past me full course, cursing you," one
Morlaix knight crowed. "Shrewsbury's man
shouted you were that hell's demon on point."

"Yes, I saw that berserker swing." Drogo's eyes
gleamed. "They ran into a grindstone when they
struck you, de Bocage."

Ingrith leaned against the side of the trembling
horse. They were all but fawning over him, they
thought him so wonderful. She was glad they were
not paying any attention to her. The lump on her
forehead hurt. She did not think she would faint,
but she was dizzy.

Someone shouted they had found bodies. Gilbert
started off with Simon. Limping, she followed
them.

The fog had not lifted. One had to come right up on him to see the mailed knight on the ground, arms flung out, his helmet split almost in two. Under him, streams of blood flowed across the dirt and into the leaves.

Gilbert bent over him. "Simon, this is your work. He's Shrewsbury's."

A few of the knights crossed themselves. Drogo said, "Shrewsbury cannot give us the blame. In the ambush, in the fog, we couldn't know foe from friend."

A knight called, "This one's not dead."

Two outlaws lay side by side in the road. They wore jerkins of boiled leather for armor. Their feet were bound in rags. Beyond them a blond giant lay propped on his elbow, looking at them. Blood ran down his forehead. He held his hand over a large gushing wound in his thigh. He was bearded, better clothed than the others, with high leather boots and cowhide armor studded with metal. His jewelry was fine, bands of copper and enamel on his huge arms, a gold torque around his throat, gold and silver rings on both hands.

"I think we have the chief of the robbers." Gilbert bent and stripped the rings from the man's hands, then the torque from around his throat. The outlaw never moved.

Gilbert would have tossed a ring to Simon but the other shook his head. He threw it to Drogo, who caught it. He stood over the Englishman, speaking Norman French.

The outlaw listened but said nothing. He looked past Gilbert, studying Ingrith with blazing blue eyes.

Simon de Bocage rubbed his face with both hands. "Get someone who speaks English," he told them.

Gilbert shouted a name. The rawboned young knight who had fixed the wain's axle came forward. He squatted down before the wounded man. After a few words he looked up.

"Sir, if you will just look in his mouth." He appeared apologetic. "I don't think the man will answer. His tongue has been cut out."

Ingrith pushed past a knight to see. This was more of their Norman justice. The English outlaw was a fine-looking man; she wondered why he'd had his tongue taken.

"Cut his throat," Drogo said.

They could see he understood. He stared back at them, unblinking.

Gilbert grimaced. "He's not mortal wounded, I would put him to the sword soon enough if he were." He was struck by a thought. "Shrewsbury's men will double back. God's death, I mislike leaving even an outlaw for Belleme."

Simon shrugged. "If you take him to Wroxeter they will hang him."

The other scratched his head. "So they will."

Ingrith stepped forward. She knotted her hands together, suddenly thinking there was no reason why they should listen to her. But before she could plead for the Englishman's life, Simon said, "Sweet Jesu, Gilbert, if you do not want to gift him for Shrewsbury's dinnertime, put him on the mule."

Drogo opened his mouth to say something. Gilbert said "Why not?" and started for his horse.

"Anything. Let us first get out of these damnable woods."

The destrier was found after some searching, also the horse of the dead Shrewsbury knight. Simon saddled the warhorse and led the limping mare. A knight led the Shrewsbury horse, a handsome bay stallion somewhat lighter than their destriers, but still strongly built. The wounded outlaw, tied, and with his head and leg bound in strips of his shirt, rode the mule, which was suddenly docile under his great weight. After a few miles the road ascended a knoll and they passed through clearings in thick stands of oaks and beeches. Here the fog clung to the ground in long flags. Above, the sunlight shone hazily.

They came to a shallow stream that emerged from bracken to seep across the road, and stopped to water the horses. Simon and Gilbert together set the broken arm of an older knight named Winebald. He was shamefaced afterward because he screamed as they were pulling the ends of the bones apart.

"Better to faint," Simon de Bocage told him, "if you can."

Ingrith watched him walk away. Those first moments after the fighting while Gilbert was talking to him it was as though he were a man dumbstruck and couldn't hear, could hardly see. Yet the other knights were worshipful, saying that he fought like a madman. Like a demon from hell.

The horses watered, a few knights stripped off their mail, then their underclothes, to stand in the ankle-deep stream and wash away the blood and dirt.

She decided for once not to turn her back.

Curious, she leaned against the trunk of an oak tree, seeing them take off their chausses, Drogo and one they called Arnuld the Frisian.

Their naked bodies were hairy and white, ropy with muscles, the Frisian particularly scarred. Their private parts had the same singular ugliness. Except, as she remembered it, Simon de Bocage's were larger.

She wondered, even now, how she had managed. How *he* had managed; he was the one who had taken her.

She watched the Frisian, wincing, scoop water onto his hurt thigh. Both he and Drogo had groins with thick furry hair and, in the middle, dangling shafts with puckered skin that covered the tip.

She stared at them. *It is better if you faint*, Simon had said to the knight when they were setting his arm. She knew now where that wisdom had come from. Had he fainted when the Saracens trimmed his cock, thinking they would cut the thing all the way off?

It was, Ingrith knew, a terrible wound. Everyone could tell how men felt about their privates. How when they went to make water they handled them, examined them, full of a constant concern. For Simon de Bocage to have one so damaged explained much. He was admired by the other knights, more than handsome enough with his black eyes, his strong, graceful body, yet he was cold-natured, always holding himself apart from the others. Perhaps, she thought suddenly, he could not get a woman to sleep with him.

She was deep in her thoughts, standing longer than she intended, watching the knights. Certainly not expecting a sharp blow that caught her in the small of her back.

# Chapter Eight

When Ingrith turned, Simon de Bocage was standing there holding the bundle of her clothes.

She lifted her eyes to him, thinking she did not have to explain that she had been studying other knights' nakedness, realizing that he had been mutilated by Saracen torture. And what it must have meant to him.

She searched his face for some sign of what he had endured. But all she could see was his cold arrogance that was strange for someone who dared not reveal the dread secret he had under his clothes.

He scowled at her. "Stay away from the knights." He indicated the forest with a jerk of his head. "I want you to come with me."

He walked away, not looking back. She waited for a moment, uncertain, then followed him. He made his way up the seepage of the stream and farther into the woods. The ground there was spongy with fallen leaves. When she looked back, she saw they were out of sight of the others. His long legs covered the ground rapidly; she had to skip a few steps to keep up with him.

"What are you going to do?" she asked. She was beginning to see this might be the chance she'd waited for. At least they were alone.

He stopped. The spring was deeper near its source, a bubbling pool of water surrounded by the fernlike bracken. The sunlight fell in splayed beams through the branches of the oaks.

"Take off that thing," he told her. He put the bundle on the ground, opened it, and lifted a folded blue cloth. When he shook it out she saw it was a linen overtunic embroidered with silk thread. He studied it for a moment, then wadded it up and laid it on the ground. He took out another.

A breeze pushed Ingrith's hair across her face. She brushed it back with her hand, fighting down something cold and nervous that rose up inside her. This was what she wanted, was it not, to be alone with him? Then it was even better, she told herself, if he wanted her with her clothes off.

"What are you going to do?" she said again.

He did not look up. He shook out another dress. It was odd to see this tall, grim-faced knight going through her clothes. He turned the dress around to look at the back of it. "Take that thing off but keep on your shift," he said.

She was silent for a moment. "I don't have a shift."

When he turned, she had already undone the lacings on the front of the green dress and slipped her arms out of the sleeves. She held up the front of the dress modestly, with both hands.

"You don't have a shift." He stared at her. "What

have you been wearing underneath?" When she opened her mouth to answer he said, "I don't want to know." He reached into the front of his jacket and took out a brush and tossed it to her. "Scrub with this."

She caught it. It was the brush he used to groom his horses, she could tell by the smell.

"And your hair," he said.

Ingrith picked a few horse hairs out of the brush. Shoulders drooping, she walked to the brook and waded out into it. Behind her she heard the jingle of mail and knew he was pulling off his hauberk. She stopped. She wondered what to do when they were both naked. This was her chance; she could think of nothing else.

With her back to him she stepped out of her gown and tossed it to the edge of the stream. When she looked he was sitting on the ground pulling off his boots and cross garters. The front of his quilted jacket was open.

She was aware of her naked skin, and it was hard not to try to cover herself. Perhaps when he started to bathe, she thought, she should turn and show herself to him.

She bit her lip. Holy Saint Mary, she did not know how to begin. Would her nakedness be enough, or should she do some of the things the bawd mistress had shown her at Malmsbury's manor house? The things any whore should know how to do without feeling wretchedly stupid.

She reached down and took a handful of sand from the stream bottom, put it on the brush and scrubbed her legs. At Castle Morlaix she had been given fine cakes of soap and the water they had brought her to wash in had been hot. It was strange how one could get used to fine things so quickly. When she scrubbed up her arms gray streams poured back into the water. The brook was so cold she dared not sit down in it.

Bending over, she wet her long hair. The flesh on her back and legs prickled with chill. She heard him wade into the water from the bank. Her heart began to pound.

Ingrith wrung out her hair between her hands, ducking her head so that she could look at him from under her arm. He had shed his quilted jacket but he still wore his hose. Sweet Mary, here she was naked, and he was going to wash in his underclothes! He splashed water onto his chest and arms, making grunting sounds. He didn't look at her.

She turned away from him to wash her feminine places. The spring was freezing. When she could stand it no longer she splashed to the bank and picked up the green gown. Before she could use it to dry herself he came up behind her and grabbed it.

"Have you no sense?" He balled up the dress and flung it away. "Don't put your dirt back on."

She backed away. "I'm not dirty, stop telling me I'm dirty!" She could not stop shaking and it was not all due to cold. "I—my family is—when my mother married she had clothes enough for four mules to carry. And many jewels!"

He stood glowering at her. "And don't wipe your hands on your clothes when you eat. It's a foul thing to do."

She shouted, "Gilbert does it."

"Gilbert is rich."

She knew he was not and started to taunt him, but instead found herself watching small beads of water run down his chest. She dared not lift her eyes, standing as she was, naked and shivering.

She felt something hot stir in her belly and was surprised. She should be doing something now if she wanted her freedom. It took courage, but she stepped closer. "I have not been given leave to bathe before this," she murmured.

The words didn't matter, she told herself. *Always look into their eyes*, the bawd mistress had said, *it's like a snake with a bird. You have to, if you want to lift their purses.*

He looked down at her, not moving.

She held out the brush. "I have finished."

When he took it she put her fingers lightly on his arm as she had done with young Aimeric. Her body was almost touching him, the nipples of her breasts a hairsbreadth away. She heard him suck in his breath.

She put her hand against his thigh. Something changed in that winter-dark look. "What the devil," he muttered.

Her eyes held his as her fingers brushed upward to the cord that held his hose. Now the tips of her breasts were touching his chest. His bare skin was warm, wildly distracting. She could feel him swelling and growing in his groin as she pressed her lower body against him.

Ah God, the cord at his waist would not give, the same trouble she'd had that night under the alder bushes! Her fingers worried it. She gazed into his eyes, fearful that he would not stand still much longer if she couldn't get the cord untied. She lifted her hand from his arm and pressed it between them to the bulge that continued to stiffen.

The moment she touched him there, he shuddered. With an oath he wrenched up his arms. "Let go of me!"

Ingrith hung onto his wrists. There might not be another chance to be alone with him before they got to Wroxeter.

He shook his arms violently but she had him by the wrists, trying to wrap one leg around him to press her body closer. The traitorous hose she had not been able to budge now began to slide down his hips.

"Sweet Jesus in heaven," he swore. He grabbed her with one hand and tried to use the other for his hose.

She held fast to his arms. "Please," she panted. "I just want to—"

"Damn you, unhand me!" He staggered in the ankle-deep water, trying to shake her loose by jerking his arms. "Did you hear what I said?"

Ingrith could feel, in spite of his dragging her from side to side, that he was excited, still swollen. His hose slid down past his hipbones. Her lower body now touched wet skin, the brush of hair in his groin.

"Stop it," he roared. "What in Satan's name are you trying to do?" He slung her violently away, and Ingrith shrieked as she lost her footing.

He teetered, fighting for balance. She held tight to him. Her weight carried him over and they fell into the spring with a great splash.

Ingrith lay stunned, the pressure of his body holding her down. It seemed she could hear someone's voice calling. Wavering and indistinct, as though underwater.

*She* was underwater! She couldn't breathe. He was lying on top of her and her head was in the spring. When she tried to shriek she only drew in strangling water, not air. The shouting grew louder.

"Simon!" Hands pulled at them. It was Gilbert bending over them. "Christ crucified, man, you are drowning her!"

The body on top of her rolled off. Gilbert's hands reached into the spring and seized her by both shoulders and pulled her to a sitting position. Beside her, Simon de Bocage got to his hands and knees and spat out a mouthful of water.

"Jesus God, Gilbert," he croaked, "the bitch attacked me."

Ingrith coughed. A little water came up in her throat and she swallowed it, blinking. She blew water out through her nose.

Gilbert hauled her to her feet. His eyes widened at her nakedness. "Ah, Simon." He shook his head. "You swore an oath on this."

The other hopped toward the bank, his hose in both hands. "Don't abuse me, Gilbert," he snarled. "She's an animal. If you hadn't come she'd have me stripped naked for her lust."

Gilbert bent over her, his face full of concern. "Are you well?" When Ingrith nodded, still coughing, he reached down and picked up the green gown from the grass and handed it to her.

"Not that!" Simon stepped between them, snatched the dress and threw it high into the trees. He took the blue one from the ground and slung it at her. "You devious slut, I ought to tie it about your neck!"

Gilbert put his arm around Ingrith's shoulders. "Peace, peace, I heard the screaming back in camp. You were ever a violent man, Simon."

"God's wounds, you're my friend, Gilbert, can you remember that?" He went about picking up clothing and rolling it into the bundle. "I tell you, she's got the Saxon itch. She has it on her mind constantly." He tossed the brush in on top and tied it. "Yestermorn she tried to tell me—"

He stopped abruptly. Shutting his mouth on the words.

Ingrith shot him a quick glance. So he was not going to tell that she'd accused him of taking her maidenhead. She shrugged off Gilbert's arm.

While the two men watched she picked up the blue gown, stepped into it and pulled it up to her shoulders. It had a kirtle made of blue linen embroidered with colored yarn in many shapes of birds and flowers. She cinched the belt tightly.

"Now you see," Gilbert said. He watched her comb her hair out with her fingers and shake it across her shoulders. "I grant you, God knows she's the devil's own temptation just to look at her. But Simon, if I were you—"

The other made a snarling sound.

"Ah, but can't you see these lusty humors rise only because of my sister?" Gilbert bent to him, one reasonable hand extended. "When you can't have the woman you care for, it's natural to look for another to ease the want."

Ingrith started back to the camp, holding her

skirts up with both hands so they would not drag on the swampy ground.

"You'll stop thinking about it," Gilbert was saying. "It is hard to bear, but if it will make it better I swear to you that I believe my sister is innocent of any notion that you have nursed a passion for her."

Ingrith listened, interested. But Simon de Bocage, his face like thunder, said nothing.

They traveled all morning, never leaving the forest. It began to rain, a summer storm with lightning and thunder far off in the Welsh hills. Sheets of water drained from the woods and across the forest track. The horses plodded, heads down. They broke into a clearing of beech trees and saw a circle of huts made of branches and twigs that were more like shelters for animals than men. A tribe of charcoal burners with long hair and wild faces appeared furtively among the trees. The women carried naked babies on their hips. They had no domestic animals about, only a pack of wolflike dogs.

Gilbert called to the charcoal burners, asking about the end of the track. Shy, they kept their distance. No one understood their language, not even the young English knight, Aelfred. Gilbert ordered a bread sack opened and Drogo threw them some bread. The wild people fell on the crusts, snatching them from the ground. Then they melted like smoke into the forest again.

Gilbert ordered camp to be made by a brook. The Morlaix knights cut branches with thick leaves to make small shelters. The downpour was steady and the cook fires would not stay lit. The knights ate cold bread and meat before they crept into their lean-tos to sleep.

No one built a shelter for the tongueless outlaw chief. He was tied to a rowan tree, his hands behind him. From Simon's bower Ingrith watched him sitting with his head bent in the beating rain. At last she got up, telling herself she did not think any of the knights would try to stop her. She went to her bundles of clothing and found the martenskin cloak. When she carried the cloak to him the outlaw lifted his head, rain streaming from the rattails of his fair hair. The downpour was cold. His lips were slate-colored.

"Here," she said in English. She crouched before him and pulled the fur cloak around his shoulders, the hood up to cover his head. "It does not fit you too well," she whispered. He was a big man, long-legged; his knees and feet stuck out of it.

She turned away from that blazing look. He never moved while she was putting the martenskin around him. She shivered, thinking about how it would be not to have a tongue. Not to be able to speak.

When she crept into the shelter she found Gilbert there, huge as a wet mastiff, crowding the space. He stripped off his mail, making the leafy structure shake.

"At least you could have offered the cover to me." His eyes teased her.

She gave him an uncertain look. He'd told her he had four sisters; Alys, who had married the Frenchman, was the oldest. From what he said he still rallied them unmercifully.

She lay down on the wet branches that had been

spread for their bed. From the expression on Gilbert's face she wondered if he was remembering what had happened at the spring.

She lowered her eyes. She was not sorry for what she had done, only that it did not work. Even if she had half drowned there might have been a chance that it would have turned out all right. She let her mind play with it, that the knight Simon would have discovered he was lying on top of her and dragged her out. And then, both naked—

Rain dripped from the ceiling of the shelter onto her hands and face. Sighing, Ingrith hunched her back, thinking that she should have kept the martenskin for herself.

The shelter shook and Simon de Bocage crawled in, wrapped in his sodden cloak. He lay down on the other side of her with a groan. There was a crack of lightning close by, followed by thunder.

"Are you hungry?" He turned his face to her, eyes dark.

She shook her head. Gilbert had given her bread to carry to the outlaw and she had eaten some of that and some cheese. On their backs, both knights lifted their hands and crossed themselves, then muttered their lengthy prayers.

Ingrith listened. The Normans were always at prayers, the knights especially, even those who were the most cruel. When he turned over, Simon's leg touched hers. He moved it quickly. Gilbert stared up at the roof, muttering curses at the raindrops that spattered down on them. Somewhere deep in the forest wolves howled.

After a while they slept.

* * *

Simon got up before dawn and crawled outside the shelter to relieve himself. He came back at once to wake Gilbert and tell him the prisoner had escaped. They roused the camp. The knight on guard, a seasoned fighter named Gulfer, had been hit from behind. His head was bloody. Gilbert stamped up and down, swearing.

The rain had stopped and the sky above the trees was moonless but full of stars. Two knights helped Gulfer to his feet. Blood poured down the knight's back, covering the shoulders of his hauberk. He staggered a few feet then fell back into their arms.

Gilbert swore again. "His skull is cracked. Now we have a knight with a broken arm and one with a broken head. It has been a foul trip through this woods, thanks to that damned outlaw and his friends."

"Not them." Simon bent to point to the marten-skin cloak, neatly folded. "Outlaws would have taken this."

The knights gathered around. Some turned to stare at Ingrith. Gilbert shook his head. "Nay, not the girl. She lay between us all night."

Ingrith did not look at them; the Normans would be vengeful with two knights sorely wounded.

"Well, he was not a prisoner I wanted," Gilbert said. "We would have enough to do in Wroxeter looking for a leech, without an outlaw to deliver for hanging."

The knights filed away to break camp. Ingrith picked up the rain-soaked cloak. Simon de Bocage walked away. Ingrith, the cloak on her arms, followed him.

\* \* \*

They left their camp before dawn, breaking their fast in the saddle. Simon rode the big gray warhorse, leading the limping mare on a rope, with Ingrith up behind him. The destrier was like a moving mountain. She was terrified at first, but the stallion kept a steady, smooth gait. After a while she stopped being so fearful.

The sun came out as they reached the edge of the forest. The track became a road that wound between rolling fields of ripening oats and barley as far as the eye could see. They passed a line of serfs' huts, an old village, deserted. One of the knights called out they were still in Belleme's lands.

It was noon before they came to a crossroads. A mendicant friar had been sitting by the side of the road and he got up and came toward them. Behind him a dwarf sat on the back of a fine saddle horse.

Gilbert reined in. "God's love, isn't it the same friar who preaches against knights? How did you get ahead of us?"

"Milord." The young friar hung back but the dwarf hopped down from the big chestnut and made a fancy bow. Ingrith craned to see. She remembered the dwarf jongleur from the wedding party. From what little she'd heard, he had a memory for truly vile tunes.

"We are making for Wroxeter with this horse," he was saying, "as a gift from milord d'Aubigny to the canon of St. Margaret's."

The horses stood in the middle of the road. The summer sun was hot on their backs after the dank forest. The dwarf wore a red tufted satin coat over worn leather breeches. He had arms and legs the size of a child's but the trunk of a full-grown man. He was not bad looking, Ingrith thought, almost as handsome as the curly-headed friar, with a generous nose. Hat in hand, the dwarf talked to Gilbert. But she noted he kept his eyes on Simon de Bocage.

Ingrith rested her cheek lightly against the mailed back in front. She was growing used to riding like this. The dwarf said he and the friar had taken a short route, off the forest track, to have traveled so fast. Gilbert asked about outlaws.

Ingrith was thinking they needed to buy food when they got to Wroxeter. The bread they'd eaten that morning was not enough. She was already hungry.

She was not, she told herself, going to think about her plan until they reached the town. And she was certainly not going to worry what the Normans would do to the man she held in her arms when it happened.

# Chapter Nine

$J$udah Ha-Kohen of Wroxeter got up from his chair and opened the door to the outer room where his son-in-law was tallying his goldsmithing accounts. The steady click-click of Elias's abacus was more than a little distracting when Joseph was measuring, as he was at the moment, small amounts of herbs. But unless one did something about it, the bottom of the house grew unbearably warm. By mid-afternoon the breeze from the river, which blew the length of the downstairs when the doors were opened, was needed if one wanted to keep on working.

While he was up he went to his apothecary shelves, searching among the jars of belladonna, colchraim, crocus, henbane, lavender, linseed, mallow, mustard, poppy, and wormwood for a bottle of gentian. A prescription for a tincture of the plant, steeped in white wine, had been sent to him by his cousin Saloman ibn Verga, a renowned herbalist who, in a recent letter from London, had recommended gentian as being especially effective for inflammations, infections, and other *mal humors* of the visible flesh.

However, Judah was thinking somewhat crossly, one's hand had to be unfailingly steady when measuring ingredients, and not anticipating the somewhat irritating rhythms of the abacus counters as they struck one another. The presence of the machine itself was enough to keep one on edge, a reminder, as always, of Jews' position in a rough-hewn and alien culture.

As used by goldsmiths like Elias, the abacus speeded precious-metal stock inventory, calculations of interest on loan accounts, and suchlike; no right-minded gold dealer would be without it. But here in the northwest reaches of the Christian island of Britain, where tallies were still kept by primitive notched sticks or knotted string, it was enough of an innovation to be regarded as the devil's invention. When there were customers in the shop, Elias put it away out of sight. When the abacus was in use, as it was now, it seemed to Judah Ha-Kohen that Elias hurried to make up for lost time.

Closing his ears to the clicks in the outer room, he sat back down at his table. He propped his cousin Saloman's letter against a candlestick and picked up the jar of dried gentian, bending close to the vellum to read the first prescription.

*Use caution*, it advised at the top of the page. Judah could not resist a snort at his cousin's favorite direction. The second was *discretion*. Not too far down the page under "Dosages" he read: *Proceed cautiously*. Followed by, under "Poultices," *discontinue with discretion*.

One had to admit Saloman's reminders had merit. When one was a Jew, a doctor, and a Norman, caution and discretion were indispensable. In a country where cooks and barbers practiced healing arts and their infamous surgery, a trained physician took his life in his hands when a patient died, unless it could be viewed as inevitable, or the treatment so obviously benign that death was judged to be an act of God. In Lincoln recently, a rich cloth merchant had been assailed by a sudden malady that rendered him blind and deaf and unable to move.

The town's respected Jewish physician, Samuel Usque, persuaded by the tears and entreaties of the merchant's family to attend him when others had abandoned the case, had been in the process of bleeding the cloth merchant when the man abruptly expired. Usque had then been rewarded by the hysterical wife and the merchant's sons, who fell upon him crying witchcraft and Jewish blasphemy, and beat him so severely that he was lucky to leave Lincoln with his life. He took a good part of Lincoln's terrorized Jewry with him.

And as for childbirth—

Judah measured out a spoonful of the dried gentian flowers and regarded it critically. Childbirth with its high level of emotion and potential for disaster was better left to midwives. Although in Italy and other more enlightened countries he had heard learned physicians had great success with cases of difficult births.

He sprinkled the dried flowers into a shallow dish and added white wine from a flask. He held the dish over the candle flame until it was hot, then dabbed his finger in it, noting the deep purple color that promptly covered the tip.

The tincture might have real and satisfactory properties against morbid inflammation, as Saloman claimed. It was also very satisfyingly colorful. Patients tended to improve rapidly when treated with a bright stain on the afflicted part.

A thumping in the front of the house made him cock his head.

He heard the bench scrape back from the gold-working table, the last click of the abacus counters rattling home as his son-in-law slipped it away out of sight.

Judah snuffed out the candle with his fingers and threw a cloth over the gentian mixture. Elias shouted through the front door, asking what was wanted. Voices in the street responded, asking for the leech.

Judah allowed himself a small sigh of relief. He took his fur-trimmed coat from its nail behind him and shrugged into it. Elias was already unbolting the door when he entered the front room. He nodded, and his son-in-law swung the door open.

The watch guard of the wool factors' guild stood there in a leather jerkin and metal headpiece. Behind the watch was a pale-eyed Norman knight, fully armed, on a tall roan.

The knight did not dismount. "I'm looking for the leech." From his manner he was obviously a captain. "We have two men hurt, one with a broken arm and the other a broken head, in the house of one Sophia Belefroun in the street of the cloth merchants."

Judah saw Elias's start of surprise.

"The house of Sophia Belefroun?" He kept his face bland. "It is empty, sir knight, shut up for many years. Although the beadle of the church of St. Margaret's is paid to do the caretaking. Did not the watch tell you?"

The wool factors' guard drew himself up. "Nay, there are many knights there now with Belefroun's son, called Simon de Bocage. Sir Gilbert of Morlaix vouches for it—that the house is Bocage's."

"Come, is there a leech here, or not?" The knight looked down at them. "We were told a Jew of Wroxeter by name Judah Ha-Kohen is skilled with bones."

Judah fixed his gaze at a spot beyond him. *So he has come,* he told himself. He was careful to let his face show nothing. But he was recalling what he had heard from certain sources in the spring that Simon de Bocage was then in Rouen. There was not a Jew in all of England—in all of northern Europe— who had not heard of the Leopard. The Turkish commander Kerbogha had called him the Archangel Michael, with his beautiful face and flowing hair. Not to mention the mad way he fought, the young Crusader knight who was the son of Jewish Sophia. Dead two years, Judah reminded himself.

"I am the physician." Judah Ha-Kohen lifted his eyes to the knight on his horse. "What bones are there to set? And who is to pay me if I come to the house of Belefroun?"

"Don't worry about that." The knight turned in the saddle to look back down the street in the direction of the wool factors' quarter. "No one is going to cheat you. We are the baron's knights from Morlaix."

"In that case I will get my assistant." He went into the house and shouted up the stair for Hagit. Then he went into the apothecary and took his leather bag from its place and filled it with the things he would need, including the splints. He added a tincture of poppy for the head wound and went out.

He met Hagit by the open door. "Carry this," he said, holding out the leather bag. "And stay behind me. We are going to a house full of Norman knights, two of them injured."

"Hurry," the knight called. He spurred his horse up the street, leaving Judah with the wool factors' watch.

At the corner they smelled the smoke before they could see it. The guard broke into a heavy-footed trot. The knight galloped ahead of them.

Judah Ha-Kohen tucked his leather bag under his arm, Hagit running at his heels. The Jewry of Wroxeter was small, no more than three houses set in a cul-de-sac that bordered the wool factors on one side and the street of the weavers' and carders' guild on the other. Sophia Belefroun had chosen to live not in the Jewry but in her Christian father's house inside the factors' quarter.

The Belefroun house was as fine as any in the town, two and a half stories, the downstairs windows set with thick blown glass, and the roof made of red clay Norman tiles. When they entered the street, dismounted knights were rushing about. One had climbed to the roof. The shuttered windows were open and black smoke boiled out. From time to time a face appeared to shout something.

The knight jumped down and tossed the reins to a knight. "What in the name of Satan!"

"Drogo, someone tried to set fire to the house." The young knight pulled the horse into the street. His face was grimed with smoke. "Sir Gilbert is upstairs, he—"

Drogo pushed him aside and plunged through the doorway.

Judah drew Hagit into the center of the street. There was not much heat, nor could they hear the dread crackle of flames, but people watched fearfully from upper windows. Two of the knights' horses broke their tether and galloped away. A bucket line of wool workers formed at the well at the bottom of the hill and started up to the Belefroun house.

A head appeared above them, a strapping red-haired man with a smoke-blackened face. He bellowed and two knights came out of the bottom of the house and gave chase after the mounts. Three knights dragged a brass-bound coffer through the front door and went back. Then Judah saw him.

The knight came out into the street bareheaded, his long black hair loose about his face. He pushed through the crowd and turned to shout something to those upstairs. A knight stuck his head out and yelled a warning to those below and dropped a chair. It landed in the street and two legs promptly split away and bounced into the ditch.

Simon de Bocage shouted to him. Judah clutched his leather bag, his arm around Hagit, as more knights pushed past them to chase the horses. Smoke began to drift away down the street. The bucket line had worked steadily up to the front of the house. It passed the water buckets to a knight who had stationed himself at the front door.

Judah watched Simon de Bocage with a feeling of elation. Sophia's son was beautiful, as Sophia herself had been beautiful. A young Joshua, a warrior from the time of Israel's kings. He saw him order his men to stand back. The bucket passers rushed inside, up to the second story.

The smoke was nearly gone. The redheaded knight stuck his head out of an upper window to bellow that there had not been much damage after all. Simon de Bocage moved out into the street to look up at him. The roof was tile, not thatch or shingle, and that was what had saved it, the man above called, rubbing his eyes. His head popped back inside.

"Sir knight." Judah Ha-Kohen stepped forward. "I have come for—"

His voice trailed away as Simon de Bocage whirled on him. It took his breath away for it was Sophia's face; one could not miss that strange, graceful mouth.

The bucket carriers came back downstairs and joined the group of apprentices and wool merchants discussing the fire.

Simon de Bocage said, "Come, man, what is it?"

Knights returned with the runaway horses. They rode into the midst of the band of apprentices, who gawked at them, envious.

Judah was thinking of the night Sophia Belefroun, Sophia de Bocage she was by that time, had come to him in the goldsmiths' part of the Jewry with this beautiful young man, then but a babe, in her arms.

A dark night; Judah remembered that it had been raining. It was in the spring. Her child had been born in the spring near the time of the Passover.

He shut his eyes to see memory's vivid images. *I want you to call the rabbi,* Sophia had said to him. Had she known then that the father, the Christian knight, would take the child away from her?

Impatient, Simon de Bocage had turned away. Judah was thinking that only he, Judah Ha-Kohen, knew that this formidable Crusader and hero of Antioch had been theirs since that night his mother had brought him to the Wroxeter rabbi.

"Sir knight," he called. "I am the physician, I have come to attend your wounded knights."

Judah stepped forward, pulling Hagit with him. He pulled back Hagit's hood and slipped the cloak away.

The street was so close-packed there were few to notice what was happening. As it was, Judah gave Simon de Bocage only a moment to look.

"And this is my daughter, Hagit," he said. "Your mother and I saw to the *kiddushin,* your betrothal, when you and my daughter were mere babes."

Then Judah Ha-Kohen drew Hagit's cloak around her once more.

# Chapter Ten

*F*or a moment Simon could do nothing but stare.

Gilbert shouted down that the fire was out. Simon barely heard him. The old man had come up to him saying something about his daughter and in the next instant had whisked away the assistant's cloak, revealing a pretty young girl. The story was his mother had supposedly betrothed them when they were babes.

He took the old man by the arm. "Not here," Simon told him.

He dragged the Jew through the front door and the bottom part of the house, which stank of smoke and was filled with Gilbert's knights getting in each other's way. They went out through the back door, past the kitchen house, into the backyard.

It was, he saw at once, not a good place for their business. The houses in the wool factors' street had cesspools in back into which chamberpots and kitchen offal were emptied. He shoved the man toward the lower garden, and the cloaked figure of the girl stumbled after them.

He had to get the physician and the girl away from the others. It was bad enough to have surprised prowlers, who had set a fire in the house as they were opening it, but now this: a Jew accosting him with some story of a supposed betrothal. They would never let it rest, Simon told himself, this taint of his mother's race. But he had not expected to see it crop up here, in Wroxeter.

He pulled the old man to a stop.

The physician was past middle age, with a gray-streaked beard that hung to his waist. Like most Jews in the north he wore a long gown of brown linsey-woolsey, plain except for a gold chain around his neck from which hung his physician's measuring spoons.

The girl was another matter. One look and Simon was back again in the east, seeing a beautiful young thing with loosened dark, waving hair held in place by a gold band. And long dark eyes that were too much like his own.

He tried not to look at her any longer than was necessary. His nerves were already on edge. "What in infernal hellfire is this about a betrothal?"

The girl cringed. But the old man said, "Oh, young sir, it is true." He stroked his beard, nervous. "I, Judah Ha-Kohen, physician of Wroxeter, know you have been raised as a Christian; it is common knowledge among us. But perhaps you would not be displeased to know it is still our Jewish law which governs you, dear sir. That is," he added, "through your mother, our esteemed Sophia, and *her* mother, you are fully born in our Jewish faith."

"Christ." Simon swiveled to look back at the house. Drogo and Aimeric were on the smoke-blackened roof, too far away to hear. And the path from the kitchen house was empty. "That is an accursed lie!" At the look on the girl's face he said more softly, "An honest mistake, physician. You want someone else."

The Jew stepped closer to peer at him. "Oh no, I am not mistaken. Your dear mother, Sophia Belefroun—Sophia, wife to the knight Geoffrey de Bocage she was then—brought you to me when you were newborn to have Rabbi bar Lev, may his soul rest in peace now these fifteen years, do the *bris*." He tugged at his beard. "In secret, though, so your father would not know of it except when it was too late."

Simon winced. A capricious fate was tormenting him vilely, yet he could not think of how to put an end to it. He saw the girl was near to tears.

"Listen—"

"Judah Ha-Kohen," the other said, helpful.

"Yes, well, Ha-Kohen." He gritted his teeth. "I was not born into the Jewish faith. I am Christian born and baptised. And if you wish to keep your eyes and your tongue you will not say otherwise."

The old Jew raised his eyebrows. "Do you deny, Samuel, Sophia's son, that you are circumcised? It was more than twenty-five years ago but I saw with my own eyes when the rabbi—"

"Didn't I say for you to shut your mouth?" *Circumcised*. He did not want to think of it. And he had not heard the name Samuel in years.

Simon whirled on the girl. She had opened her cloak with a shy smile in spite of her tears, and stood in her sumptuous purple velvet gown, dark, wavy hair spilling over her shoulders, the band of gold and red stones upon her head. The effect was exotic, quite lovely.

Inwardly he groaned. The physician was obviously lying. The girl was nowhere approaching thirty. Which she'd have to be if they were betrothed in their cradles.

"Your father has deceived you," he told the girl. She kept smiling at him. "Besides, why would you want to marry me?" he said, desperate. "I am poor, a knight who lives by the sword. Of worldly goods I have nothing."

That should have taken care of the preposterous affair. But as Simon turned to go, the physician stepped in front of him.

"Oh, but you are not poor, dear sir," Ha-Kohen told him. "Profits from Belefroun factoring have been well held by my son-in-law, Elias ben Ezra, for these past two years. There are investments in Bruges in Flanders, and with the varied loans overseen at above an advantageous twenty-four percent—"

"God rot it! Will you stop?" The girl had laid a pleading hand on his arm. Simon tried to pry it away.

He looked around, thinking he couldn't go back to Gilbert and the other knights with the Jew nattering at him about his mother's wool trade and how rich he was, and that he was betrothed to his daughter. It would be the utmost folly, and besides, none of it was true. The girl was not over fifteen if she was a day. The whole thing was some kind of extortion.

Exasperated, he stepped toward the old man, who stepped back, eyes wide.

"Listen, Ha-Kohen, I have heard these claims of my Jewishness before and I reject them. Although my mother was of that faith, she married my father, who was *not* a Jew."

"Nevertheless, you should believe me, young Samuel, sir. I saw your *bris* personally!"

It was the last straw. Simon grabbed him, harder than he'd intended; the Jew's head banged against the boards of the kitchen-house wall.

"Listen, Ha-Kohen, whatever you think you know or do not know," he growled, "you will keep it to yourself." He gave him an extra shake. "Do you swear it?"

The man's face was gray. Beside him his daughter wrung her hands, whimpering. But Judah Ha-Kohen held his ground. "When you go to London, Simon de Bocage, those you seek will know you are one of us."

*"What?"* Simon let him go and stepped back.

"Why are you surprised, someone like you? That we know where you are bound, and why?" Judah Ha-Kohen rubbed his throat. "You have been to foreign shores, you know the way of the world. Did you never think these Christians would use you for their own purposes one day?"

Simon stared at him. How could they learn of something here, in Wroxeter, when he had not yet been to London? "You know nothing," he said.

"Do I not?" The girl handed her father a kerchief and he wiped his face, then his neck, gingerly. "We fear this journey to Prince Henry will do us ill— although it is to be admitted, we are not sure how.

Tell me," he said, squinting at him, "why do you want to be a Christian? Their knights go about slaughtering each other in the name of courage, a madness which they call a virtue. But with their carnage these Christians are a plague on the earth. Even their priests preach against them. On the other hand, if you are a Jew—"

He nodded to his daughter, then tucked the kerchief in his sleeve, his face composed. "We Jews do not have to prove our bravery and manhood each day. What we love in this life is peace, our families, good trade at a profit. Also study, and learning. We seek enlightenment, a thing Christian knights know little of. It is said that you are bookish, a good scholar. Samuel Sophiasson, do you know how a scholar among Jews is greatly revered?"

Simon had been waiting for the old man to finish. *He wants money*, he told himself. There was no other explanation. He had not thought his mother would do this to him.

Gilbert came to the back window. He stuck his head out and shouted down something about the leech.

The physician took his arm. "Stay with us, I beseech you, young Samuel." His voice was urgent. "Listen to me, give up this strenuous Christian life, marry here in Wroxeter, beget many Jewish children, enjoy your books and be happy. You need go no farther, it all awaits you here."

He shook him off. And the girl, who'd been hanging on him again. "Sweet Mary, why do you insist on it? That I am a Jew, when I am not?"

"We need the leech," Gilbert was bellowing. "Simon, what are you doing down there?"

He wrenched his arm away, then disentangled the girl's hands. Looking down at her, Simon was suddenly struck by the little Jewish girl's loveliness, her sweet and pleasant demeanor. The physician's daughter was a rare rose, velvety and tempting. And not, he thought somewhat sourly, some gawk of a Saxon with an unearthly beauty and a lunatic disposition.

The old man was right. His life *was* a hand-to-mouth affair, and like any knight's, subject to violent death at any unforeseen moment. For a brief instant he allowed himself to think of what it would be like, married. Safe, comfortable. Pursuing his dreams of study just as Ha-Kohen had described, with this pretty young thing beside him.

He shook off the strange fantasy reluctantly.

"Physician, go and do what you were called here to do," he said. "Which is tend our wounded. But if you mention this to any of the others I will have your damned tongue."

The Jew looked at him as though still thinking to persuade him. Then he sighed.

Resigned, Judah Ha-Kohen picked up his leather physician's bag and pushed the girl ahead of him toward the house.

Simon waited.

His mother had not betrothed him to Judah Ha-Kohen's girl, he was sure. But that the Jews wanted him to stay in Wroxeter was plain enough. And they knew more than was thought, from what the old man had said. Or else all England, even the Jews, longed for a new monarch.

But whatever else there was, Judah Ha-Kohen

knew what his mother *had* done. He had been an eyewitness at his circumcision. Or so he said.

Under his breath, Simon swore.

Ingrith left the kitchen as soon as she heard their voices on the path, and waited by the cesspool until she was sure the leech and his daughter were inside the house. When she came in she found Gilbert looking for her in the back passageway.

"Where have you been?" He held her while he looked her over. "Are you all right? You did not breathe any of the smoke?"

"I am not damaged." He always treated her like this. Like cargo. "I went for a broom."

"A broom?" He looked down and saw it in her hand. "That is not what you are here for. No one wants you to sweep." He took it away from her. "And you are not supposed to be wandering. Someone should be watching you, girl. You wouldn't want to run away from us, would you?"

He steered her ahead of him. The hall that ran the length of the wool merchant's house was narrow, with barely the space to pass. The front room was used as a counting house. He threw open the door, ducked under the low lintel, and pulled her inside.

Simon de Bocage was sitting at a wooden table. He looked up when Gilbert said, "If the girl says she does not want to go to London, then someone should be guarding her."

"They're your knights, Gilbert."

"It's you they listen to. The great paladin."

Gilbert pushed Ingrith to a bench. He sat down beside Simon at the table and helped himself to wine. They discussed the house, the Belefroun wool factoring, and the accounts that had been kept in Wroxeter since Sophia Belefroun's death.

Simon pushed the papers away. "I am no merchant, Gilbert, but I am told there is money here, in the house and the business. The Jews have overseen a part of the profits. So has St. Margaret's."

Gilbert raised his eyebrows. "Stay, then, in Wroxeter, and be rich. Don't go to Paris."

"Hah." He lifted his eyes and looked at Ingrith. "Your father has already seen to my task."

They began to choose the knights who would go on to London, and those who would return to Castle Morlaix with Gilbert.

Ingrith hunched forward, elbows on her knees. She was hungry. She thought a knight had been sent to buy food, but he hadn't come back and no one had asked about it. They had not yet had their midday meal. Her stomach clenched with hunger.

She was glad Gilbert de Jobourg was going back to Morlaix. When he started for Welsh marcher country she would lie with Simon de Bocage and prove to him that he had had her in the forest that night, and that she was no longer a maid. All she had to do after that was wait for his punishment.

She looked around the room. She had never been in a house like this one. It was more elegant than the lord and lady's rooms in a castle. The walls were plastered, then painted with limewash. There was also a window with panes of thick glass that let in the light. Upstairs, where someone had set the fire, there were three rooms for sleeping.

The house belonged to Simon de Bocage's mother, she'd been told. And her father had been a rich merchant. The room was covered on three walls with shelves holding baskets and wooden paddle carders, some with stacks of counting sticks and string tallies. On the fireplace wall there were willow rods with hooks from which hung swatches of wool for grading. Anyone who had ever been to a sheep country fair knew what they were: the wool merchants carried the long sticks with their sample tufts of wool when they came to buy the new shearing.

This house in the middle of the town was surrounded by noises: carts rolling by in the street, people talking in the gardens next door, the sound of a church bell ringing somewhere. It was exciting. She'd noticed even ordinary folk were busy, well dressed, nearly all wearing shoes, not like in the country. To live in a big house such as this would be as fine as even the nobles' manor houses she'd seen.

"Not Drogo," Simon de Bocage was saying.

"He is my father's man, I wouldn't give him to you. Take the English knight, Aelfred." Gilbert paused, thinking. "And Aimeric."

"Aimeric. God's face, the tadpole's already in love with her."

"We seem to have that trouble." Gilbert turned to look at Ingrith. She returned his stare with a lift of her chin. He laughed.

They went back to discussing the knights. Gilbert did not want to give more than four for the London journey. Winebald, with his broken arm, would go back to Morlaix at speed. Gulfer, if he lived, would have to be left at the guest house at St. Margaret's church.

Gilbert yawned and rubbed his face with his hands. "We might have lost some more men here if we had not discovered the fire. By the Cross, who would think to set it with wool?"

"It burns well enough if the sheep grease is still in it."

"Yes, and stinks. You cannot breathe upstairs." He twisted in his chair, stretching out his long legs. "Jesus in heaven, two men out as well as an ambush. In which we may well ponder who was attacking whom. Now a fire, and the burglar who set it jumped onto the roof and got away."

"And a broken wain."

Gilbert looked at him. "I had not thought about that."

"Think about it, then." Simon drew his dark brows together. "No sooner is the fire put out than the old Jew comes to me and says my mother betrothed me to his daughter, and I must marry and live here in Wroxeter and be a Jew."

Gilbert stared at him. "Your mother betrothed you? God's wounds, Simon, your mother is dead." He crossed himself quickly. "May God rest her soul."

"It was a trick. I did not give him time to ask me for money." He looked down at the table, still frowning. "I tell myself it is not the girl they want, there have been too many chances to take her. Or kill her." He thought a moment, his face bleak. "The same for me."

Gilbert was confounded. "Nay, I swear to you, Simon, you are—"

"Gilbert, that would be King William's way.

Think about it. Kidnap or kill. But since that has not happened, what is it?"

Gilbert shook his head. "I know how you have lived has made you cynical, Simon, but 'tis no plot. It was a burglar who set the fire here. These are lawless times, but you are making too much of nothing."

He wasn't listening. "It seems they cannot make up their minds. Or perhaps they are merely stupid. Like Saxons."

"Saxons?"

At that moment a knight came to the door with a message for Gilbert and he got up and went into the hall. He came back to say the physician wanted to see him about the injured knights. "Simon, I will go with you to London." He looked troubled. "With all my knights, I cannot leave you alone with this if you truly think there is danger."

"No." He drew a sheet of parchment from a pile on the table and began to write on it. "Go see to the wounded. I have a lamed horse. Ask the leech for some balm for it."

Gilbert hesitated. He started to speak, then changed his mind and went out.

Simon continued writing. Ingrith saw him bend his head to the parchment, quill in hand. His dark hair fell forward at the sides of his face.

One had to be very clever to learn to cipher and read as he was doing. People said to read and write was to be more clever, even, than the nobles.

People did not regard her as clever. Gilbert de Jobourg and his cousin talked of the king of England as though she weren't there; as though she could not understand simple words. This was the way they always treated her, as though she were little better than their horses.

Ingrith scratched her arm where she'd snagged it on some briars. There seemed to be more to this journey than bringing her to London to be some great Norman's leman. In the back of the house there was the Jew with his daughter wrapped in a cloak so that one could not tell whether she was a man or a woman; he was telling Simon de Bocage that the girl was betrothed to him. She'd watched them through a crack in the kitchen-house wall: the tall knight with his padded undercoat stained with the fire, and the physician who wanted him to wed his daughter. He had said Simon de Bocage was a Jew, too.

She scratched the back of her hand. She had never seen a Jew and was not sure what they were. But to be one was not, from the look on Simon de Bocage's face, a good thing.

"Are you hungry?"

She jumped. When she looked up he was studying her.

Uncertain, she shook her head. *No.*

"Then stop grabbing your belly." She took her hand away. "Why can't you keep your shoes on?" He stared at her feet and she tucked them under the bench. "Do you cook?"

Cook? She turned his question over in her mind, not sure what to say. She hoped he did not want her to fix any food; Gilbert had not wanted her to sweep, or help clean up after the fire. You're not supposed to do this, Gilbert had said.

She nodded.

"Saxon cooking?"

She watched his face. The corners of his mouth curled up.

There was nothing wrong with Saxon cooking, even though the Normans made fun of it. As she opened her mouth to say so, Gilbert came back into the room.

"The Jew says the broken arm will mend well enough. Gulfer goes to the guest house at St. Margaret's and the brothers' care." He picked up the wine and poured a cup. "He wants to speak with you, Simon. In the hall."

"No." He did not look up.

"Simon."

"I'm writing a letter to your father about this house and some money that is in trust with the Jews here." He picked up another sheet of vellum and stuck the quill pen in the inkpot, shook it and began to write again. "Tell Judah Ha-Kohen there is nothing to speak about."

Gilbert put down his cup and went out. They heard his voice in the hall. Aimeric came in with a wooden tray with bread and cheese and sausage.

Simon got up and crossed the room and took it from him. He carried the tray to the table.

"Come," he said over his shoulder, "have something to eat. If I know you, you are starved."

Ingrith came to his side and he poured her a cup of wine. She looked over the rim at him as he fixed a slab of bread and put cheese and a piece of the sausage on top.

"Here," he ordered, "sit down like a decent person and don't put it all in your mouth at once."

He took his dagger and cut through the bread and

cheese and meat several times, making small pieces.

She watched him cut up her food, trying to think of something to say about Saxon cooking. She wanted to say that she could not only fix food but hunt, set snares for small game, and fish. She could take care of herself, she was not as stupid as they thought. But she was hungry; she could not talk and eat at the same time.

Forgetting, she put more than two pieces of bread and meat in her mouth. The corners of his mouth turned up again.

Ingrith made herself sit there, slowly chewing, until she could swallow. Hating him.

"Much better."

She lifted her head and saw the strange dark in his gold-spangled eyes. Like a woods pool, black, with specks of sunlight. She knew his skin was sun-darkened except for the private places on his body, and she could remember very clearly the feel of him, smooth and heavy with muscles. By the stream he'd shuddered when she'd touched him. She distinctly remembered what he'd looked like without a fore-skin. It was not so ugly, she supposed, now that she'd seen Drogo's and Arnuld the Frisian's. One might even grow to prefer it.

Thinking about it, she realized her eyes had been on his crotch. She looked up. He was watching her, eyes narrowed.

She looked away.

The afternoon was spent cleaning the upper part of the house. Some knights took the horses to be stabled at the ostler's, leaving the rest to do the work of hauling out the burned furnishings. At last, after the evening meal, they went upstairs. The sun was just setting, it was still light. Gilbert eased off his boots with a groan. "One still cannot breathe up here. 'Tis a stink that takes long to fade."

The marks of the fire were on the walls. Over the bed it had burned through the plaster and down to the beams. Gilbert said the wool guild would catch the burglars and punish them. He said he did not believe it was Saxon mischief.

"You didn't have anything to do with it, girl, did you?" he asked Ingrith.

She didn't answer him. She climbed into the middle of the bed. The bare slats had been spread with saddle blankets. She lay down, pulling her marten-skin cloak over her. The fur was still damp and it stank, but with the smell of the fire one could overlook it.

In the twilight, both men lay down together on either side of her. They held their hands clasped before them and rumbled their prayers. This was the first time since they'd left Morlaix that they'd slept under a roof. Ingrith had grown quite drunk with traveling, she who had never been more than half a league from her family's hut. She had almost gotten used to being in a different place every day.

They would begin the journey again on the morrow, before dawn. And sleep somewhere else the coming night, but not in a house. Not unless they stopped at an inn.

She remembered the knights said there were houses in London finer than any in Wroxeter. Finer even than Baron Malsmbury's manor house, where she'd been held for a sennight, and which had fireplaces in every room and a great hall and a solar. How good it would be to live this way, she thought with a sigh.

She lay watching the light fade on the fire-blackened walls. Gilbert was already asleep, he had begun to snore.

The physician had wanted Simon de Bocage to marry his daughter. She was pretty; Ingrith had seen the Jewish girl's face when she threw her hood back. She tried to imagine Simon and the Jewish girl married, doing the things married men and women did when in bed.

All sorts of pictures flitted through her head. She found she did not want to think of him doing anything like that with the Jewish girl. Married or not.

Such thoughts about men and women had made her skin tingle. Ingrith moved her leg. It touched the one beside her and he moved it slightly away.

Simon de Bocage was not asleep. She lay there listening to his even breathing. He knew too that she was awake.

Unbidden, the memory of his wet and naked body that day at the spring came to her mind. He was a handsome man, gracefully made, she could not deny it. She did not know why it rose up now, to trouble her.

*Tomorrow*, Ingrith told herself. Tomorrow they would not have Gilbert.

# The Roman Road

# Chapter Eleven

"So this is Watling Street," the English knight said. He reined in his horse. "I have never seen it."

Simon de Bocage and the four Morlaix knights rode ahead past the marker of a moss-covered stone pillar of cross and wheel. It was some sort of shrine. The stepped base was littered with offerings of wilted flowers and fruit. A basket filled with a sheaf of green oats had been put there for the coming Lammastide, the first day of August when loaves of bread were made from the new grain.

Beyond the cross, the ancient Romans' stone highway went through the rolling plains like the slash of an ax. This was middle England, where Saxons had fought and conquered Britons, and then felled the forests to plow the heavy clay soil. As far as the eye could see, the corn fields were yellowing. In the distance, figures of men and women with scythes were already at work.

"The Saxon tribe of Waeclingas levied tolls here

once," Aelfred informed them, "and gave the road their name."

"Saxon *kingdom*," Ingrith said. "Not tribes. The Saxons had kings."

The young friar smiled at Ingrith over his shoulder. Since Wroxeter, she had ridden behind him on his mule. Simon de Bocage was at the column's head on his gray destrier, leading the lamed Saracen mare. Ingrith was glad to have company on the road. When the knights were not passing the time singing Norman war songs, the Benedictine brother, who said his name was Enguerrand of Domfront, told stories. The dwarf, who was the Earl of Chester's jongleur, sang and related scandalous jokes. Simon de Bocage had wanted to refuse them their travel, saying the mule and the dwarf's donkey would slow them down too much. But in the end she knew the friar had given him money.

They saw Simon lift his hand and give the signal to turn. When he issued an order the knights jumped, they were so eager to please. His back was straight and he was unhelmeted, wearing the mail hood that covered all of his head but his face. Her mind turned to that night he'd lain with her, remembering his naked body, in his crotch the ramrod sex upthrust against a mat of black hair.

Her cheeks flamed. She didn't know where such ideas came from but this was not the first time her thoughts had strayed. She was surprised the memory of lying with him could be so lasting.

The mule's shod hooves made a loud noise on the stones. Curious, she leaned around the friar to see.

She'd been told the road ran the length of England from Chester in the north to London, and beyond that to the southern coast and the sea. It would cross two great tracks, Fosse Way and Icknield Way, that ran east to west across the kingdom. The knights said these were even older than Watling Street, having been built long ago before even the Romans, in the days of the giants.

Ingrith felt a shiver deep in her flesh. She was in strange country, among unknown people. It was good in a way that the friendly young friar was with them.

The mule stepped into a hole in the paving and stumbled. Ingrith tightened her arms around the friar. Before them, the Romans' road went for miles with two grooves in the middle where wagon wheels had run for so long they had eaten away the stone.

All traveled Watling Street under the king's peace. It was proclaimed from King William Rufus's court twice a year that no outlaws, robbers, or other lawbreakers could violate the king's peace without harsh and swift punishment. But in real fact, it was better to beg safe conduct from a troop of knights, as the jongleur and the friar were doing.

By midday they had passed two villages, one with a market fair where they stopped to buy bread and wine. There the friar preached a short sermon, standing on a tanner's barrel, denouncing the deadly sins of pride, lust, and avarice, but promising a revolution at hand. God and his earthly servants were about to punish the enemies of the church.

Ingrith looked around, startled at the friar's words, but saw the peasants only nodded, agreeing.

There was some shouting from the back to the effect that they'd know the ones to punish.

The crowd did not like the dwarf, Anorlyx, when he told a few jokes and sang songs. No coins dropped into the hat he had put down. When he did a few cartwheels and other tricks there were comments about his deformed arms and legs. Women who were carrying turned their backs or went away, afraid to mark their babes by looking.

The friar finally rescued him. "Come," he told him, taking him by the arm and pushing him through the sullen peasants, "they are not worldly enough here to laugh at good stories."

Anorlyx hung his head, breathing hard, and didn't answer.

When they were on the road again the dwarf took out his comb and brush and tidied his hair and neat, golden beard. Except for his hooked nose, his big head was handsome, and suited to his deep voice. Ingrith watched him, fascinated. He had worked hard, his velvet coat was stained with sweat, and the villagers had not even dropped an apple or a piece of bread into his hat.

She leaned over to him. He rode next to the friar; they were the last in the column. "Is it often like that?" she wanted to know. "That you give them jokes and tricks, and they give you nothing?"

He did not look at her. "If I had a woman as beautiful as you," he said harshly, "I would make much money. Women always take the cap around. The better looking the woman, the more the hayheads give." He lifted his chin and took the comb and raked under it, untangling the bright curls. "At night, I would charge a silver mark for a special show, to let them watch what I do to you. I have a cock bigger than any of those shit hoppers back there."

Ingrith's mouth dropped open. She could not believe what the dwarf had said in his elegant-sounding French. She knew the friar had heard it; she'd felt his body stiffen.

Anorlyx tucked comb and brush back in his purse. "I could make much money from you alone." His amber eyes were expressionless. "I could teach you some things I have learned in Paris and in Italy that would make a lord pay a fortune to have you in his bed."

With an effort, Ingrith turned her face away and studied a field of oats where reapers were working. She could not pretend that she had not heard. But she hoped he would not speak to her again.

They rode in silence, the donkey trotting beside the mule, the dwarf staring fixedly at her.

After a while Ingrith told herself the Earl of Chester's court was a corrupt and evil place, as bad as the king's in London. Perhaps that was what was the matter with Anorlyx.

She rested her head against the friar's back. There was something about the dwarf that did not seem right to her. For that matter, the friar made a strange roadside preacher. She wondered if she should speak to Simon de Bocage about them. He would probably not believe her.

On the road between the villages they met a line of hay wains coming from the harvest. The column of knights went up on the bank to give them way. The hot July sun beat down on their heads and backs. The knights doffed their helmets and pulled off their tunics, leaving only their mail.

They ate the noon meal in the saddle, and spied a troop of knights coming north. Aimeric called out that they bore the standard of Tamworth Castle.

They went up onto the bank again to let the Tamworth knights pass. The knight captain looked up from the sunken road. "Simon de Bocage," he shouted.

They saw him turn his head. He shouted back, surprised, "Julien de Marmion."

The Tamworth column did not stop, but the leader saluted Simon with his fist to his helm. "Antioch! Antioch!" he bellowed.

A few of his knights gave the Crusaders' cry, "Deus Volt!" *God Wills It.*

Simon de Bocage rode on as if made of stone. The Morlaix knights looked straight ahead, their backs stiff with pride. But the dwarf made a face. "Christ's wounds, we have a hero among heroes."

The knights around them stiffened, scowling. "Peace, peace," the friar said quickly. He took the mule back down the steep bank. Ingrith clung to him, her eyes closed, as the mule slid onto the roadway. To soothe her he said, "Do you want me to finish telling you about the death of old King William?"

She nodded eagerly. The friar knew endless stories; he was better than a troubadour. She especially liked tales of the last English king, Edward, whom people now called the Confessor (which meant priest), and stories of Great King Alfred, who fought the Danes. She even liked to hear of William the Bastard, Duke of Normandy, who had conquered England. Brother Enguerrand had been telling them how the old king had split his kingdom among his two sons, Duke Robert, and King William Rufus of England, and left the youngest of his nine children, Prince Henry, only a modest sum of money.

Aelfred and Aimeric fell back to listen. Up front they were singing another verse of the Normans' favorite, the *Song of Roland*. The dwarf took off his velvet coat and rode in his undershirt, his white, muscled arms exposed to the sun. Ingrith tried not to look at him.

In his later years, the friar was saying, the great Conqueror grew old and grossly fat, no longer the iron-fisted warrior who had subdued England. His oldest son, Robert, tormented him every year by raising barons in Normandy against him in bloody rebellions. Finally, challenged by the rumors that he was too old and unfit to fight, the Conqueror mounted a campaign against King Philip of France, who had encouraged Duke Robert against his father. The war went well, although William suffered greatly from his age and his great bulk.

It was an accident with his horse, the friar said. The king was riding among the smoldering ruins of Nantes, a great victory in which he had destroyed that once-prosperous town, when his horse shied at something and reared, throwing him against the pommel of his saddle.

"A ruptured bowel," the dwarf put in.

The old Conqueror's belly had gone soft. His doctors had long worried that it was no longer supported by strong muscles because of his gross flesh. King William was carried from Nantes to his capital at Rouen. His two loyal sons, William Rufus and the youngest, Henry, called Beauclerc, because he was scholarly, were sent for.

"He was a long time in dying." The jongleur sat sideways in his saddle as his legs were too short for stirrups. "All summer, from July to the beginning of September."

Aimeric nodded. "That's a belly wound. They are slow to kill."

The friar said, "They carried him out of Rouen because the noise of the city bothered him, to the priory of Saint-Gervase. During the long burning summer the king struggled with his wound, with his physicians, Gilbert, Bishop of Liseux, and Guntard, the abbot of Jumieges, beside him."

"I have heard," Anorlyx said, "the stink was terrible. But nothing like the stink when he was dead."

Brother Enguerrand gave him a reproachful look. "King William repented much, blaming the horrors of his fatherless childhood for his cruelty. And he confessed his repentance for the terrible destruction of England in the north, where he had caused so many to die."

The English knight looked grim. "Yes, when William the Bastard put down the great rebellion of Seventy-six, he burned and wasted and turned out to starve every man, woman, and child. My father would say people tried to give their children away but no one could take them, they were starving themselves. So the English lay down to die in the fields, in the roads, with their babes in their arms. Thousands of them." He looked around, challenging them. "William the Crippler did well to repent."

The friar crossed himself. "My grandfather, the

thane Leofwine," Ingrith said, "swore himself to Prince Waltheof, to put a Saxon prince again on the throne. But my grandsire was tortured and killed, and the rest of my family scattered."

Aelfred said quickly, "Leofwine, King Harold's man?"

She nodded, surprised that he knew.

The dwarf broke in. "Come, are you going to tell us or not?"

The friar quickly said, "Of course I will tell you. Now Robert, the Conqueror's oldest son, was given the duchy of Normandy, which King William had held before he conquered England. To his second son and favorite knight, William, the Conqueror left England itself. And to Henry the clerk he gave five thousand silver marks."

While Prince Henry was busy counting out his silver with the help of his friends, King William had called for the crown and scepter of England, and given it to his weeping son William Rufus, along with a letter to the Archbishop of Canterbury. The king told William Rufus he must leave at once and not stay for his death, but reach England and seize the throne before the people knew of it.

The friar said, "There are many in England who still believe Duke Robert should have Normandy and England both, as his father held it."

Ingrith rested her cheek against the friar's back. "There was no one left with the king when he died."

He turned to look at her. "You have heard the story."

"No." But she could see it in her mind's eye. "They would leave him, all those nobles, when the king was dead."

It was true, the friar admitted. King William the Conqueror died at dawn, his great, gross body rotting with ruptured vitals. Bishops, his friends, even lowly monks deserted him. Only one knight, named Herluin, the friar told them, carried William back in an ordinary cart to the small church in Normandy to be buried beside his wife.

"God bless Herluin." Aimeric looked approving. "A knight who knew his duty to his lord when all others had abandoned him."

The dwarf hooted. "Oh, noble, dutiful knights." He spat into the dirt.

Aimeric said, "That is a knight's oath. To honor duty above all else."

"Only when it suits you." Anorlyx began to sing in his rich tenor, a Breton song about the beautiful maid Iseult of Armorica, the bride of Cornwall's King Mark.

Anorlyx sang very well. Even the knights riding ahead stopped their talking to listen. In the song King Mark's trusted man, brave and handsome Tristan, was sent to bring the Breton princess Iseult to Cornwall. But instead of delivering her to his liege lord, Tristan fell in love with Iseult, and she with him. As a consequence he broke his oaths, and they ran away together.

Some of the verses describing the lovers' passion were very bold. When Anorlyx finished there was silence.

Ingrith said, "They were not Saxons."

The dwarf pushed his donkey close to the friar's mule. "They were Britons. King Mark was king of the southern Welsh, and his promised bride was from Brittany."

She gave him a scornful look. "If a Saxon had sworn an oath to deliver his king's bride, he would die rather than break it."

The friar laughed. "Ah, you see our beauty does not believe in love!"

"Why should she?" The dwarf stared at her with his tawny, insolent eyes. "For what she does, she has no need of it."

He pushed the donkey up the road to ride with the others. Ingrith's cheeks burned. Aimeric started to spur his horse after him but the English knight caught his reins.

"Pay no heed," Brother Enguerrand said to Ingrith, "he is a bitter man." After a while he turned to her and said softly so the others could not hear, "It is not your wish to go to London?"

She stiffened. In front, Aimeric and the English knight talked of the forest of Arden they had left behind and how many outlaws it was said hid there.

The friar said in the same voice, "In the north there are those of your own people who would care for one of Leofwine's kin."

She held him around the middle, her cheek pressed to his back. She knew that was not the way a friar should talk—hinting that she could escape.

She decided to pretend she hadn't heard him. "I was there in the camp when we were first traveling," she said, "when you were preaching, do you remember? When you spoke of the Truce of God."

He twisted in the saddle to look back at her. She held tightly to him as she leaned back to look into his face. "But you did not say what the Truce of God was."

He stared at her for a long time. Finally, he turned

around again. "The Truce of God," Brother Enguerrand said, his back to her, "was that the lords of France should stop their warring on the second and third days of the week, Monday and Tuesday. And on Easter, Christmas, and Whitsuntide. And allow their vassals to till the soil and tend to the business of their demesnes."

"And they didn't?"

She felt him sigh. "No one wanted to be the first to leave the field. And give up his place."

"Oh," Ingrith said.

# Chapter Twelve

Nevertheless, Ingrith thought about escape as they turned off the Roman road to Tamworth Castle. She knew if she asked young Aimeric to help her he would. But Simon de Bocage was too fierce and able a knight not to chase down and catch anyone who sought to escape, and she would be punished, along with her family. And Aimeric, or the friar or anyone else who helped her, would most certainly be killed.

The sun fell low in the sky, and the byway led them down into Tamworth village. Here the two rivers, the Tame and the Anker, came together. Above them rose Tamworth Castle, built on a high mound of dirt that had once been the site of the ancient fort of Saxon kings. Stretching out in both directions were the earthworks, giant mounds and grass-grown rings of the old fortifications.

Anorlyx wrinkled his nose. "Tamworth's a wooden pigsty," he proclaimed. "I played here once, and the only good thing was that the old Conqueror's steward, who was the lord here then, had built the great hall in the middle of the bailey, away from the garbage heap."

They saw the dwarf did not exaggerate. Tamworth Castle was a homely structure of wood. The keep stood as it had since King William's day, surrounded by earthenworks topped with a high wooden palisade. It looked very primitive. It looked, one of the knights remarked, still Saxon.

"Didn't I tell you," Anorlyx said. He kicked his donkey to ride up ahead.

On the way in, they were overtaken by the Tamworth troop that had passed them on Watling Street, returning from collecting taxes. Julien de Marmion, brother to the lord, rode stirrup to stirrup with Simon, urging him to stay more than a night. Although horses and men were in need of a rest, Simon shook his head, saying they were late enough as it was to make London. The tall knight all but dragged him from his destrier.

"Nay, would you deny me precious talk with another Crusader?" he bellowed. "There are six of us here, thirsting for comradeship in a place where no one knows Emperor Alexis Comnenus or William Grant-Mesnil from a turd. Which, come to think of it, they are." Julien de Marmion stared at the Saracen mare. "What's the matter, is the Arab horse lame? Good, all the more reason. The stable knaves will soak that leg. And a night's rest will make her more fit to travel."

As they approached Castle Tamworth they were challenged by sentries shouting down from the portal gate. The hail was only a formality, as their escort rode with the de Marmion device of a running bear flapping in the wind over their heads. Simon shouted their identity. Just as formally two gate guards, trumpets blatting, filed out to meet them. It was a grand show for a castle made of wood. The Morlaix knights hid their grins.

Once inside, Simon went off with Julien de Marmion to the great hall, leaving Aelfred and an older Morlaix knight, Renaud, to take Ingrith to the kitchens.

The cook house was hot as a bake oven with not one but three roaring fireplaces going at once. The new de Marmion lord had married rich there in grain-growing country: food for the evening meal was heaped on the tables and cooks, undercooks, scullery girls, and kitchen knaves ran back and forth to the fires with panniers of vegetables, upending them into the pots.

A huge cook with a carving knife in his hand came up to them. He looked over the knights, scowling. "Sit out of the way," he shouted over the din. "We've little room here, what with taking in all the riffraff from the roads."

The back of the kitchen was full of travelers not of sufficient rank to eat in the lord's hall: peddlers with their bags, a miller and his helpers, a ruined monk with his tonsure growing in. And, standing out of the way, the same troupe of mummers who had followed the d'Aubigny wedding party. When they shouted his name, Anorlyx went to sit with them.

Ingrith sat down at a table of kitchen girls chopping summer marrow and onions. Aelfred and Renaud climbed over the bench to sit on either side. One of the big-breasted cooks came up and said something in Norman French. Aelfred answered at length, too low for Ingrith to hear. The woman's expression changed. She looked hard at her, then went off.

Renaud and Aelfred were so eager for the food they didn't stop to make the sign of the cross over it. The women cooks and scullions stood watching them eat. They stared at Ingrith, talking behind their hands.

At last one of them said, "Is it true, girl, that they are taking you to be some Norman lord's whore?"

Ingrith looked at Aelfred. Now she knew what he had said. Her mouth full, she could only nod.

"Saxon, are you?"

When she didn't answer, one of the women cooks went away. She came back with a pot full of fruit pudding made of apples and currants cooked in honey and beer.

The biggest cook leaned over her. "Ah, you poor young thing." She patted the top of Ingrith's head. "At least they've not bound you like the one we had here not so long ago. She was a pretty little bit, but they'd tied her hands and feet so's she wouldn't run away. One knight that was with her, he never let her out of his sight."

Ingrith kept her eyes on her food. She didn't want to hear their stories. She didn't want to think about what happened to other women when some Norman wanted them.

A man-at-arms came into the kitchen shouting that the mummers were wanted in the hall. The swarthy men and the two women picked up their maypole with ribbon streamers, the top with a shape like a huge male organ that they used to make wicked fun of the May season. One began to beat a drum. They had asked Anorlyx to join them; he marched out, waddling on his short legs.

Renaud scraped up the last of his pudding. Mummer's women were whores, he told them, their men sold them to anyone who wanted them after the entertainment. Ingrith remembered what Anorlyx the dwarf had said to her, about teaching her things that would make any lord want to pay much silver to take her to bed.

The kitchen women clustered around the big, rawboned English knight, pouring his beer and chattering. One of the scullery girls fetched a comb. Before Ingrith could push them away, the undercooks undid her hair and combed it out, exclaiming over the color. They wanted to know if she'd been given clothes to wear other than the ones she had on. Aelfred got up from the table and walked to one of the fires, sipping his beer, his back turned to them. Ingrith watched him as she told the cooks and the scullions about the martenskin cloak.

When the music in the hall started, Aelfred and Renaud got up from the table. Putting Ingrith between them they went to stand in the kitchen doors to watch. They were in the way of the food bearers, who cursed them, and the knights cursed them back. They stood through the mummers' scandalous maypole play. Renaud roared at the worst parts. Aelfred sucked in his cheeks, looking sidelong at Ingrith.

She paid little attention. In spite of wooden walls, Castle Tamworth took its meals in style. There was a long high table set on a platform for the lord and his family. Pages and squires knelt to serve their masters. One ran back and forth only to fill the wine ewers.

Below the high table were trestles for knights, then chamberlains, reeves, tallyers, and other castle officials, men-at-arms, armorers, stablers, and houndmasters. Behind them sat ordinary folk, and women and children. The castle chaplain and the lord and lady's confessor were at a table near the front with Brother Enguerrand.

"Not a love match," Renaud said, watching the high table. The new lord, Roger de Marmion, sat next to his wife.

"On her part, no," Aelfred said. They had heard the gossip.

Roger de Marmion was very attentive to his pretty wife. The former widow, very pretty with a long neck and smooth black hair tucked under her coif, only seemed to endure her new husband's doting looks. When he put his hand over hers on the table she waited until the roast was served before she took it away. He looked sideways at her, frowning.

"Besotted." Renaud laughed. "One marries a castle, and promptly surrenders."

Ingrith saw Simon de Bocage seated there with the lord's brother, Julien. They looked down on a table full of knights who shouted to get Simon's attention. Once he laughed and Ingrith saw a flash of white teeth in his sun-darkened face. He suddenly lifted his head and looked around the room as if seeking someone. Then his eyes found her.

It was as much a surprise to him as it was to her, for he quickly looked away. But Ingrith had found herself trembling.

She had not been able to forget the dwarf's song of the knight Tristan and his king's intended bride, Princess Iseult. The thoughts ran through her mind that Iseult had not wanted to be delivered to an old man, even though he was a king. Perhaps Iseult had planned that King Mark's knight Tristan would be tempted to take her maidenhead before they got to Cornwall. Then, of course, she could no longer be brought as a bride to a man she did not want.

As she stared at Simon de Bocage's bladelike profile Ingrith found she understood that perfectly. She would have done the same thing in her place.

"Ah," Renaud said, "they are going to do tumbling." He took her arm, pointing. "I saw them do this when they camped with the wedding. The blond girl is very good."

Ingrith shook off his hand. She watched the tumblers. Iseult's plan had worked. Except, of course, the fool knight, Tristan, had fallen in love with her.

Brother Enguerrand saw the Saxon girl standing in the doorway as he bent to speak to Tamworth's chaplain. The sight of her strangely fascinated expression, bent on Simon de Bocage at the high table, distracted him enough to make him lose track of what he was saying.

"His Holiness," the chaplain prompted, "believes in primogeniture in such claims."

"Yes." Enguerrand was trying to remember the question. The girl's eyes were fixed on de Bocage at the high table. He told himself he would give a silver penny to know what was in her mind.

"But shouldn't the claim be what the king," Father Hildebrand was saying, "has determined? There is the root of the problem."

"Yes, according to the law, the oldest son is given all." He put his mouth to the chaplain's ear to be heard over the shouts encouraging the acrobats. "That is the rule of western Christendom, despite the deathbed vagaries of a sick king. Remember, it was six weeks that King William lay dying. In that time the mind weakens much."

The chaplain murmured his sympathy at the thought of the king's terrible ordeal.

Enguerrand leaned even closer. He was not sure he could win support for Duke Robert's cause here in middle England where William Rufus was hated, but perhaps not enough. The king had put down his barons' rebellion so bloodily five years ago that there was not much stomach left for one now. And if there was one fault with the king's brother, the Duke of Normandy, he thought with a sigh, it was that Robert was never in the right place when wanted. Even if a plot could be fostered in England with the throne as the prize, the Conqueror's oldest son was still on his meandering way home from the Holy Land.

Brother Enguerrand leaned to the chaplain's ear and said, "There are those who would argue that England belongs—has always belonged—to Duke Robert. And not to a ruler that only a saint, our blessed exiled Archbishop Anselm, keeps the holy church from excommunicating."

Across from them the de Marmions' confessor looked sour. "Not only the ruler," he snapped, "but also his friends. Would that we could excommunicate and expel Robert of Belleme. Whom we suffer here in England without justice, when this monster is so enamored of Godless cruelty. Belleme is a disgrace to knighthood." When Enguerrand looked at him the priests said, "Oh, aye—Goderic of Helmsford is before Belleme's gates now, demanding the return of his son that the perverted Satan has captured for torture."

Enguerrand looked properly concerned. In his soul he heartily wished Duke Robert would renounce his old friend, Belleme. It would win more support for their cause. But it was not likely.

He looked back to the Saxon girl. "It is said Robert of Belleme behaves like a saint in the company of the duke, who may well be all unknowing of his friend's sins."

He didn't believe that himself. Even the chaplain looked unconvinced.

The confessor snorted outright. "Let Duke Robert look to the waste and warring he has brought to his own lands. How can he rule England when he does not rule well in Normandy?"

Father Hildebrand said, "Seint-Omer, I had heard that you took holy orders since you returned from Outremer."

"Not final orders, Father." The tumblers had gone, replaced by the dwarf jongleur, Anorlyx, carrying a harp. "I am as you see me, still a lay brother."

One of the mummers brought a stool. The dwarf sat down on it and began to tune the harp. The noisy crowd subsided.

Enguerrand sat back on the bench. If Anorlyx had been more beautiful his voice would have made him famous and rich, even loved. It was what Anorlyx said himself, over and over, when he was drunk.

The dwarf began a Norman love song and the

hall grew still. His bright, pure voice soared, his listeners hanging on every embellished note.

> *Perchance I see her but a day;*
> *Yet maketh my heart so free*
> *Her beauty so rejoiceth me,*
> *A full month after I am gay.*

Enguerrand Seint-Omer was telling himself it was hard to forget Anorlyx would do anything, including murder. Hugh of Avranches, the Earl of Chester, another great friend of Duke Robert, had made his jongleur available for what they might need of him.

He sipped his wine, thinking if he had not learned Simon de Bocage's real mission in England by the time they reached London, he might yet be forced to use him.

Ingrith grew tired of standing. She felt as though she could go to sleep leaning up against the door. After the dwarf, two young boys, the castle bailiff's sons, gave a recitation, part of a poem about the Normans' great battle of Senlac. Roger de Marmion took his wife's hand from the table and placed it on his arm, clasping his other hand over it. She turned and looked at him. He smiled grimly, watching the bailiff's boys return to their seats.

At last it was over. The tables and benches in the Tamworth great hall were moved to their places against the wall and the dogs turned out for the night.

When Ingrith lay down, the kitchen was half dark and still smelled of meat and onions. The kitchen people, stable knaves, single men-at-arms, curled up on the benches and went to sleep. She couldn't. The benches were narrow and hard; she kept feeling as though she would fall off. Stretched out on a bench beside her, Renaud watched her through half-closed eyes. She turned over and put her back to him.

At last, when everyone was sleeping, some drunken knights came in. She heard them among the benches, rousing the scullery girls.

"Ah, here it is." One stumbled back against a table, then fell over Ingrith, shouting he wanted to see the most beautiful tits in Christendom. The scullery girls screamed.

Ingrith struggled to get out from under him. It was a Tamworth knight, not anyone she'd seen before. She threw him off and jumped onto the bench. One of his companions tried to drag her down, the others waiting. But Aelfred had come up from his bench, sword in hand. At the front, the big bald cook roared to his feet.

Ingrith kicked at one of the drunks, aiming for his belly, and sent him reeling. The kitchen women were running about, shrieking and snatching up pots and other things to throw at the intruders.

Where was Simon de Bocage? They needed his help. She looked around, then remembered he was with his noble friends, not caring what went on in the kitchen among the drunks and common folk.

Aelfred and one of the Tamworth knights were battling with drawn swords. With his fists, Renaud drove the other knights, stumbling and cursing, toward the center of the room where the big cook and kitchen knaves lay waiting for them.

One of the kitchen women pulled Ingrith down beside her. "Let them fight," she told her. "They are always after the girls back here, the filthy Norman dogs."

The Morlaix knights and the cook and his people drove the intruders to the door, then pushed them out into the ward and slammed the door shut and drove home the bar.

The kitchen was in an uproar. Aelfred and Renaud came back to their benches, breathing hard. In the corner the kitchen girls wailed they could not sleep in peace anywhere. The cook went off to his bench shouting about drunken riffraff.

Renaud and the English knight began arguing over Ingrith. Aelfred said, "She did nothing; they came for her. Besides, one has only to look at her."

Renaud looked over at her. "Come sleep on the bench with me," he said. "I will protect you."

Ingrith lay down and drew the marten cloak about her. She turned her back and tried not to think what would have happened if the Tamworth knights had dragged her out of the kitchen. At least Renaud and Aelfred had protected her. Inside the cloak she shivered, although the kitchen house was sweltering.

Gradually the kitchen quieted. Aelfred lay watching Ingrith. It was the last thing she remembered, his eyes on her, before she fell asleep.

Then it was as though she had slept just a moment. Hands shook her awake. She opened her eyes to see the women cooks standing over her.

It was still dark. "It's too soon," she mumbled, pulling the fur back over her.

"Nay, your young knight captain is outside," one
of the women said. "This very moment."

Aelfred sat up, rubbing his eyes.

They began fussing over her again. A cook brought
out a comb and tied her hair. "It's true, you're
Saxon, aren't you, girl?" someone whispered.

She pushed them away. In the next minute they
had hauled her up and were hurrying her across
the kitchen still filled with sleepers. They pushed
her into a corner by the storerooms. One of the big
women took the hem of Ingrith's skirt and yanked
up her gown. It stuck at her shoulders.

"What are you doing?" She was frozen with fear.
Mother of God, they had been kind to her before,
now they were stripping her naked! She thought of
screaming for Aelfred and Renaud.

Gathered around her, they giggled. "Ah, she's a
beauty, that's the truth. No wonder the knights
wanted a look." The biggest cook pulled Ingrith's
gown all the way off and held it clamped to her
body.

Ingrith tried to cover her breasts with her hands.
They looked her over, avid.

"Ah, yes, you'll do," the big woman said. There
was more muffled laughter. They turned her around
several times so they all could see.

"She has a mole there," one of the younger
women said. "On her belly."

"Bah, I don't see any mole," someone said. As
quick as they had taken them off they yanked her
clothes back on.

Ingrith stood helpless as their hands worked at
her. Then they took her by the arm and pushed her
out into the hall. When she sat down at the table

with Aelfred and Renaud, someone fetched a bowl of oat porridge. A hand reached over her shoulder to drop a piece of butter into it.

Simon de Bocage came in. Renaud got to his feet, yawning. Simon said something to them in a low voice. His black eyes looked Ingrith over. "Are you all right?" he asked her.

She looked down at the bowl of porridge with the butter melting in it. A pulse in her head was pounding. She did not want to go anywhere with Simon de Bocage. He had probably been with a woman all night, he and his high-born friends. And the way people treated her, even the English, as though she were a whore and a slave. God in heaven alone knew what would have become of her if the drunken knights had raped her.

Her arm pressed against something hard in her skirt. She straightened up in her seat and put her hand to it.

Even as she met his eyes she knew it was a dagger. A small one that fit the hand, what the Normans called a *demi-poignard*. One of the cooks had stuck it in the waistband of her drawers when they put her clothes back on.

She did not have to look. The women standing around her were grinning.

# Chapter Thirteen

*T*hey saddled up in the dark in the ward among wagons and sleeping grooms. Because of what had happened in the kitchens Simon decided to take the Saxon girl up behind him again. They were riding the destrier because he wanted to give the mare a rest, even though she was no longer limping.

Before they started he called Renaud and the English knight to him. "They came looking for her, the drunks? And she did nothing to encourage them?"

The knights looked at each other.

"Sir Simon," Aelfred said, "I have never seen the demoiselle do anything to encourage anyone. If anything she is"—he saw him lift skeptical brows—"unfriendly. Except with the friar, Brother Enguerrand."

The friar, he saw, had climbed up on the mule. The dwarf trailed him on his small mount. Simon was struck by what a motley procession they made: six mailed knights, a preaching friar on a mule, a dwarf on a donkey, and a barefoot girl riding a pillion with him, their captain. It was a wonder the de Marmions had let them in.

"Whatever," he told them. "She will ride with me from now on."

He swung into the saddle. Some of the kitchen women had come out to watch them leave. A cook stepped forward with a brace of rabbits and held them up by the ears. The meat was welcome; fat coneys would make their midday meal. Before he could tell one of the knights to take them, the girl leaned down with a cry.

"Ah, how pretty!" She put out her hands.

The kitchen woman lifted up a kicking rabbit. In a second she had it in her arms.

"By the Cross." Simon turned in the saddle and saw she held the thing clutched to her breasts like a baby, its long ears lopped over her arm. "Give it back."

"No. I want it." Her eyes were wide, defiant. "I'll name it King Harold."

"You'll name it food." He couldn't reach behind him to take it from her without unseating them both. "Give it to me. And there was no cursed King Harold."

Aelfred led his horse up. "She means King Harold Godwineson."

He didn't need anyone's help. "It's a damned rabbit." He groped behind him with one hand and touched a round, warm thigh. Then he could feel her shrinking back, out of his reach. "And Harold Godwineson was never king."

Aelfred looked up at him. "The English crowned him, Sir Simon, before the Conqueror came."

Behind him the girl piped, "Yes, he was the last Saxon king."

More women came out into the ward, a horde of scullery girls and knaves behind them, yawning and rubbing their eyes.

The girl said, her voice defiantly louder, "I want to keep King Harold."

Looking at the crowd, mostly English, Simon knew he would have to dismount, drag her down and pry the thing away from her. He expected she would howl. And it would be risky to beat her, in front of these people.

All over a rabbit.

"Let her keep it, sir." A big cook came up to the destrier. "It's little enough for her, the lovely. Look, I will fetch you another."

"No." He motioned for Aelfred to take the other animal. They had been given sacks of bread and a small cask of ale, the de Marmions' gift.

Simon touched his spurs to the flanks of the destrier and turned its head, pushing the warhorse to the front of the column. The guards came out of the portal gate to let them out onto the drawbridge.

Damned infernal country, Simon told himself.

Behind him the Tamworth kitchen people waved and called out godspeed.

Between Tamworth and Berkhamstead the land was open, fields broken only by small forest preserves to provide firewood and the lords' hunting.

The weather continued hot. The travelers they passed on the road, two monks on foot going to St. David's priory in Wales, a band of nobles from Stafford Castle to the north chasing the deer, complained of the heat. But Simon preferred it to the rain. So did the Saracen mare. She was feeling frisky in the hot summer sun. Now that her leg was better she pulled and kicked behind them, wanting to run.

By mid-morning they had come to the crossroads where the Roman road met the ancient track of Fosse Way. The other road was not paved, a path for the ox-drawn harvest wagons that appeared regularly from fields in the west. These were piled high with not only hay and grain but the harvesters themselves, brown-faced and cheerful.

While they waited for a flock of sheep to cross Fosse Way, they saw another line of wagons coming east. The oxen that pulled these had their horns painted crimson and blue, and the beasts were crowned with oak wreaths. The carts were full of villeins, mostly young people, shouting and singing. Everyone seemed slightly drunk.

Aelfred was told by one of the peasants in a strong Briton dialect that they were going to a feast in the fields.

In the last wagon a plump young girl in a linen shift sat on a great mound of millet sheaves. She wore a wreath of field flowers on her head from which dangled a veil of ribbons that, from their dirt, had been used many times. Her long brown hair was combed out to fall about her shoulders and arms. Her cheeks and the tip of her nose were red. She too looked rather drunk. When the knights grinned at her she giggled without stopping.

Aimeric and the English knight were riding just behind Ingrith. "I had thought this custom gone from these places," Aimeric said.

"Yes, it's the corn queen, going to the fields," Aelfred told him, "but not, thank Christ, in the bad old way. Although I'll bet half a farthing she gets more than she's expecting from that group of young louts around her."

The dwarf trotted up on his donkey. "I ought to go with them," he said, smirking. "She's a pretty little piece."

Aimeric said, "It's to celebrate the harvest."

The English knight nodded. "Yes, after the sheaves have been cut. In the old days they would take her out to the fields and the men would have her until all of them had done it. Then they would strangle her, cut her up, and plow the pieces into the furrows. To make the next year's crop bountiful."

"Jesus in heaven." The young knight looked at him. "They don't do that now?"

They turned south on Watling Street. Aelfred looked after the retreating wagons. "No, now they'll take her out to the fields and all the young bucks you see following the wagon, they'll have her. And precious more than she wants, too. She'll be a sorry thing when they come back this eventide. But if what comes of it is that she's carrying a babe in the spring, then that will be a good omen for the crops."

Ingrith had been listening, watching the red-faced girl swaying tipsily on her perch of sheaves. Now she asked, "Does she know what's going to happen to her?"

Aelfred rode alongside the mare for a while without answering. Then he said, without looking at her, "Do you?"

Ingrith stared at him.

\* \* \*

The air grew sultry, brewing a storm, but the sun on their heads was fiery. They saw several villages on the horizon but did not stop. They were traveling fast now; something had been said about making London in two days. When they stopped briefly to water the horses at a roadside well, they ate the Tamworth bread and drank some ale. Ingrith sat on the ground and pulled grass for King Harold to nibble while she ate her portion of bread. No one asked about cooking the rabbits.

The horses watered, they hurried steadily south. For long stretches they passed fields where the grain had been harvested. Clouds of blackbirds and crows came down to glean, and rose with a noise like rain when they approached.

The wind died. Insects came up from the new-cut fields. They were soon slapping and itching. The horses grew skittish. Two knights began to argue over something. When their voices grew loud Simon de Bocage shouted for them to be quiet. After that there was a long silence while the storm clouds piled up in the west.

Ingrith pressed her face against the mailed back in front of her. As they rode she thought of the little corn queen and what was probably being done to her. She thought of Gudrun's rape, Gudrun's baby with a father no one could name. With the corn queen it would be something to praise; a good omen for crops, the English knight had said.

They began to see the old stones more than a league south of Fosse Way. First they were solitary standing pillars of granite, rough-hewn, like the shapes of tall men. As they rode the knights talked about who had put them there. Since the time of the giants, Aelfred said. Before Britons, before Saxons and Danes. And before, of course, Normans.

The sky grew dark with the oncoming storm. A vixen and her kits, trapped in the open fields, bounded off toward the west. Some of the knights, superstitious, crossed themselves. Purple rolling clouds mounted into the sky. There was only a band of light, the setting sun, against the horizon. Against it they began to see clusters of ancient stone tombs like little flat-topped houses. In places there were so many they were like villages. Of themselves the horses picked up their pace to a fast trot, hurrying ahead of the wind.

Along the black underside of the storm a bluewhite bolt of lightning cracked, boring into the earth. The ground shook. One of the horses bolted, taking its knight up out of the sunken road and across a grassy field before he could rein it in.

The wind began to batter them in gusts. Renaud rode up beside Simon de Bocage. "We will have to seek shelter soon," he shouted.

Simon nodded. In the distance a dirt track led from the Roman road up a small hill. The remaining bright strip of sky outlined a huddle of house graves at the top. He gave the order to leave the road.

Aimeric rode up. "Sir Simon, there is someone already there."

He grunted. He'd seen them. At the hill's top there were a few pack mules, a wagon, and a tent. Whoever they were, they would have been better off to have camped on the lee side out of the wind.

The knights cantered into a broken circle of tall stones. Simon was surprised to see women—nuns, their habits blowing like sails, trying to get their camp in order. Other women, seemingly servants, were trying to help.

The wind scoured across the knoll with a sprinkling of rain. The sky rocked with another lightning bolt. An older woman, holding her blowing veils back from her face with both hands, did not seem happy to see him.

"Sir knight," she shouted, "I am Ermengard, prioress of St. Ronan's abbey." She came up to the stallion's side. "As you can see, we are camping here to wait out the storm." Her eyes slid past him to the Saxon girl.

"My lady prioress," Simon shouted back, "allow us to be of help. First we must find shelter and see to our horses."

He saw two nuns struggling with the tent, which was about to rip free of its stakes. The wind was howling like a wolf. Strangely, he thought he heard a baby crying.

A crash of thunder shook the air. The top of the hill was not the safest place for the nuns but Simon did not feel like arguing. He turned and trotted the mare down the lee. The knights followed, their horses shying even with the wind at their backs. The friar and the dwarf on his donkey stayed behind.

They came to the ancient stones, low to the earth. Dirt and sod had built up to their roofs, making them look like animal burrows, but they were sturdily made with slabs on three sides and another for the roof.

Ingrith was afraid. He could hardly pry her hands loose from around him.

"Get down and seek shelter," he shouted. He

pulled her down from the mare, then shoved her under the lintel of the nearest stone house. It was low and it was dark; she had to stoop almost double, then step down. But the inside was dry enough; the sandy dirt floor was sifted with dried grass.

"Look for badgers, bears, whatever might be living there," he told her. She shot him a look of terror.

The sound of the wind and the storm was loud even under the stones. He saw in the half-light she was eerily beautiful with her great azure eyes, white skin, the long sheath of gold hair. He saw her clutch her breast. The damned rabbit, he remembered. Under her cloak.

"Don't be afraid." Simon was sorry he'd frightened her. He considered saying something more, but could not think of anything. She sat down on the sandy ground and drew the cloak around her.

"How fares the coney?"

She looked up, surprised to see him still there. She slowly drew back the cloak. He saw the rabbit was nestled against her breasts, its feet tucked in, its ears folded back to make a neat black and white ball. It looked warm and safe there in her bosom.

She stroked its head, murmuring its ridiculous name. The thing opened amber eyes, then half closed them, content.

Stupid rabbit, Simon thought. Of all animals they were not noted for genius. He knew he should see to the escort and his own horses but instead he stood there watching her, thinking of the softness and warmth of her white skin.

She looked up at him. "It is well," she whispered.

There was nothing else to be said. He told himself she'd be safe enough.

He went out.

Aimeric had tethered the mare and the stallion in the lee of the stones. The others, the knight told him, shouting over the wind, had already gone to help the nuns. Simon swore under his breath.

The gale swept up the knoll from the darkened plain and blasted around them. Overhead, the sky boiled with dark clouds.

"Sir Simon." Aimeric leaned to him, yelling. "Give me leave to speak."

Simon untied the bundle of clothes from the saddle, then his own kit. "What about the horses?"

"They are all secured below here, on the other side of the hill." The boy gave him a strange look. "Sir, these people camping here. They are postulants, did you not see how they are dressed? St. Ronan's has a bad name."

No, he had not noticed how they were dressed. He looked up the knoll. He saw figures running about, supposedly chasing their blown tents.

Suddenly, he was not so sure. "Postulants?"

There was another crash. Aimeric flinched. "Aye, St. Ronan's is a place where husbands send their wives when they want to put them away. Or fathers with lame, ill-favored, or otherwise unmarriageable daughters. You know." He hesitated. "They never take final orders, these women. Most of them live well in the priory, they wear nun's clothing but they are not pious, they, ah—"

The servants, Simon thought. Nuns did not have

an army of maids. And he was positive he'd heard a baby.

Sweet Mary, now he remembered. Aimeric was right, some orders of nuns were mere dumping grounds for unwanted women, rich or poor. Undisciplined. Unruly. Some were famed for their lechery.

"Where is the cask of ale from Tamworth?"

Aimeric gave him a blank look. Ale and food, Simon thought, now they had both in plenty. It was more than enough when mixed with men who had not been with women since Morlaix. Not this kind, anyway.

Cursing under his breath, he started toward the top of the knoll. Aimeric ran beside him. The storm crashed, bolt after bolt of blinding light. No rain. Not yet.

The wind made them bend double going into it. When they got to the first standing stones they could make out knights and women running about in the wind-ripped gloom. The ale cask was nowhere to be seen, but with the gale one could smell it. People ran past, screaming or laughing, but there was no sound, all drowned out by the racket of the storm.

Simon squinted against the blowing dust. It was a scene straight from hell. In the dark, it was hard to tell what was going on. Christ in heaven, already some of them had no clothes on.

"Here you, Turold!" He grabbed at a knight charging past, and missed. "Hermer!" He lunged at another one. "I command you!"

They were not listening. Or they could not hear him; the storm was right overhead. The first rain came spattering down.

Beside him Aimeric cried, "Sir Simon, fear not, I will never—oof!"

Two half-clothed women threw themselves at the boy. Before Simon could come to his aid they were dragging him away, outside the stone circle.

Simon started after them at a run, but at that moment the skies opened up. In the blink of an eye the stone ring was empty of everything but lashing rain. He looked around. God and only He knew where Morlaix's knights had gone.

He started back down the knoll, half-blinded by the torrent. He came upon a pair coupling furiously in the flooded grass. When he looked up he saw the Saxon girl standing there, staring at the knight and the woman on the ground as though she were watching a murder.

Simon stepped around them. From the way the two were going at it they would either have their pleasure, or drown. He hoped for the latter.

He took her arm, jerking her away. She hung back, yelling something. Trying to look. He couldn't hear, the rain beat around them with a roar. Tired of struggling with her, he bent and picked her up in his arms.

God's wounds, he'd forgot she was hardly light. He could barely manage her, carrying the bundle of her, clothes and his own saddle kit, which contained the dry clothes, food, flint and tinder they needed. When they came to the stone house he staggered under the low lintel, slipped on the wet stones, and hit his forehead a resounding crack.

Simon fell to his knees. The girl spilled out of his arms and onto the floor. He could not see for a moment. On his hands and knees, he shook his head to clear it.

It had been the devil's own night, he told himself. He would have to send the escort back to Morlaix. They were useless, now, for command. He could only hope the prioress did not cry rape. Or assault. Or robbery. God knows what was going on out there. Perhaps the storm would kill them all.

When he looked up, the Saxon girl stood in front of him, a dagger held in her hand.

# Chapter Fourteen

*T*he next he knew, she had pushed him flat on his back.

The Saxon girl leaned over him, the blade gleaming in the dim light. Swiftly she hauled up the bottom of his hauberk with one hand, and with the other began to saw away on the waist cord that held up his sodden hose.

Simon closed his eyes.

Since he'd set foot in England a hellish fate had conspired to give him no rest from his relatives' plots, marriage-minded Jews, and now a lust-crazed Saxon. At that moment he wanted to throw Prince Henry's would-be whore out in the storm to join the crowd of St. Ronan harpies.

But, cautious, he lay still. It was so dark he could barely see, and the little poignard she was waving around was close as sin to his privates. No need to alarm her, Simon told himself. Or make her start, or jump, or whack away at something other than the waist cord by mistake.

From under his eyelids he could see her cutting

through what was left of the top of his hose, then dragging it down to expose his strap. Intent, her fingers worked at the codpiece. He could see enough of her face to glimpse the tip of a pink tongue held between her teeth.

What did she think she was doing? he wondered. From what they said she never assaulted the others. He saw her put the dagger beside her on the ground, no doubt thinking he was still addled from cracking his head.

Well, by the Cross, it was time to put an end to it! He was sore weary of being attacked. But just as he lifted his arm, his hand stretching out for the knife, he felt her fingers close around him.

Simon's body went rigid in a spasm of feeling so great he could not get his breath. Shock reverberated through him down to the roots of his teeth. Not to mention that part of him she now stroked in her soft, warm hands.

This girl was no virgin, he realized with that part of his mind that was still working. He was not surprised. If Malmsbury had only her word for it, why shouldn't she lie? But certainly no tender maid, innocent of a man's body, could have such bold and expert hands. They teased him, featherlight across his crotch. Fingers explored the inside of his thighs, the backs of his knees, then quickly trailed a path between his legs to cup his agonized flesh.

Ah, she knew what she was doing, he thought with a groan. Little nail flicks on his rising flesh marched around the top, then made grooves of lascivious pressure along the shaft itself. Before he could recover from that, she bent her head.

Her dangling wet hair fell across his legs. He

shuddered as her tongue lightly touched him. A moment later her mouth moved away up and down his inner thighs with warm caresses until he rose to even harder, more bursting life.

She slid her hand under his backside to hold him and he felt the faint scratch of her nails, the muscles there contracting painfully. She held him as his cock pulsed, rising out of his groin as rigid and invincible as any biblical sword of justice. If that was what she wanted, Simon thought with a shuddering gasp, he hoped she was satisfied.

She suddenly sat back on her heels. He heard a rustle in the darkness and gathered she was pulling off her gown. They were both wet as drowned cats.

Simon hauled himself upright. He heard her indrawn breath. Then, quickly, she babbled something in English about her mother and sisters.

The whole family, Simon thought. He supposed it was, in all charity, what they'd had to do to survive. No matter, he was on fire with what she'd so artfully accomplished.

He wrestled his hauberk over his head and she scuttled to the side, out of his way. He reached for his kit and dragged it to him for flints and a candle.

As he pulled out a wad of tinder he marveled that the devil of it was, he had no great way with women, his life from childhood on had been spent learning the knightly arts. War and duty had been his dedication, and the love he bore for one sweet maid who'd had his heart since they were children.

There had been precious few others he wanted to remember. Perhaps the two girls in the harem in Palestine who had been lent by a Saracen pasha, but that had been some time ago. Outside of these, one could hardly say he was a slave to his senses.

Until now. With the most beautiful woman—girl—he'd ever seen before him, he could hardly think.

He leaned foward to blow into his cupped hands. When the tinder sprang into flame he lighted the stub of candle. The eye of light sprouted in the dimness.

The Saxon girl, naked, crouched before him, long pale hair falling against her gleaming body. At that moment he thought he heard the faint, lustful howls of the carousing knights and women in the storm outside. It did not help.

"I must tell you something," she was saying in English, "about that night, when we stopped in the woods with the wedding."

He wanted to kiss her, he thought, distracted. She held both hands raised, fingers spread, to cover those truly astonishing breasts. She was tempting enough to stir a dead man's blood, and his cock now felt as though it would burst.

He no longer wondered why she pursued him, why she found every opportunity to touch him each night, putting her legs against his when they lay down to sleep. He wanted only to hold her, possess her, bury his burning flesh in her. It was the first time in his life that he'd wanted a woman almost past reason.

"You are no longer a virgin," he said, wanting to make sure.

"That is what I am trying to tell you." She lifted her hair back from her face with both hands. With the movement her rounded thighs shifted and her breasts thrust out, rosy tipped.

Without moving his eyes, Simon tore off the rest of his clothes. Malmsbury and the rest might think her untouched, but he knew differently. She was greatly experienced; he'd wager his Saracen mare on it.

He reached out and pulled her to him. She came willingly, saying something about some alder bushes in the woods.

"You were drunk," she told him, pushing him far enough away so that she could look up into his face. "That is what I have been trying to tell you."

"Never." He bent his head and his mouth traced the silky curve of one shoulder. "I would remember something like that."

He felt her violent start as his lips closed on a rosy nipple. "Stay, stay," he murmured as he pried her hands out of his hair. "I will not hurt you."

She was sweet, and tasted of flowers. Holding her in his arms made his head spin. He knew he could stand little more. He lowered her carefully to the sandy floor. Her hands, fingers spread, moved against his back, his shoulders, uncertain. He shifted to roll her under him.

A piercing scream ripped the darkness.

Simon jumped as though he had been stabbed. He came to his feet, crouched and wary of the low roof, casting around for whatever it was that had shrieked.

The girl had wrenched herself out of his arms. She dove for the bundle of the cloak under them.

"King Harold?" She dug into it and held the animal up, its legs kicking. "Oh, poor bunny! Did we hurt you?"

"Sweet Jesu."

Simon sat back down on the floor. Any lust in him should have been quenched but he saw, wincing, he was still rigid. More than that. He was in torment.

He reached out for the rabbit, rolled the cloak over it and tossed it into a far corner.

She howled, turning on him like a fury. "You are trying to kill him! Poor King Harold!"

"God take it!" He caught her hand before she could hit him. "Stop calling the cursed thing King Harold!"

Holding her flailing hands, he pulled her down to him and covered her mouth with his. She squirmed, knocking her nose against his. While he kissed her, she held her breath.

After long minutes he pulled back, looking down into her flushed face. He saw her take several loud gulps of air. One would think she had never been kissed before.

On the other hand, Simon knew bawds had rules about it. He'd heard they almost never kissed the men who paid to lie with them.

He watched her, the pulse throbbing in her white throat, those magnificent breasts heaving with some emotion. *Poor beauty,* he couldn't help thinking, she was the most ravishing thing he had ever beheld. And in a sorry estate; given a choice, he doubted any girl would choose to be a whore. He touched a strand of her hair with his finger. It was beginning to dry. Fine gold threads framed her face. Her eyes were like woods violets, deep and true.

"Are you going to do the rest?" she breathed.

God's wounds, she was insatiable.

"Yes, I'm going to do the rest," he murmured.

He lowered her to the floor. She all but leaped out of his arms when his fingers touched her tight, moist cleft. He was suddenly sure no man had ever pleasured her. For all her bold cleverness she was still curiously untried. For once, he vowed, he would not let her provoke him.

His kissed her again, long and thoroughly, teaching her to open her lips. It was an ascent into sweet perdition, smoky and hot, spiced with her whimpers of discovery.

He pulled himself away with an effort. The more she responded, the more it inflamed him. He did not think he could be this aroused and still live.

He kissed her again. This time her mouth opened eagerly. But when he tried to press her knee down, to make way to enter her, it jerked up, hitting him a blow in the groin. That, too, should have stopped him. But, amazingly, he was still on fire.

Hurriedly, he inserted one finger into the tight, slippery channel of her femininity and stroked gently. She looked at him under half-closed lids. "I want to tell you about that night," she moaned. "The alders—"

"Shhh," he murmured, pulling himself over her.

She looked up at him, so beautiful, so childishly trusting, that a rush of unfamiliar emotion surprised him. He had no time for it. His own body trembling, he pushed into her. He was instantly sheathed as she squirmed against him. Her arms wound around his neck. She pressed her mouth to his.

"Wait," he tried to say.

But she lifted her hips and moved—awkwardly. And yet it was enough. A thousand sparks burst behind his eyes. He lifted her in his hands, roared into her, felt her surge to match him in his frenzy. He found himself falling among stars. Clutching her.

He heard her cry out as his own peak ripped through him. He lowered himself against her, sweating and shuddering. Struggling for breath.

What they'd had, he thought a moment later, was a wonder of the world. It was past belief.

"I am no longer a virgin," he heard her whisper.

He lifted his head to look down at her. Her mouth was swollen with his kisses, her hair spread out in a golden web. She was the most wondrous vision he'd ever seen.

She ran her tongue over her lips. "Now your Norman in London will no longer want me for a whore."

Softly, Simon kissed the tip of her chin. "Why is that?"

He saw her frown. An instant, undecided. "Because you will not lie about it, on your honor as a knight. That you had me, and found me no longer a virgin."

Simon gazed down at her, trying to understand what she so wanted to tell him. He could not believe that this sweet, piercing moment when he had almost lost his soul to her was only a sorry device for some idea she had. That Prince Henry would not want her if she could prove she was not a virgin.

And that he was her proof.

He cleared his throat. "Prince Henry will not care."

She pushed him away and sat up. She turned to him, naked and ravishingly beautiful. "Prince Henry? You were going to take me to a *prince*?"

He shut his eyes, thinking that he would forbear no matter what. "Not 'were.' I *am* taking you, nothing has changed." He put his hand on her wrist and tugged at it. "Come, lie down again."

She yanked her hand away. "He will not want me, I have been despoiled," she yelled. "*You* have had me!"

He caught her wrist again. "Prince Henry is no collector of virgins. I tell you, it will make no difference."

If it was cruel, it was no more than what she had done. He knew she did not want to go to London, but there was nothing to be done about it. Still, he found himself less than satisfied himself with the thought of her in Prince Henry's bed.

"How can you do this?" Tears filled her eyes to brimming. "How can you take me," she wailed, "despoil me, and then bring me to another man?"

"God's wounds, stop screaming." He sat up. He had hoped to lie with her again before the night was over, but he could see this prospect was fading. "Stop saying I've despoiled you. There was nothing to despoil!"

"Nothing to despoil? Norman murderer!" With a shriek, fists raised, she launched herself at him. "In the alder woods you raped me!"

He caught her hands before she could land a blow. He turned his head, listening.

"Be still," he told her. There was something outside.

She kept on howling.

"Shut up!" He shook her so that her long hair flailed around them.

He no longer heard the sound of the rain, the storm had subsided. But there were running feet. The clang of swords. Shouts, someone crying hoarsely for Morlaix.

Simon flung her away from him with a sweep of his arm and scrambled across the floor for his sword. He barely had it in hand before the first shape appeared at the dark opening of the doorway. He gave her a last shove into a corner and launched himself at the opening.

It was a bad defense. The attackers had the advantage, whoever they were, in that they were in the open, flushing him out of the stone tomb. He had only the cover of dark.

He hurled himself through the doorway into the night. He was lucky enough to roll under the first blow and met a dagger, not a sword. He wondered who they were. An arm locked around his throat from behind. He staggered backward and fell.

A body fell with him. He heard a scream as he brought the sword down. His last thought was of the girl. And who would be left, now, to take her to Prince Henry in London.

Then there was only blackness.

# Chapter Fifteen

"**D**emoiselle," Aelfred said. "Come out, quickly."

He held up a lantern.

Ingrith stepped out of the stone house with King Harold in her arms. She could hear sounds of fighting. In the distance, a horn blew.

"Hurry," he told her. He took the bundle of her clothes and Simon's saddle kit from her. Behind him she saw a tall, fair-bearded man in a sheepskin coat. There was something familiar about him. Staring, she almost tripped over the dead man just outside the door.

She staggered back when she saw the corpse had taken a sword thrust that almost severed him in two. Anorlyx lay in a flood of blackening blood. "Blessed Mother," Ingrith cried, "what has happened?"

The English knight tugged at her arm. "Duke Robert's assassin. And better off dead." He said something to the bearded man that she didn't understand.

She shuddered. "Duke Robert's assassin? What does that mean?" She looked over her shoulder as he pulled her away. She still could not believe it. "The dwarf?"

"An evil little man, he murdered for hire. The friar escaped, they are looking for him now."

The friar, Brother Enguerrand. Ingrith could not believe that, either.

They hurried down the side of the knoll, away from the ring of standing stones. She stumbled again, thinking of what Aelfred had said. They were almost running; it was hard to ask questions.

Where was Simon de Bocage? Her heart rose in her throat when she thought of what had happened in the stone house. Did any of it mean anything to him? Was he even alive? She hadn't moved, crouching in the dark, since he'd left her.

The cold dawn wind scoured the treeless hill. There was no sign of the rowdy nuns of St. Ronan's priory. Their campsite was deserted; only a few tent stakes were left in the mud. A horn blew again. In the distance a voice called out something in the name of the king.

Ingrith dragged the English knight to a stop.

"I will go no farther," she gasped, "until you tell me what is happening. The Morlaix knights are fighting. Why are you not with them? Where is Simon de Bocage?"

He looked over her head at the other man.

"Ingrith Edmundsdaughter," Aelfred said, "the Crusader knight de Bocage has been taken with a warrant from the king's court in London. But this is no affair of the Saxons."

*"What?"* She was glad he was not dead. But she did not know what else she felt.

He had lain with her, treated her sweetly, tenderly—but then he had thrown her away from him before he charged out into the night. Across the floor and into the wall. Her shoulder still hurt.

The other man said something again.

Aelfred nodded. "Ingrith Edmundsdaughter, we do not concern ourselves with these Norman plots. The Normans seek to overthrow their king. It is nothing to us." His grip on her arm tightened. "Come with us. We will see you safely away."

"No." She pulled away from him. "What do you want with me?"

"Have we not just said?" The tall man in the sheepskin stepped to her. As he spoke he pushed back his hood.

Ingrith gasped.

"Aelfred and I will take you to the north," the tongueless outlaw told her. "In two days we will be beyond York minster, in the country of true Englishmen."

She knew him at once, remembering their little play in the forest, Aelfred telling Gilbert de Jobourg the outlaw's tongue had been cut out.

"He can speak!" she blurted out.

"This is Halfdane of Arden," Aelfred told her. "An outlaw now, but a good Saxon. His father was *huscarl* to your grandsire, Loefwine."

"We will carry you away," the outlaw said, "to your friends who do not wish to see thane Leofwine's granddaughter taken as a whore for some Norman."

So that was it.

The cold gale blew up the hill. The sounds of fighting had faded. "You have meant to do this since Arden forest," she said.

The outlaw nodded. "Since Malmsbury, Edmundsdaughter. Your grandsire's old friends have schemed to take you away so the Normans could not boast of it, a Saxon girl of good birth given to one of them. Like a slave."

Not for herself. But for the honor of Saxons.

Ingrith shifted King Harold into the crook of her arm. She still could not believe that the outlaw had a tongue and could talk. They had taken a great risk in the Arden forest lying about it to Gilbert.

"I cannot leave. I am pledged to go to London." They did not know about her mother and sisters, but she did not find it necessary to explain. "I gave my word at Morlaix."

"That is foolishness." Aelfred glanced at the other man. "Girl, you must listen to wiser heads. The king's men are seizing de Bocage's knights, there is no reason to stay." He took her by the wrist. "When we are far from here we will discuss all this."

"No, we will not!" Ingrith broke loose from his grip, and started up the hill. She set her mouth stubbornly. She was not going to let them take her away to the north to people she did not know.

She could hear them following, talking in low, urgent tones. She had only gone a few steps when she saw another dead body in the grass ahead.

She stopped short.

Aelfred came up. He swore under his breath.

Ingrith made herself look. From the look of his tunic, the dead man was a Morlaix knight. She could not tell who it was; the bottom of his face was missing. But it was strange to think any of them could be dead, the Morlaix knights she had ridden with for so many days, had taken meals with, had listened to. Under her breath she said a quick prayer.

The outlaw said something to Aelfred in his guttural Saxon. The knight nodded. He stepped in front of Ingrith.

"Come, we do not have time to stand here arguing. Is it because de Bocage slept with you last night that you do not want to go away with us?" When she turned to stare at him he went on, "We will take you to a safe place, where this will not happen again."

At the top of the knoll the Morlaix knights were throwing down their arms. Ingrith did not know what would happen to Simon de Bocage. *A king's warrant.* Perhaps they would kill him.

"Come," Aelfred said. He held out his hand.

She did not even see it. Lying with Simon de Bocage had not been what she'd expected. He had ridden her hard and she was still sore in her tenderest parts, but there had been passion and something more. She could not explain that to anyone. She could not even explain it to herself.

Halfdane scowled at her. "Look you, girl, you have nowhere to go. The Leopard is under arrest. The Morlaix knights will take you back to Baron Malmsbury if they find you."

She turned to meet that fierce stare. She was not afraid of him, nor of Aelfred. They were English, Saxons, her own kind. But one was an outlaw. The other a false knight. She was a thane's granddaughter.

"You will not call me girl," she said. "You know my name."

He opened his mouth to speak and she said, "Firstly, do not tell me you will save me from something that has already happened. If there are Saxons who worry for their honor, tell them I account for my own and no others."

"Now, girl—"

She gave him a look that froze him.

"And if you do not let me go," Ingrith said, "I will scream to the Normans up there that they must come and help me. That you would have your base way with me, when I am to be taken only to Prince Henry!"

He stepped back and looked at Aelfred. "Prince Henry?"

The other shook his head. "I know nothing of this, Halfdane, I swear."

Ingrith had made up her mind. There would be no escape unless she went to London and explained to Prince Henry. It was only fair, now, not to let them kill Simon de Bocage.

"It doesn't matter what you know," she said. "The knight de Bocage who was to bring me to him did not deflower me, only that he was drunk, and I made him do it." She stopped, thinking it sounded confused. Well, no matter. "Even then he thought I was his true love, the Norman girl, Alys," she finished.

There was a silence.

Aelfred cleared his throat. "The knight de Bocage deflowered you, demoiselle?"

Let them think what they would. "That is what I said."

Ingrith shifted the rabbit to her other arm and held out her hand for her clothes. She looked down at Simon's saddle kit. She supposed she should take it with her but it was heavy. She picked it up.

Leaning a little with her burdens, she walked away toward the knoll. She heard the outlaw say, "Would she lie about such a thing?"

She did not hear Aelfred's answer.

She held King Harold on top of the bundles, managing her blowing skirts. The wind bent the tall grass ahead of her.

The king's knights wore red and gold tunics with the running leopard of Normandy. It was less easy to find the outnumbered Morlaix white and green. A gray first light was showing under the low clouds, striking sparks on chain mail and arms. The Morlaix escort had laid down their swords. There were only four, now, but they had fought bravely. Two had dripping wounds. She saw Aimeric's brown head, bent, as he looked down at the ground. Under flapping banners the king's knights stood around a naked man, his hands tied behind him.

The naked man was Simon de Bocage.

It was the way he had run from the stone house, Ingrith remembered, to do battle. Some of the king's knights looked at her, grinning.

The wind blew his dark hair about his face. His hands were tied behind him. The black curls in his crotch, the big, dangling shaft drew her eyes. He looked naked, goatish.

A man in a close-fitting mailed hood strode up to her. He was tall, with gray eyes. "Demoiselle." He looked down at the rabbit, her load of bundles. "I am Raymond of Hesiden, king's justiciar. What do you here?"

Ingrith looked past him to the Morlaix knights. "God keep you, milord." She could not understand why the king's knights and a justiciar had come to arrest Simon de Bocage. And this hard-faced man did not look as though he would tell her if she asked. "I—I am traveling with the knights you have taken."

Beyond them she could see the king's party, staring, talking to each other. The Morlaix knights did not look at her at all. The two injured men were helping each other bind up their wounds. Aimeric stood with his chin on his chest, his shoulders drooping. She remembered the night she had stroked his hand, to cozen him, so they could go to the road to watch the wedding.

"Good sir, have you charged the Morlaix knights with any misdeed?" she wanted to know. "Other than"—Simon heard her. She saw him lift his head—"that naked one there?"

The justiciar studied her, expressionless. "They are Morlaix's knights, demoiselle. I do not detain them."

Ingrith felt a surge of hope.

"My lord, by your permission." She was so nervous she stumbled over the Norman French. "I ask leave to speak to the escort to ask if they will see me safely to London." She shifted King Harold to her other arm and looked up, beseechingly. "I have no money, milord, I must beg charity of the Morlaix knights to get there."

He was watching her closely. "And where do you go, demoiselle, when you get to London?"

She remembered her story. "To the house of my lord husband, good sir. He is a rich merchant there."

She saw Raymond of Hesiden did not believe a word of it. It was plain he thought her a whore, the way she was dressed. And all alone. If she'd truly been a rich merchant's wife the escort would have defended her, and not run off to the lecherous nuns. Nor would she have been sleeping with the naked man they routed out when they attacked.

He said, impatient, "Go speak with the escort. As it is, they are on their way back to Morlaix."

He turned on his heel, striding off.

Ingrith studied the Morlaix knights. She could persuade Aimeric. But he was young and inexperienced. She needed one other. And she needed money.

She suddenly thought of looking in the saddlebag. There would be money there; Simon had it for travel.

Now she was glad she had not listened to the Saxons. They cared nothing for her, only what they saw as the disgrace she would bring to Saxon pride.

She must follow the justiciar and his men to London, with two knights, if she could persuade them. She did not know what Simon de Bocage was wanted for in the king's court, but she would find out if she could. She needed to make the rest of the journey to Prince Henry, it was her chance to throw herself on the prince's mercy, and justice.

Suddenly she was plunged into despair. Everyone remarked over and again on how young she was, they would not leave it alone. When in all truth she felt old as death. Prince Henry would have to know that she was no longer a virgin. And with her maidenhead lost, that she was no candidate for his bed. She did not believe Simon de Bocage when he said it would not matter.

She did not want them to kill him; she had changed her mind about that. Even as she thought about it she saw she did not know how to do any of this. She would have to trust to the goodness of God, the saints, and luck. But all she wanted was to sit down on the ground and weep with the difficulty of it all.

She wondered if Prince Henry was familiar with the story of the knight Tristan and the Breton princess, Iseult.

# Chapter Sixteen

"The Jews wanted him," Raymond of Hesiden said. "We should have murdered de Bocage on the road as the sheriff of Repton urged, but the bishop could not bring himself to do it. Now we have the king's court intervened with a warrant for the Leopard to appear and defend himself against the charges of, God help us, a Jewish marriage contract. And the girl and the damned Morlaix knights are following. A veritable circus. That does nothing to advance the cause of Duke Robert in all this."

The justiciar and the friar stood in the shade of London tower's curtain wall that sheltered stables and a new knights' barracks. It was late morning, and the sun was hot. Beyond the green grass the river Thames had begun to steam, obscuring the trees on the far bank.

They stood watching as four armed and mailed knights, the tower guard, brought the prisoner up from the cells.

"The girl is not a harlot, Raymond," the younger man said. "You are mistaken in your opinion of her.

But I grant you, she is beautiful—if she chose to follow a whore's profession she could make a fortune here. Or in Paris, for that matter."

The prisoner strode forward, his quilted jacket, his boots and hose, showing the effects of a night spent below. They saw him lift his face hungrily to the sun.

As well he might, Hesiden thought, watching him. Even a short stay in the prisoners' tanks gave one a taste of what it was like to be without air and sunshine.

"He may have taken her by force," Brother Enguerrand was saying. "There was a storm, the St. Ronan's women were being unruly, it would be a time to catch a maid helpless and frightened and, ah, have one's way with her."

The justiciar smiled sourly. "As God is my witness, the Saxon girl was scarce helpless and frightened. When I first saw her she had the look of a woman well tumbled. And he, as you have heard, was caught running about in his skin."

The tower guards dragged the prisoner to the cistern and gave him a bucket, indicating he should strip and put his hair and body in order. The chief justiciar of England and holy Bishop of Durham, Ranulph Flambard, before whom the prisoner was shortly to appear, did not tolerate the stinks of the dungeon at his hearings.

Simon de Bocage peeled off his jacket and hose. The hot wind blew his hair about his handsome, hawklike face. When stripped, his body was like that of any good swordsman: broad-shouldered, lean in the trunk, with long, well-muscled legs.

Hesiden's eyes narrowed. "What could the Jews

be wanting with this man, that they pay good money to have him brought under arrest to the king's court in London? Other than he does not leave his skills behind him in the Holy Land. If there is one thing on which all agree, it is that he is dangerous."

Seint-Omer nodded. He had followed Simon de Bocage from Calais, since Duke Robert's spies knew that the Leopard had been in Rouen, and that he carried a letter to Malmsbury in the Welsh marches. For the Duke of Normandy's supporters the question had always been not where the Leopard had been in England, but where he was going. One did not send for a man like this one merely to escort a trollop southward.

Would to God they could get rid of him, Enguerrand Seint-Omer was thinking. De Bocage was a dagger pointed at them until they could discover his true purpose. The Jews too were just as alarmed.

"We tried to kill him," he murmured. "Or at least your little assassin did."

Hesiden frowned. "It was never my intention to use the dwarf. You see what good it has done us."

"It was not a matter of using him, Raymond. Anorlyx was a difficult little beast. It was his own fancy he chose to attack de Bocage." He studied the tall knight. "It was a blunder. As for those damned women from St. Ronan's—as God is in heaven, I had nothing to do with them! They are an uncommon menace."

The justiciar turned his face slightly away so that they would appear to be discussing nothing weightier than the hot summer weather. "Nevertheless, they served their purpose, did they not? It is the problem we face now that worries me."

When the other turned to him he said, "Aquitaine has sent an embassy. They addressed themselves to King William at Stafford before he left the hunt there. Duke William of Aquitaine wishes to borrow money from England's king so that he may also crusade to the Holy Land with no less than two hundred thousand men. I am told he will pledge Aquitaine and all his lands in return for a great sum of money."

Seint-Omer looked around the grassy ward of London tower. Other than the knights and their prisoner there was no one near. "Then the King of England will have most of France in pawn to him. Does Duke Robert know?"

The other snorted. "The duke is on his glorious honeyed moon with his young bride and does not worry overmuch. He leaves that to us, his friends here, who risk our lives to make him England's next king."

Seint-Omer turned his head away. "God's wounds," he groaned, "there will be no duchy of Normandy when Robert returns. Excepting that it belongs to William Rufus. And now he will hold damned Aquitaine too, from the looks of it."

"Peace, Seint-Omer, it has not happened yet."

The justiciar watched Simon de Bocage water down the front of his jacket and then rub parts of it together to get out the spots, a soldierly tactic born of living in the field. Then he saw him douse his hair in the bucket, wringing it out with both hands.

When de Bocage was finished he was not what

one would call well turned out. The Leopard was lacking his mail, his helmet, and his weapons, but he was surprisingly presentable. The man was good-looking in a dark, raffish fashion. They would shortly meet the Leopard before the chief justiciar and see him for what he was: a first-class fighting man, steely, impressive, daunting.

Hesiden took Seint-Omer's arm. "We cannot account for the Jews, let them have the Leopard for now. But nothing must happen until Duke Robert can reach Normandy. Once on his own lands the duke can raise the nobles, declare his sovereignty, and challenge this king all England hates."

"Then what of this hearing before Flambard? God's blood, Hesiden, tell me why the Jews are so uneasy."

"Jews are in a constant state of unease; it is how they survive." They started walking toward the tower. "Ah, they are taking him in. It is time for us to go."

Seint-Omer stopped. "Hesiden, wait. Tell me the fate of the girl. Grant me the favor, speak to the bishop and the others for me."

"The fate of the girl?" He raised his eyebrows. "The *Saxon* girl?"

Enguerrand Seint-Omer crimsoned. "Yes." His eyes slid away. "Hesiden, tell them I would take her under my protection."

Hesiden dismissed this with a hoot. "Enguerrand, licentiousness does not become you! I prefer you godly, in your friar's habit."

"Hesiden, I beg of you, treat me fair. She is too fine and beautiful to lose in this mad game."

"Fine and beautiful? The young slut they are

sending to the master lecher himself, Prince Henry? That is not the real reason our Leopard is here, to do Henry's pimping."

Seint-Omer started to speak but he waved him into silence. Simon de Bocage was being marched away between the tower guards.

"Say what you will," Chestershire's justiciar murmured, watching him, "for all that he is a Jew, yon Leopard makes a brave, parfit Christian knight."

As the party from the London Jewry came near the tower, urchins darted out of side streets offering to hold their horses for a price. The mounted band tried to ignore them; this was usual close to the courts and the buildings of government. But when the boys saw they were Jews, they skipped along in the rear of the rabbi's party, shouting threats as to what they would do if they did not throw them a copper. It was all Judah Ha-Kohen could do to keep himself and his horse between the unruly little knaves and his daughter.

"They do not like us, Father," Hagit cried, looking over her shoulder.

"Bah, they want money, the ruffians." Judah had been to Paris, and to Rome. "It is the same everywhere."

The six armed knights employed by the rabbi of London endured the rabble for a while, mindful of the discreet behavior Jews preferred. But the mob followed them down the hill to the Thameside, howling for money and growing in numbers until finally, at a signal from Rabbi Hezek ben Ibrahim himself, the knights plunged their horses into their midst and drove the ragged children away.

By that time they were at the bailey of the London tower. It was filled at that hour of the morning with the company of guards, provision wagons, knights, horses, and lawyers and king's subjects gathered for the chief justiciar's court.

The view from the knoll overlooking the Thames was fine even in the hazy heat. The river spread out before them with ships and small craft making their way to the sea. From this hill to the north side of the old Roman wall, William the Conqueror had built a tower that would not only defend the city but control London's river. Now London tower was both a jail and courts of law, surrounded by stone government buildings.

The grooms dismounted first; Jews could not ride through the king's gates on horseback like nobles. They carried around footstools for London's chief rabbi, the delegation of elders, the two leading goldsmiths from the Jewry, and Judah Ha-Kohen and his daughter.

Judah pushed the grooms out of the way and held the stirrup for Hagit to dismount. As he did so he saw over his horse's back a young woman standing flanked by two young knights wearing colors of the de Jobourgs of Castle Morlaix.

The girl was probably, Judah realized, the most beautiful female he had ever seen. Her remarkable hair was the color of palest gold, worn in the Saxon style of two long plaits twined with ribbons. She was tall; she would have overtopped some of the Norman knights in the bailey. But not a harlot, he decided; even though in her purple and red silk gown she was dressed as one.

He pushed his daughter ahead of him so that Hagit walked between moneylenders, grooms, and horses. Even so the girl managed to approach him before they reached the gate.

"Kind sir." Her Morlaix knights shouldered aside the rabbi's grooms. "Kind sir, may I speak with you?"

She was a harlot after all, otherwise she would not have called a Jew "sir." But those blue eyes, that grave, straightforward air entranced him.

"Sir, I have seen you in Wroxeter." She spoke Norman French with a strong Saxon accent.

He motioned to Hagit to go on. "I have never seen you, girl. I do not know you."

"I was at the house of the wool merchant with the Morlaix knights in Wroxeter, sir. It had caught fire." She put out her hand. "I saw you talking with Simon de Bocage. Oh, can you tell me why they have brought him here? And what is to become of him? They will not kill him, will they?"

*So the Leopard has a leman*, Judah thought. He felt his dismay in the pit of his stomach.

The day was not well begun. It had been that way since Judah had first risen. First the London moneylenders had come to the rabbi's house openly nervous about the hearing with Flambard, the king's minister, with whom they dealt weekly on the matter of royal loans. Then Hagit had observed a bad omen, a bird in the chief rabbi's garden with a broken wing, and could hardly be persuaded to go. It had taken hours of tearful threats and arguments.

On top of it all, London's chief rabbi was incensed at what the hearing, the writs—the bribes—were costing. Two hundred silver Flemish marks. It was a fortune, even though the London Jewry, sensing unknown peril, had said they would pay it willingly.

Judah thought of his own daughter. God help him, he had sacrificed Hagit too.

"Kill him?" He could not bring himself to be kind; he spoke what was in his own heart. At that moment he wished he had never heard of Sophia Belefroun or her son. Judah said over his shoulder as he hurried away, "Who knows?"

The delegation met their lawyer at the foot of the tower stairs. He was an Italian from Rienzi whose manner was lofty because they were only Jews. He carried a large package of their sworn testimonies under his arm to give to the royal clerks. A youth followed with more vellum rolls sealed with ribbons and wax. Judah knew they were paying the Italian lawyer a fortune too.

The Italian led the way. The stairs were crowded with court clerks, young monks with shaved heads carrying armfuls of writs who barely stepped aside to let the Jews in their fine silks and jewelry pass. Ranulph Flambard, the king's chief minister, chief justiciar, now Bishop of Durham by royal act, was shouting in the big hearing room above. They could hear his voice, strident, full of impatience.

Judah had to virtually drag Hagit the last few steps.

On the landing a man in a long blue wool coat approached them and said, "I am Raymond of Hes-

iden, justiciar for your district. Wroxeter, is it not?"
He took the writs from the lawyer, motioning them
inside.

The hearing room was the tower's gray stone,
unrelieved by rugs or wall hangings. The large window, shutters thrown back this warm day, over-
looked the river. Ranulph Flambard, his arms
propped on a littered table, was reading a pile of
vellums surrounded by tonsured clerks. It was said
the chief justiciar could manage Latin, but only
barely.

Flambard signed the last of some work, the clerk
at his elbow holding down the parchment to keep
it from rolling back up.

One of the moneylenders whispered something to
Judah. He shook his head.

The king's justiciar, Bishop of Durham now that
he had bought the see for one thousand marks, was
singularly baseborn, one of many children born to
a poor parish priest in Bayeux. Flambard was richer
than most of the king's magnates, and all-powerful:
London loved to whisper about his mistress, the
beautiful Aelgifu, the daughter of a wealthy Danish
merchant family of Huntington, by whom he now
had several children. Since he'd been raised in the
old Conqueror's court with his many brothers, it
was said Ranulph Flambard knew every vice.

Judah saw Simon de Bocage standing between
two tower guards and remembered the girl in the
street. In spite of his somewhat dirty clothing, the
tilt of the man's head and his dark, burning look
brought once again to Judah's mind the invincible
warriors of the ancient Jews. The Leopard, yes, he
could see it. Would to God he were theirs, now, he

thought, to claim openly, and dispel their awful fears.

Patience, Judah told himself.

Flambard pushed away the signed parchments. His eyes passed over the group, then rested on Hagit long enough to make Judah feel uneasy. There had also been an ugly story about Flambard attempting to rape his wife's niece, the saintly Christina of Markyate.

The lawyer stepped forward, speaking Norman French. Hesiden, the king's justiciar of the western marches, submitted more writs, taking them from the arms of the assistant, the statements of the five required witnesses, including the Jewish elders and the goldsmiths.

Flambard put down his pen and leaned back in his chair, his eyes on Hagit. The lawyer, Federichi, read a description of the complaint. When he came to the names of the moneylenders, ben Hama, and the goldsmith Ezra of Toledo, Flambard appeared to recognize them. The minister got up and came around the table to speak to them.

While Flambard was speaking to the moneylenders, a young clerk took a writ from Federichi and began to read the testimony by the five witnesses to a marriage contract.

Flambard turned, frowning, and waved him away. "Stop, I am familiar with the charges." He strolled over to Simon, who was standing between the guards. "So this is Simon de Bocage. The one they call the Leopard of Antioch."

He looked him over from the top of his head to his boots. At forty, the same age as his friend the king, Ranulph Flambard was handsome, tall, and well made, with a reputation for surpassing cruelty. *Flamma*, they called him in the vernacular. The Torch. *Flambe*. The Scorcher.

He said suddenly, "When Duke Robert sent you to negotiate a truce, I heard the Turk ibn al Ashir was much taken with you, de Bocage."

Simon looked down his nose at him. "I was not sodomized, milord, if that is the story."

The minister gave a shout of laughter. "Good, you have wit! I do not expect it in dour fighting men."

He turned and went back to the table. "Well, Leopard, know that the Jews swear you are one of them, and have produced witnesses that your mother was a Jewess from Falaise, as was her mother."

Simon said, "Milord—"

"Shhh." The other held up his hand, every finger covered with gold and silver rings. "Although it is written here you claim you've been raised as a Christian by your Christian knight father."

A clerk leaped forward with a vellum, his finger pointing to the place.

"Where is Hesiden, and the lawyer?" When they stepped forward, Flambard bent to the writ. "Therefore, these Jews testify that your mother made a contract with one Judah Ha-Kohen of Wroxeter whereby you will wed his daughter, Hagit bint Judah, this contract legal and binding among Jews." He looked up. "The argument is that you are a sworn Jew."

A young monk slid forward to put another vellum in Hesiden's hand.

Flambard went on, "This dispute of the wedding contract and the Jewishness of Simon de Bocage, knight, has been ruled on by the chief of the London rabbis, Hezek ben Ibrahim." He looked around. "He is present?"

The chief rabbi, his glittering robes swaying, made a gesture.

"Ah yes, there you are. And you have so signed," Flambard said, consulting it. "You write Latin, ben Ibrahim?"

"And Greek and Hebrew, my lord."

"How interesting." He turned back to Simon. "So the Jews have had their rabbi declare you one of them, de Bocage. What say you to that?"

There was a pause. A chamberlain went out, returned with a candlestand and candles, which he lit and placed on the table.

Simon said, "My mother was a Jewess, milord, I do not deny it. But my father was Christian and raised me as such."

Flambard raised his eyebrows. "De Bocage, you are a handsome fellow. By her look the little Jewess likes you much, but her father claims you do not want her. Tell me, on your oaths as a Christian, do you renounce Jews as heretics?"

The group from the Jewry seemed to shudder. There was a small silence.

Flambard paced up and down. "Well, de Bocage?"

Simon met his stare stonily. "Milord," he said in an even voice, "they are my mother's people."

Flambard stepped closer, half turned to look at the Jews standing there, the rabbi, the goldsmiths, Judah Ha-Kohen. "And?"

Simon's look did not waver. "No, milord, I do not renounce them."

"God is merciful," the rabbi whispered.

Dramatically, the king's minister picked up one of the writs and waved it. "You are not one of them, de Bocage, but you do not renounce them?" His eyebrows shot up even farther. "God's face, man, do you know what they are offering you?"

Simon looked wary. "I have been held prisoner here in the tower, milord may be gracious enough to remember."

Flambard's stare challenged him. Then he turned away, saying, "Federichi, read your sworn settlement."

The lawyer stepped forward, unfolding his writ. "If it be considered by the favor of Almighty God and his son our Savior, Jesus Christ," he read, "and the court of our most noble king, William the Second, and his chief justiciar, His Grace, Bishop of Durham, Ranulph Flambard, that one Simon de Bocage, son of Geoffrey de Bocage, who is also known in other parts as Samuel Sophiasson, be accounted a Jew and will as ordered marry Hagit, daughter of the physician Judah ben Ezra, both of Wroxeter, then this Simon de Bocage will receive such sums of money from Judah Ha-Kohen and other members of that family as will take him to the colleges of Paris there to live and study until he is accredited of his desired knowledge."

Simon stood stunned.

"Dear sir," Judah called out to him, "in the name of God, accept." Hagit was holding out her hands. "Look you, my daughter wants you, poor child. We have granted your most desired wish. We will arrange for you to be a scholar."

There was a silence. Flambard looked from one to the other, enjoying it hugely.

"Ha-Kohen," Simon said, "I denied this marriage once, even though your daughter is a woman any man would want. I will not do it now, no matter if you offer to send me to the universities at Padua."

The chief rabbi said quickly, "You prefer Padua? That can be arranged."

Simon's eyes flickered, incredulous. "Do you believe I will agree to be a Jew in order to go to Padua?"

The goldsmiths broke into excited conversation. Ranulph Flambard walked up and down the room, his hand on the heavy gold episcopal chain at his breast. "I have read the testimonies, the charges and the writs. And it is my judgment that we are dealing with not one matter but two."

The talk stopped. The elders looked at one another. Judah took Hagit's hand.

"The first issue is to discover whether under Holy God and most noble and valiant King William of England, the knight Simon de Bocage is a Jew as his mother's relations claim. The second is that if he is a Jew, whether a true marriage contract is effected. But all parties should take note that in the king's court, before his chief justiciar, a fee has been paid for only one hearing." Flambard inclined his head to the young monk at his elbow. "How much was that, Gilles?"

The clerk, his hand on the writs, did not bother to look. "One hundred Flemish marks, Milord Grace."

The Jews stood frozen. Simon gave Judah Ha-

Kohen a quick glance. The old physician had gone white as milk.

"Say that there are two hearings," Flambard went on with relish, "of which this is one, to determine the charge that Simon de Bocage is a Jew. Would it now seem fair that for the second hearing on the wedding contract a similar sum of money is owing?"

A breath, anxious, dismayed, seemed to leak out of the Jewish delegation. Through the window there was the sound of a horn from one of the ships on the river.

"Milord," Hezek ben Ibrahim said in a choked voice, "it is beyond our meager fortunes to pay for another hearing. Consider that for your most gracious attention here today the one hundred Flemish marks we have already paid is a most serious sum. We could not repeat it."

"Yes, yes." Flambard changed like a chameleon. No longer smiling, he was sudddenly brisk, implacable. "So, de Bocage, you say you are not a Jew." Hands under the back of his robes, head thrust forward, he paced the room. "That you have lived as a Christian and wish to remain one?"

Simon met his stare. "Milord."

"And do you repudiate these heretics, the Jews, your mother's people?"

His profile was like stone. "Jews are not heretics, milord, according to holy scripture. Christ himself was a Jew. You will allow I could not repudiate Him."

The king's chief justiciar whirled. "Damn you," he shouted, "are you arguing holy scripture with a bishop of the church?"

Simon's expression did not change. "As my lord is the church's holy bishop, only he can answer that."

Seemingly angry, Flambard cleared the piles of writs from the table with a sweep of his hand. The clerks scrambled to retrieve them from the floor.

"De Bocage, I can throw you back in the foul tank that you've had a taste of this past day, and let you rot! Now tell me, do you denounce Jews as heretics or no?"

They stood with their eyes locked.

Simon said, his lips hardly moving, "My mother came from godly people. On both sides. I will renounce neither."

Abruptly, Flambard flung back his head and shouted with laughter. The Jews started, violently.

"By the heavens, you are doughty! They told me that. The Leopard would challenge the devil himself."

Flambard turned back to the monks. "I swear by God and Saint Mary, I will settle it, then. My judgment is that as Saint Paul chose on the road to Damascus not to be a Jew because he desired to be a Christian, so do I declare Simon de Bocage to be wholly Christian for the reason that he like desires it. For a hearing on whether he has broken a just marriage contract, the Jews of London must decide if they wish to pay one hundred Flemish marks more."

Judah winced. The rabbi turned in anguish to the lawyer, Federichi, who looked away.

"Milord Bishop, Your Grace." Hezek ben Ibrahim could not keep the outrage out of his voice. "I plead that this is no judgment. For us, the one hundred marks we have already given is a fortune. What you have said is no resolution to this matter."

Flambard went behind the table and sat down again. "God's face, I didn't promise to rule on this," he drawled, "only hear it."

The clerks moved to stack the writs around him again.

"One hundred marks for this hearing. Now, if you have one hundred more"—the minister lifted his eyebrows, devilish—"we will hear the pleadings on the marriage contract."

The rabbi stood staring at him in disbelief. One of the elders took him by the arm. Ben Hama and Ezra of Toledo were already backing toward the door.

Judah pulled Hagit toward the door, jerking her arm when she would have looked back at Simon de Bocage. The money was lost, and ill-spent at that; it was no mystery to any Jew why Flambard the Scorcher was well hated.

In the stairwell Judah grabbed ben Hama.

"Hurry ahead," he told him. "Do not let Simon de Bocage leave London."

# The King's Forest

# Chapter Seventeen

*T*he Jews, gesturing and shouting, came out of the tower gate. Seeing the disturbance, the rabbi's knights quickly rode up, bringing their grooms and horses. The Morlaix knights who had been waiting at the gates thought it was a riot. They drove a wedge into the crowd, shouting for Simon de Bocage.

Ingrith ran forward, vastly relieved to see him alive and whole. "We have your horses, your mail, and your arms." She thrust the jacket at him. "All the knights stayed, and I bought you a new coat in the market."

He gave her an unfocused look. "Suffering God, let us get out of this. If the damned Jews will let me go."

A crowd had collected in the street. The money-lenders fell back, their knights around them. Ingrith followed Simon de Bocage thinking he did not look as though he had been treated ill, although he was dirty, and worn. She had never seen him with a stubble of black beard.

"We spent the night in an inn." She turned to look back. The London Jews were staring helplessly after them, their knights riding in a circle, keeping the crowds away. "I paid with the money in your saddle kit."

He strode up to the Morlaix knights. "You dare look me in the eye." When they turned their heads away, he told them, "No matter, you are going back, anyway. The king is hunting in New Forest and the prince is with him. I will go on to meet him with the girl." He looked around. "Where are the horses? Let us get out of here before the Jews send their men for me."

Aimeric said to Ingrith, "Do not worry, demoiselle. He is harsh, but he is right. The night he was captured credited us ill. Gilbert de Jobourg will not be pleased."

Someone handed Simon his saddlebag. He began to give them their pay as they hurried in the direction of the ostler's. When they reached the stables Renaud and the others mounted and galloped off without looking back.

Ingrith walked behind with Aimeric. She'd been mistaken to think Simon de Bocage would be pleased that they had come to London. He was cold to the knights, and he had hardly spoken to her.

The ostler's boys led out his mare and destrier. Simon bent to examine the horses' feet and looked into their mouths before he paid them. Ingrith walked into the street to wait and young Aimeric followed her. A market was setting up booths of fresh vegatables and fruit.

Aimeric looked around several times, hesitated, then suddenly dropped to his knees on the cobble-

stones. Some peddlers pushing a water cart stopped
to watch.

"Demoiselle." Aimeric clutched Ingrith's skirt
with one hand, head bent. "God has not favored my
sentiment for you with any good fortune. But if you
would find it in your heart to think of me—"

Simon came up, leading his horses. "Sweet
mother of God, what is this, Saint Mary and the
angel? Get up," he told Aimeric. "Else I will drag
you up."

"No, stay." She didn't want Aimeric on his knees
before her, either. A crowd of idlers was gathering.
But she said, "He's done no harm. Why does he have
to leave?"

Simon said something under his breath. He took
Aimeric by the arm and hauled him up and led him
to his horse. The young knight stood, downcast, as
he spoke to him. Simon gave him his money. He
took it, looking over his shoulder at Ingrith. Finally,
biting his lip, Aimeric mounted, wheeled his horse
once, still steadily staring at her, then went off at
a trot down the street toward the river.

Ingrith watched him go.

"He only wanted to bid me good-bye," she burst
out. "Aimeric was not like the others. He told me
he didn't run off with the nuns, they were the ones
who dragged him off and had their way with him,
against his will."

He gave her a black look. "Against his will." He
had donned his mail and belt and sword. "The pup
wants to marry you. He's a jelly of lovesick
emotion."

Marry her? Her mouth dropped open. She turned,
wanting to say something more, but Aimeric was

out of sight. "But he wanted to go with us," she cried. "So did Renaud and the others. They were dutiful."

"Dutiful in hell." He climbed into the saddle. "Besides, do you think I mean to kill them all?" He leaned down and held out his hand to pull her up behind him. "We would be badly outnumbered in a fight. The other night proved that. As we are, just the two of us, we may be able to slip away and follow the prince."

She backed away. "You are lying."

He made an exasperated noise. "God rot it, girl, if they have done this much to keep me in London, do you not think they will try again? An escort of knights can only stand and fight."

He reached for her again. But she walked away.

She was not going to ride up behind him, holding him in her arms, when he had not even thanked her for the jacket she had bought him in the thieves' market in London. Nor had he given a thought to how tormented she had been to know that he was in the tower dungeon, perhaps being tortured, perhaps to be killed. When as it turned out the whole thing was nothing more than being arrested because of the Wroxeter physician and his Jewish marriage contract!

"You have driven them all away," she yelled. "You are cold and cruel. You think nothing of what others have done for you!"

"Cold and cruel?" He sat on his horse, watching her. "Cold and cruel? Dammit, girl, who held you in his arms two nights ago?"

She had stopped in the roadway, her breasts heaving, glaring at him.

"Was that nothing?" She stood there, biting her lip. "Now come get up behind me," he told her.

She shook her head. "No, not until you tell me who you say is pursuing us. Is it the Jews?"

"No, it is not only the Jews." He frowned at her. "They are merely terrified."

She looked up at him, eyes wide. "Terrified of what?"

"God rot it, they won't talk to me, but they don't know. Neither, I suspect, did your friend the friar and his murderous little dwarf. But none of them want us to reach Prince Henry."

She stared at him, amazed that at last he had explained something to her. Although she didn't really understand it. She was still thinking on it as she walked to the side of the horse and allowed him to pull her up.

He turned the horses. The destrier, rank after a night stalled, tossed his big head and yanked at the lead. Ingrith grabbed Simon tightly. After a while she asked, "Where is New Forest?"

"In Hampshire." He kicked the mare forward. They started for the river. "We go south."

Beyond the street of the markets they turned to the Thameside looking for the ferry.

Ingrith said, "Well, if it is not the Jews, then who is it?"

She heard him snort. "I will tell you when I know myself."

From London they took the Stanes Road that ran east of Windesoras and turned south into Sudrie. This was well-settled country with fruit orchards and pasturelands, the old Saxon realm of Wessex.

Simon pushed the mare at a hard gallop. When the horse tired they stopped, and saddled and mounted the destrier. Hanging on to his belt, sometimes with her arms around him, chafed by the scrape of his mail, all of Ingrith's muscles ached. She clenched her teeth, knowing enough not to complain.

He had changed somehow in London. Perhaps being a prisoner had made him more bitter, more reckless. He was already cynical.

Now he watched her when he thought she wasn't looking, a black, steady regard. She thought of Aimeric. It was not the same.

In the afternoon, blue towers of thunderstorms rose in the sky. After the first shower Simon dismounted and, with water from a puddle, got out his razor and shaved.

"It is heaven to get off the dirt of prison." He looked into a small metal mirror and pursed his mouth to see what he'd done before he wiped his face with his shirt.

While he shaved Ingrith pulled handfuls of grass and sat on a small stone with King Harold in her lap to feed him. When she thought of that night they had lain together in the stone house she could hardly bear to look at him. *Was that nothing?* he had shouted at her. She didn't know what to think. Suddenly a lump came up in her throat and her heart began to beat, hard and hurtful.

She bent her head and picked at King Harold's thick fur, looking for little black dots of fleas. Although she was not sure rabbits had fleas like dogs.

Out of the corner of her eye she saw Simon take off his mail and lay it out on the grass to clean it. She wondered when they would begin to ride again.

She considered that he had been in such a hurry to get out of London, telling her that someone followed them and wished them ill, that it could have been a lie, to make her obey.

Ingrith stroked the rabbit's velvety ears. It didn't seem to be such a bad thing to be a Jew; they appeared to be very rich and important. The Jews had paid many silver marks, the knights said, for a hearing before the king's court. But then the knights also said the Jews were heathens and heretics and that the holy mother church preached against them. When Simon called to her to get back on the mare she was still thinking about it.

Sometime later, heavy showers rolled across the moorland to overtake them. Ingrith sputtered as the first rain hit. Simon turned his face up to it. "This will wash the stink of London tower off me," he shouted over the downpour.

He turned to look at Ingrith sitting drenched, the purple and red dress sticking to her body and clinging to her breasts so that the points of her nipples showed. He stared a long time. Then he turned the mare's head again to the south.

The fine, steady rain was warm. The horses snorted and blew. There was almost no wind. Under an overcast sky the fields glowed a vivid green. They saw villeins clad in straw raincoats coming along the road like moving haystacks. Simon took the horses across a field to avoid their stares. The saddle and the mare's back grew slippery with wet.

Ingrith put her arms around Simon and clung with all her strength to keep from sliding off. The motion of the mare's gallop thrust her lower body rhythmically against him.

She closed her eyes, remembering the look on his face as he stared at her, the silk gown sticking to her nipples. A warm place grew and tingled where her thighs clasped his hips. After a while she heard him groan.

He reined in so suddenly she slipped to one side and almost fell off. He jumped to the ground and pulled her down after him. The rabbit, spilled out of her arms, hopped away.

"Don't say anything." His face was set. "In God's name don't *do* anything."

He took her up against a tree while the horses watched, still holding the reins, her wet skirts hiked up around them. He pushed down his hose and, careful of his mail against her, thrust into her at once. She was too tight. When she cried out he shuddered to a stop.

"I hurt you," he whispered against her mouth.

She shook her head. She put her hand on the back of his neck, under his wet hair, and his body quivered. She stroked him, his skin warm to her fingers. She touched his face, the hard line of his jaw, then his warm neck, enjoying the feel of him.

He held her. He was in her but still not moving. "You pet me like you pet that rabbit," he murmured.

"Ummm." She stroked his mouth, softly.

He pulled her fingers away and roughly covered her face with kisses. "In Flambard's dungeon this was all I could think of. To have you again."

He plunged into her. She tightened around him, gasping. It was savage and sweet. He rocked her and lifted her with his wild thrusts. The tree ground into her back and water shimmered down on them from the leaves. For Ingrith all else faded. He was in her, driven to have her until there was nothing left. She heard a throaty, squealing sound and knew it was her own peak, but she could not hold it back. She drew her legs around him so she wouldn't fall.

He seized her mouth, bruising her lips, thrusting his tongue into it. The world rocked. They were in it and melting together, uncaring. He held her bottom with both hands and she felt his body pounding her, the convulsion of his legs and hips. Then he bucked, stiffened.

"Aaaagh." Between clenched teeth he groaned, plunged violently, then slowly subsided.

They held each other until the world came back again.

Ingrith opened her eyes and saw the sun, a white ball of steam above them. She was sticky, her thighs were cramping. But when she moved, he held her. "No, not yet." He slid in and out of her slowly, measuring her shudders, watching her. "I like the feel of what I have put in you." His voice was husky. "You are tight, anyway, and now you feel silky."

He had propped her against the tree with his hips. His hands found the laces of her dress, then her breasts, the skin damp and cool with rain. Stroking into her, he kissed her mouth. His fingers pulled her nipples into hot buds. "I would put my own seed into you," he whispered, "before I take you to Henry."

Ingrith opened her eyes, seeing his black-lashed gaze in hers.

"Then he would have one bastard he could not truly claim."

She watched him for a long moment. That handsome face, that curving mouth softened now with his kisses, those black eyes intent in hers.

She pushed at his shoulders with the heel of both hands. "Let me go."

"Shhh, girl—"

"God rot you, do you not yet know my name?" She squirmed until he slipped out of her. Her legs slid down his thighs, then she was standing. His warm rod pressed against her bare skin.

He was breathing hard, holding her, staring at her. "Is it so bad to have something of you?"

She wrenched her hands away. "Sweet Mother of God, but you are like the rest! You are worse than a whoremaster. You take what you want, but you can do nothing else!"

Black eyes bored into hers. "Girl, I can't help you, don't you understand? Not out of this."

A wordless cry burst out of her. She wanted badly to hit him. She looked around for something, a stick, a rock, but there was nothing. "God curse you! You would be well served to go back to your friends the Jews! Since they are the only ones who want you!"

She lunged away, sobbing, through the wet greenery. He did not follow. Ingrith did not care, she had to get away from him. She felt as though her heart would break. She could feel it pounding, hurting, in her chest.

She flung herself through a coppice and out into a field that bordered an apple orchard, then over a stone wall made of rocks picked from the field.

He was a cold and heartless man. He was the only one she'd slept with, he'd taken her maidenhead, yet he treated her like a whore. Just like the others.

She sat down on the stone wall, pressed her hands

to her face and sobbed. He meant nothing to her, she tried to tell herself. He was only a murdering Norman. Being a Jew made him no different. For what the Normans had done to her family, to her father and brothers, she should hate him.

She wiped her eyes with her fingers. Tears had run down her chin, she'd cried so hard.

She rubbed her face on the back of her arm, sniffing. In the orchard a herd of deer were grazing on the leaves of the trees. She did not know who owned the land, but they could ill afford to have the deer come out of the forest and graze on their trees and the young apples.

If they were the king's deer it did not matter if they were in the forest or here, on cleared land. The penalty for killing any deer in any place was blinding and castration.

Ingrith lifted the hem of her skirt and carefully dried her eyes. Even before she had her womanly flux she had hunted in Malmsbury's woods, taking Gudrun with her. They were just little girls then, barely able to lift and carry a haunch of venison once they had killed. One time, in the dead of winter, they'd killed a roe with a fawn that ran away, and Gudrun had cried. She and Gudrun had to dig a hole in the frozen ground big enough to bury the dead roe after they'd cut their meat from it. It had taken most of the day and into the night, but they had been terrified to leave any sign. It will freeze in the ground, Ingrith had told Gudrun. We can come back to it.

But some days later when they'd gone back to the spot for more of their meat, someone, perhaps charcoal burners or other forest people that were always near to starving, had dug up the roe and carried it off.

She had not remembered that in a long time. Hunting the king's deer in the forest in the dead of winter with Gudrun.

Ingrith gave her nose a final wipe and got up from the stone wall. She was not living like that now, hunting deer to keep her mother and sisters from starving. She was sitting in some villein's woods in a fine silk dress, on her way to a different life. She was not sure how to feel about it. What she wanted to think about was Simon de Bocage. And how he could make one feel so wondrous lying with him, when he was so cold, and soulless.

When Ingrith came out of the woods she saw the mare and the stallion grazing, trailing their reins. Simon leaned against a tree, holding King Harold.

He looked at her, stroking the long ears that folded back over his arm. The rabbit looked content, eyes closed, nose twitching.

He said, "You can ride the destrier. I will put the saddle on it and lead you."

He didn't want her to ride up behind him. Ingrith stared down at the ground. "I don't want to ride a horse that way."

There was a silence. When she looked up, he was still watching her.

"Very well." He gave her the rabbit to hold and went for the horses.

Simon gathered their reins from the grass and mounted and cantered over to her. He reached down and pulled her up behind him.

He turned the Saracen mare's head toward the road. The destrier followed. It suddenly crowded close, making the mare shy. The warhorse reached out its massive head and butted Ingrith's shoulder with its nose, playfully.

She cried out. She grabbed Simon de Bocage so tightly he turned and looked behind him.

It was only a look. When he turned back again Ingrith clutched him even harder. The horses climbed the bank to the road south and picked up to a fast gallop. She rested her head against the mail links of his back.

Crying so hard had made her head hurt. She tried not to think of leaving him when they reached New Forest.

But she knew when they got there Prince Henry would know what had happened. And they would punish him.

She started to cry again.

# Chapter Eighteen

*A*s the day wore on they stopped several times and Simon dismounted and knelt, his ear to the earth, to listen for hoofbeats. But there was nothing.

They were headed south and west at a steady gallop for New Forest, the king's hunt and Prince Henry. It was the last day of July. The next day, a Wednesday—still called by the Saxons in Sussex Wotan's Day—was Lammas. They passed roadside shrines with the first loaves baked from grain of the new harvest. Many were decorated with the flowers and ribbons used for the old pagan gods.

The roads were thick with harvesters and their families going to the Saxon market town of Bodhlem for the Tuesday fair. They met a Norman knight *dapifer*, holder of a manor under the local lord, with his escort of ten knights and his household.

The knight's party, especially his wife and daughters, was full of questions about who Simon was and where they were going. The half-grown sons made eyes at Ingrith, who ignored them. Simon asked about the way to New Forest and was told they were on the best road, and the king's hunt but a day away. As soon as he could Simon left them, bypassing the fairgoers and striking south on country lanes bordered with high hedgerows.

In the long summer twilight the horses slowed to a trot. They ate while traveling an evening meal of bread and cheese, and drank the last of the Morlaix wine. The warm air was filled with birdsong and the steady whirring of locusts. It was still wild country: several times they saw wolves hunting in the harvested fields for mice and voles.

When it was too dark to travel farther, Simon trotted the horses into a field dotted with haystacks. He got down and pulled Ingrith down after him, and then went about putting the horses to graze on the stubble.

"We'll sleep here," he told her.

While she watched he picked the largest haystack and punched a large hole in it, hiding the hay pulled out skillfully around the bottom. When he was through he motioned for her to get in, and went around the other side of the haystack to relieve himself.

Ingrith crawled into the stack. The cave he had made was big enough to sit up in, sweetly fragrant, the green hay not as prickly as it would be in a month or so when it dried. Villeins often slept in haystacks when they were working in far places and could not return home at night. She curled up, her arms around her knees, to wait.

She did not want to sleep with him and she would tell him so. He treated her no better than a whore. He would use her lustfully as many times as he

could before he gave her to Prince Henry. She would
be a fool to endure it.

He stuck one leg into the burrow and climbed
into it. Ingrith's heart leaped when she saw he had
taken off his mail. She did not expect him to sleep
in it, but then he had slept in it before. He was a
tall man, broad-shouldered. When he sat down
there was not much room for their feet and knees.

A pulse was pounding in her head. She kept her
hands in her lap, her head bent.

"Ingrith Edmundsdaughter," he murmured.

She could not look at him. She trembled all over.
She knew why he'd used her name. Still, where they
were going, the bitter words that had passed between them, where they would be on the morrow,
hung over them.

It was with something like a sob that she let him
pull her into his arms. He tilted her face up to his.

In the dim light his eyes were somber. "Ah, Christ
in heaven," he murmured, "would that I could stay
away from you!"

He covered her mouth with his, a long, sweet kiss
that grew hungrier as she opened her lips. He drew
her tongue into his mouth. When the kiss ended he
pulled back. "Sweet, so sweet." His hand touched
her hair. "It is a miracle that one woman—a tender
maid—should look so much like an angel."

He let her go only long enough to pull off his
jacket, then his hose. Ingrith untied her hair and
loosened it to fall about her face. It hid her burning
cheeks as she lifted her arms and slipped out of the
silk gown.

He never took his eyes from her. "Where is the
rabbit?"

She gave him a quick glance. "Outside, in my cloak."

"Yes. God save me from sudden shrieks."

Head bent, she smiled. Seeing it, he quickly pulled her down beside him. Naked in their cave of fragrant grass, they fell into sudden, wordless passion. He caressed her throat, her swelling breasts, then his fingers probed the fleshy fold between her legs. As he opened her and stroked the hard button there she fell back in his arms, lost to a deep, drowning pleasure. Quickly he pulled himself over her, thrust her legs aside, and was in her.

For a moment he was more than she could bear. He crowded her into a breathlessness that eased as he lunged deep within her, big body drawing and releasing like a hunter's bow. "Put your legs around me," he whispered.

She tried to match his movements. After a while the fire seized her. She bucked, seeking it, trying to quench it.

They were wild. The haystack shook and green hay tumbled down around them. When she began to writhe with her own pleasure he stopped, sweating, still shivering, watching her with his hooded eyes while she reached her peak. When she lay quiet he gave over to his own. Teeth clenched, he called out something. Then he collapsed on her.

He was heavy, but she held him tightly clasped, drifting in a weightless place. She was blissful, feeling his breathing push against her stomach and breasts. After some while she lifted her hand and brushed at his dark hair that touched her face. Little sticks of green fell out of it.

He propped himself on one elbow, taking his

weight from her with a groan. He looked down at her, the corners of his mouth deeply indented, and lifted a still-shaking hand to wipe hay from her face. They were sticky and covered with sweat. Every piece of green stuck to them.

He brushed back her tangled hair. "Jesu, you are beautiful. The court ladies would gnash their teeth if they could see you like this, tumbled in a haystack and still so lovely."

Slowly, they pulled apart.

"Hah, green loves you, too." She pulled a twig out of his hair. "You look like one of the Old Ones."

He rubbed around the aureoles of her nipples with his fingertip, and the pink buds rose tightly.

She studied him. She was beginning to see something in him she had not noticed before. When he looked up she said, "Wotan gave a good eye to have wisdom, and knowledge. It is true, isn't it, that you are a scholar?"

He didn't answer. His hands were scarred with sword cuts. She ran her fingers over the ridges, and the half-healed place on his thumb where she'd bitten him. He lay sprawled in the cramped space, his legs too long to stretch out, a dark, graceful, sinewy man. His black eyes stayed on her as though he couldn't stop watching her. His great weapon lay to one side, dark and flaccid. He caught her hand before she touched him there.

"How old are you?"

She looked away from him. "I am seventeen." She was, almost.

His look was speculative. "You are two years past your marriage year."

"My sisters and I would not marry villeins." She

253

ran her fingertip up a scar in his side. "I like naked bodies. These wounds mar them." She bent over him, holding back her long hair with one hand so that she could look into his eyes. "Why do you have to be a knight?"

"Is that all this means to you, naked bodies?" He smiled his crooked smile. "What a heathen you are."

She opened her eyes wide. "Nay, I am a Christian."

He stroked her hair, which in the half-dark was a pale, tousled shadow across her bare shoulders. She shifted to move out of his reach.

"Why do you have to be a knight? That Jew in Wroxeter said you were one of them, a Jew. And that to be a Norman knight was madness."

His smile died.

"Why am I a knight? My father took me from my mother so that I would be one. First he took my mother's money, then me." He looked away, his expression suddenly bleak. "Poor pretty lady, she wept as though her heart would break when he came to take me. All I remember of her was that she was warm and soft." He stopped. "Like you."

"Oh, why not be a Jew, then," Ingrith cried, "if you do not want to be a Christian knight? Are the Jews not good people?"

"I did not say I didn't want to be a Christian knight."

"They seem rich, and the physician said Jews love learning." She tried to twine her hands around his neck. "They wanted you to stay with them because you are learned, too. Would it not be better—"

He held her wrists and pulled her away. "Where did you learn all this?"

"In Wroxeter." She sat back on her heels, not knowing why he was vexed. "I was in the kitchen house when you were talking to the Jew and his daughter in the back. What did they want of you in London?" She was struck with a sudden thought. "Holy Mother, the Jews did not make you marry the girl, did they?"

"God's wounds, don't screech! No, they did not make me marry her. What makes you think such things? Do you always listen at doors?"

"It wasn't a door. I told you, I was in the kitchen."

She put out her hands to him and this time he did not stop her. Lovingly, her fingers caressed his face, the line of his jaw, his mouth. Then she kissed him softly. He sat staring at her, not moving. He was right, she thought with a sigh, she did love to pet him.

"If the Jews want to give you things, why do you refuse them?" She smiled at him, meltingly. "That old man, the doctor, he offered you much."

He abruptly lay back in the hay, putting his hands behind his head. He looked at her from lowered lids. "Sweet Jesu, I have never lain with a woman like this. To wheedle and argue the whole time."

He hardly looked unhappy. "We're not arguing." She leaned over him. "What other women have you lain with?"

"Not all that many." At her look he said, "Ah, once I was given two women by a paynim pasha, ibn al Ashir for a night's entertainment."

She made her mouth a round O.

His hand stroked her bare thigh. "If you are that surprised I am hardly flattered."

"Why did they want to give you anything?"

"To reward me, of course." He propped himself on his elbow. "You have not heard of the reason for my great fame there, before Antioch?" When Ingrith shook her head, he said, "I was chosen to carry a letter to the Turkish commander, asking a parley. But I was captured in spite of my flag of truce—the paynim do not like 'Franks' as they call us, since they regard us as dirty and barbaric. A opinion, in all truth, that was not unearned."

"You were captured!" It was only what she had suspected.

"When I was caught I was stripped naked for torture. But my captors found to their great amaze that I was marked like the rest of them, and my cock not properly tasseled, like a Christian's."

Her eyes grew wider.

He smiled. "This was considered a great marvel, as they knew me only as a bold Christian knight, although I could speak a little Turkish and Arabic, which I had studied since Constantinople. So I was dragged naked once more to the tent of the great ibn al Ashir. Who decided after some thought, and because I did not correct him, that I was Circassian, born in the Caucasus, and a true Musselman."

He reached out to touch the underside of her breast with the back of his hand. "Ibn al Ashir fed me, and we played chess. When I let him, after a great false struggle, win at it, he was so pleased he sent me to his harem and gave me two of his favorites. After a few days al Ashir released me, gave me many gifts, told me to walk always in the true path of Allah. And oh yes, gave us the parley."

Ingrith leaned to him, bare skin gleaming, lips parted. "But they tortured you. There." Her eyes dropped to his crotch.

"I told you—" He stopped, following her eyes. He looked baffled for a moment, then he gave a shout of laughter. "Is that what you thought, that they'd circumcised me full grown?"

He fell back on the hay. He tried to stop laughing and could not. He started again.

She looked at him, biting her lip. It was astonishing that anyone so glum could laugh that hard. Everyone talked of it, circumcising, as though she knew what it was. "Well, Holy Mother, there *is* something wrong with your shaft!"

He pulled her over to him. "You are a wonder." He kissed her on the tip of her nose. "So you thought I'd been tortured."

She looked away, pouting. "Tell me what they did to you, those two women."

"What they did?" Now he drew her down to him and nuzzled his face against her belly. "Ah, they did many things. One was a feather used to stroke— tickle—my most sensitive parts."

"A feather?" She pulled back to stare down at him. "A feather?"

"A long feather, from a peacock. When they were done, the harem ladies put it in a place which was even more sensitive, and left it there. So that I must turn over very carefully, and take it out to lie on my back once more."

She frowned. "Was that all they did? Tickle you

with a feather? Hah, I learned much more than that from the bawd mistress at Baron Malmsbury's!"

He closed his eyes. "No doubt."

"It is true, I think it's stupid to want to lie with more than one woman at a time. Although when I did it I did not really lie with him, nor did the bawd mistress. They were only showing me what to do since I was still a virgin."

He leaned back against the hay, his arm over his face. "Oh, yes, a virgin. I had forgotten. And who was the man? What did he do?"

"He was there. That was the purpose of it, for me to show what I had learned and to please him." She bent her head, fingering tangled bright hair that had fallen over one breast. "I did not like what he did."

He took his arm down and looked at her.

"He kissed me there," she blurted out, "in my womanly places. I did not like it at all, but the bawd mistress said I must. That it gives some men great pleasure."

He said something under his breath. "Devil take it, who was this man?"

She looked surprised. "Why, the lord who took me from the knights who had captured me, have you not been told? I was not willing, but then when I came to Morlaix, the barons said I must say that I was, because my mother and—"

He grabbed her by the bare shoulders. "God's wounds, who was this man?"

"B-Baron Malmsbury."

"Malmsbury." He stared at her.

She pulled his hands away. "I didn't know people did such things to each other. But I was to be taught what a whore does, with a man, yet remain a virgin. Why do you not believe me when I tell you these things? I told you I was a virgin until you took me that night when we camped in the woods with the wedding and you got very drunk!"

His face had gone rigid. "Stop yelling."

"I told you that morning when we wakened that you had taken my maidenhead, and you said you had not! That I was still a virgin!" She rubbed her shoulders where his hands had gripped her. "And then, later, when you had me again in the place of the ancient stones, I was no longer a virgin then, and you said Prince Henry would not care!"

Simon put his hands over his eyes. "Drunk."

Ingrith said, "Yes, you went to look at the wedding party and came back with a whole skin of wine. You drank every drop."

He was very still, thinking. Then he took a deep breath. "God help me, yes, I remember now, it was on my clothes. I thought I had a wet dream."

"Well," Ingrith said. He believed her, she could see it; she should have felt more satisfied. She watched him, frowning.

He still did not look at her. "Demoiselle," he said finally, "you must forgive me."

Ingrith opened her mouth, then slowly closed it.

She knew what he thought, that he had ravished her. When in all truth she'd had to drag him under the alder bushes, and then chase him into the copse when he rolled into it. And after that, haul him about until she could accomplish the thing. She could hardly bring herself to admit it, but it was she who had taken him, and not the other way around.

This knight, the man with whom she'd lain in the woods by the wedding party, had never even known who it was seduced him!

Ingrith studied him, thinking she knew more about him now, this tall Norman whom all the other knights admired, and who had been cruelly taken from his mother when but a babe. His mother had wept, he said, her heart broken. Then, almost as cruelly, the woman he loved too well had been given to another to wed.

Perhaps, she thought with a great rush of guilt, someday he would recall that night and truly think he had made love to *her*. His Alys.

"By the Cross, I will fix it," he was saying. "I have done this to you, and it is your right to claim your due for such an injury. But first I must take you to Henry. My oath holds me to that."

She hardly heard him. His dark, curling hair fell to his shoulders full of green specks of hay. His bare arms and shoulders were tensed, his hands in fists. She stared at him, remembering their lovemaking just past, thinking that if he were to kiss her as Baron Halmsbury had done it would not be repulsive but perhaps very interesting. In a rush, her body told her she wanted to lie with him again.

He said, "How do I explain to Henry, though, how I have failed him. That I broke my oath."

His oath to his prince. "Oh, you have not broken it," Ingrith told him. She put both her hands on his shoulders and stroked lightly down his arms. His skin was smooth, slightly hairy. She kissed his collarbone. "You will still be taking me to him."

He looked distracted. "Nay, it is a different thing."

Her fingers played with his hair. "Well then, once an oath is broken," she murmured, "there is no harm in breaking it again, is there?" She put her hands in the middle of his chest and pushed him back against the hay.

He looked up at her. "God is my judge," he muttered, "but you are the very devil in a woman."

He took her by the hips with both hands and swung her over him. His hard flesh already stood erect, reaching up for her.

"How can you be an angel one moment"—he pulled her down on him and heard her gasp—"and like this the next?"

But she was already moaning.

Ingrith woke before dawn. She did not bother to put on the red and purple dress but slipped down from the haystack and stretched, enjoying her nakedness. To have made love all night gave one a languorous feeling.

Outside, long tags of mist lay over the hayfield. The air was cool. She squatted around the far side of the haystack. When she straightened up she saw King Harold had wandered loose and was nibbling on dew-drenched grass at the edge of the woods.

She hurried to catch him, striding bare, the low mist swirling around her. She lifted her arms and danced a few steps. The sky was just turning light at the edge of the earth. Above, the stars were still riding high.

They had made love all night, and he had been fierce, and insatiable. And still she could have wanted more.

She bent down to pick up the rabbit. Its soft fur

was spangled with dew. She stroked its velvet ears and kissed them, then held it up so that she could look into its eyes. In that light they looked black, like Simon de Bocage's. She kissed its nose.

"I have been struck with love," she whispered.

Not once when Simon de Bocage was making love to her had he whispered the Norman girl's name as he had the first time. She knew he still believed his love had married a good man.

"He doesn't love her anymore." She put her face in King Harold's silky fur, rubbing her nose against it, and the rabbit kicked, protesting. "He will love me. Perhaps he loves me now."

Something moved at the corner of her vision. When she looked, a man stood at the edge of the woods, watching.

For a long moment Ingrith could do nothing but stare. When she turned to run he stepped into the field, putting himself between her and the haystack. She looked about for a place to escape. She was naked. She had nothing to cover her. She clutched the rabbit.

"Wait," he called. "Demoiselle."

She stopped. The voice was familiar.

He strode toward her, a slim figure in a black and red velvet coat and long cloak. The cloak blew out in the dawn breeze, showing a lining of gold satin. Against the green stubble and mists of the hayfield he was a magical figure. Too much so. Under her breath Ingrith gasped a prayer to the Virgin.

"Demoiselle." His tonsure was growing in, a brown prickle of hair across his head.

"The friar!" She could hardly believe it. She supposed he had always been handsome with his vivid eyes, the slash of dark brows, curly brown hair, but she had never thought of him as other than a monk. "Brother Enguerrand?"

"Demoiselle, my name is Enguerrand Seint-Omer. I am not the friar you know." After one look he quickly averted his eyes. "But I am no common spy. I am well-born; I hold a manor of my cousin, Walter Tirel, Count of Pois in Normandy."

Ingrith held the rabbit to cover herself as best she could. Numbly, she nodded.

"Demoiselle Ingrith, it is dangerous for me to come here. And dangerous for you, which is why I have done it."

She started walking away from him. "I am with Simon de Bocage."

He put out his hand as if to touch her, then drew it back. "Dear sweet lady of my heart," he burst out, "I beg of you, come away with me!"

She turned to him, startled. He did not fall on his knees, as had young Aimeric, but it was the same. Ingrith clutched the rabbit tighter.

"Do you believe me when I say that I dream of loving you?" His handsome face was impassioned. "The wish of my soul is to keep you with me always, to—to give you children we may both love!"

She began walking again. She was afraid to look at him.

"It is beyond my power," he said, following her, "to marry you considering your humble estate, but as God is my witness, you will be my wife in all other ways. I will protect you, I will cherish you, I will care for you."

The dew was drenching her legs from the thighs

down. She knew he was staring at her. "No, I will stay with Simon de Bocage."

He took her arm, pulling her to a halt. "Demoiselle, hark to me." He looked desperate. "There are those who will not let the Leopard reach where he thinks to go. I—I cannot tell you, on my oath, but consider that when lowly villeins plot they do so with axes and hoes in their clumsy fashion. But with nobles and kings, their schemes are done subtly, with daggers of gold. You cannot know the extent of your circumstance, dear demoiselle. Only hark to me, and come away."

She shook free. "You are mad," she told him. "Simon de Bocage is an honorable knight. He has done nothing!"

"Honorable? He is a dangerous man," he warned her. "Leave him, I beg you, and come away with one who loves you. I will give you my heart, forever."

"Holy Mary," Ingrith cried, "he has done nothing and there are those who are still afraid of him? What do they think he will do?"

He didn't answer her.

When she turned away he called, "Come back, demoiselle, dear God, I beg of you! It means your life."

Ingrith began to run.

# Chapter Nineteen

*T*he old road from the haying fields wound down to the edge of New Forest. They could hear the distant sound of hunting horns that meant the king was in the forest early, seeking the fat young bachelor stags. It was the first of August, the beginning of the great killing of "grease time."

"They will not attack us so close to Brockenhurst," Simon said. "If they do, they are more desperate than I think."

Simon had saddled the destrier; it was the mare, now, on the rope lead. But the stallion's stride was not so smooth nor so easy as the Saracen's, and Ingrith had to keep her hands in his sword belt and King Alfred tightly tucked in her cloak. When they turned from the road to pass some sutlers' wagons, the big warhorse pounded heavily through the undergrowth, trampling bushes, ripping off leaves.

Ingrith had not had time to explain all of what had happened. Only that their friar, who had been Brother Enguerrand, was really a courtier in velvet and satin with another name. And that he had appeared in the hayfield to beg her to go away with him. It had been more than enough. Simon had hurled himself out of the haystack shouting to her to gather her things while he readied the horses. Once beyond the hayfield, they had traveled at full gallop.

The woods opened. Before them were the ruins of a stone church, its bell tower still intact. Ingrith remembered what people said, that the old Conqueror had destroyed English villages there in Hampshire to make way for his hunting grounds, still called the New Forest.

Beyond that they came up a little rise. Sunlight splayed through the trees. Three riders blocked their way. They were dressed in rags like outlaws, but underneath they wore mail.

She barely had time to see. With an oath, Simon dropped the mare's lead and dug his spurs into the destrier. The big horse leaped forward like an arrow from a bow, neck stretched. At the same time he reached back and with one arm swept Ingrith from her seat.

She landed on her bottom in the middle of the road, the breath jolted out of her. Her spine felt as though it had been driven up into her skull.

Ahead, his sword drawn and arcing above his head, howling like a banshee, Simon was taking the huge destrier in full course toward their attackers.

Ingrith got to her knees in the road, clutching King Harold, unable to think fast enough to know all that was happening. One rider had turned his horse before that mad charge, uncertain. The other two braced themselves, horses cocked on their hind legs.

The gray destrier hit them like a hammer blow. One rider went down, his horse rolling over, squealing. Like a demon, Simon turned on the other two. The big stallion rammed the nearest horse. The eyes of the knight went wide, then he was wheeling his horse, sword dropped, head and arm gushing blood.

Simon backed the gray horse and rammed again. The other rider fought to keep his mount from bolting. As it reared, Simon brought his sword down on him from behind. The man fell from the saddle.

Ingrith sat back down again in the dust. She tried to pray but her mouth was dry, her lips wouldn't move. One man was screaming from his wound. She shuddered. It was three against one. No one, not even her father and brothers, had fought like that, as if nothing could kill them.

One rider galloped his horse off into the woods. The other lay on the ground under his horse. The bleeding man was trying to mount. Simon brought the sword down on him again.

Ingrith closed her eyes. She prayed for the wounded attacker to get away.

Suddenly it grew very quiet. The high chirp of a hunting hawk came from somewhere above the trees. The mare, trailing her rope, trotted out of the woods and onto the road.

Ingrith opened her eyes and saw Simon walking toward her, leading the destrier. One of his hands was bleeding a steady stream.

He stopped and looked at her, breathing hard.

She could not tear her eyes away. The blood alone was enough. But she had watched the way he had fought.

He saw it in her face.

"Yes, now you see me." His voice was hoarse. "As I am."

Carefully, Ingrith put down King Harold and pulled up large handfuls of grass from the bank. She went to Simon and began to wipe his hands with the bunches of green grass. He watched as she lifted them one at a time to scrub at the blood. Parts of his face that were not covered with the helmet and nasal were speckled with red.

Ingrith threw the bloodied grass away, lifted the edge of her skirt and dabbed at the bloody spots on his mouth and cheeks.

There had been madness in that blind, howling assault. She wanted badly to put her arms around him but she knew he would not let her. She wanted to stroke his hair and his face, to kiss him and comfort him. She knew he would not let her do that, either.

Now you see me, he had said.

She bent her head, thinking she saw only what he had been made by others: his father, who had stolen him from his soft, loving mother, the men who had been with him since childhood. He was the parfit Christian knight the rest of them feared, and envied.

"We still have some bread." She looked at his gashed hand and the stream of bright red, trying to think of what they could use to bind it up. "The wine is gone, but there is cheese. And I picked some of the apples from the orchard. They are green but they can be eaten."

His hard face was unreadable. She did not even know if he listened.

"I am hungry," Ingrith said, "even if you are not. And we have not broken our fast this morning."

She turned from him to chase King Harold, who did not want to be caught. The big black and white rabbit hopped across the road and almost into the woods before she managed to grab him by the leg. On the way back she picked up the Saracen mare's rope. To her surprise the horse turned and walked, docile, behind her.

"Let us go on," Ingrith told him. The worst was not over. She had not forgotten they must still see Prince Henry. "If we find a stream we will have water to go with our meal."

There were two dead men on the ground behind them, and she tried not to look. When she turned again, she saw he was still standing there, studying her.

"I will find something to bind up your hand," she said. "And I do hunger."

Slowly, the rigidness went out of him. The look in his eyes changed. He said, "You are always hungry."

He held out his good hand to her.

On the edge of the king's forest, at the hamlet of Brockenhurst, they again turned from the road to come a roundabout route through the sutlers' camps.

The Norman nobles had hunting lodges in the town. Banners flew from the log and thatch houses, their devices showing those who had come with King William Rufus to hunt: the Clares, friends of Prince Henry, William Giffard, a sturdy soldier who had just been promised the see of Winchester and who would be yet another knight-bishop, the Earl of Warwick, the Earl of Northampton, Walter Giffard, the Earl of Buckingham, the king's constable Robert of Montfort, Roger Bigot. And Eudo the king's steward, which the Normans called *dapifer*.

It was August first, Lammastide, also known as Saint Peter's Chains. The red-deer season would end on the Feast of the Exaltation of the Holy Cross on the fourteenth of September. Nobles and magnates had come from all over England and France for the best hunting time of the year, the killing of the young bachelors for the thinning of the herds.

Brockenhurst had two streets, the main one and a back alley lined with great oak and beech trees. Here, behind the hunting lodges and town dwellings were the stables and ostlers' camps, pens for the hunting dogs, huts for the drivers and beaters and royal and noble huntsmen, bowmakers, horse grooms, fletchers—all the great crowd which followed the royal hunt.

Food and wine peddlers had opened their booths. Under the trees taverns with trestle tables and benches had been set up, crowded with knights and village folk and the court's attendants. All along this back street, sitting on stools that lined it, were the whores, calling out their wares to passersby in language surpassingly unrestrained. They promised to do everything.

Ingrith craned so far out from the mare's back to see the whores, that Simon reached behind him and hauled her upright again. So this, she thought, avid, was what she was supposed to be!

Some of the girls were even younger than she,

hardly budded, flat breasted, almost children. A few of the older ones called out lewd remarks to Simon.

Then there were the boys. At first they seemed to be but pretty girls, but their words and looks were even bolder than those of the trollops, and they wore more paint. Ingrith stared so long at one of them, not sure, that he stuck out his tongue at her, then pulled up his skirt to show a mat of black hair and his long, dangling shaft.

They had begun to attract attention themselves. A knight ran out of the tavern shouting after them, offering money for Ingrith. Then a Frenchman on a fine big roan horse rode up beside Simon and argued with him in a low voice, looking back continually at her. At last Simon roundly cursed him, threatening to run him through, and the Frenchman rode away.

At the end of the alley the king's lodge and royal tents were clustered. A knight with a squire following on a handsome Spanish jennet rode out in front of them.

"Leopard!" he shouted. "God has blessed me with eyes to see you again."

Simon reined in. The horses stood side by side in the street.

"Neville Chateauneuf," Simon said. They reached over the horses' necks to clasp hands. "It is a blessing to see you. God has helped our common cause."

The big knight was bareheaded in the August sun, his mass of fair hair like a lion's mane. His mail was polished steel. Around his neck he wore a gold gorget crusted with rubies and sapphires. On his blue cloak he wore the cockleshell badge of the Crusader.

They continued to talk, hands clasped. The big man's squire, a pretty black-haired boy, abruptly rode his jennet in between their horses, glaring at Simon.

The golden knight only smiled. "It has been some time, dear friend, since Jerusalem." His look that traveled to Ingrith was pleasant, unchallenging. "What do you in Brockenhurst?"

Simon gave him some answer. The squire pushed his mount between them again petulantly, saying that it was late.

The big knight shrugged. "Come look for us, Leopard. We are here, all Normans. The English never went to Outremer, you remember. Although now they are loud to say how they will go on Crusade next time." At Simon's look he said, "Ah yes, there is talk of another war for the Holy Sepulcher." He lifted his horse's reins. "Come, I am with Buckingham. Anyone in his camp will tell you where to find me."

They rode off, the pretty squire leaning to the tall knight, his hand on one rein to pull his horse to him, gesturing angrily.

Simon kicked the destrier forward.

Ingrith rested her face against his shoulder. "The boy was like a girl to him, and he did not try to hide it. And jealous." She waited a moment before she asked, "Is that what they mean when they talk about the king?"

They rode into a field of wagons where women were cooking bread dough dropped into pots of grease. The smell of hot mutton fat was strong.

Screaming children ran along with the horses, begging for farthings.

He said over his shoulder, "Neville Chateauneuf is a far better man than King William Rufus. The best, the most noble. In the east he was a shining star for us all."

She tugged on him to pull him around to look, but he only turned the side of his face to her.

"No," was all he said.

Ingrith sat back again.

Simon counted out the coins into her palm, four copper farthings and a silver penny. It was a lot of money.

"So you won't get hungry." He didn't smile. "There is a man selling oats, buy two measures, one half-measure for the mare, the rest for the destrier. I have given the cook woman her money. She is supposed to watch over you until I return."

Ingrith looked at the cook bending over the kettle of steam and popping grease. "Take me with you," she begged.

He didn't answer. He had already told her he wanted to see Prince Henry first, speak with him, before he brought her to him. All day Ingrith had been certain he knew more than he was telling her.

Simon finished dressing, buckling on the leather belt and scabbard and his dagger, putting home the big sword. He had gone to the stews below the butchers' quarter and come back some hours later with his hair trimmed, freshly shaven, smelling of strong soap.

He looked very handsome, she thought, watching him. He had put on his mail, over it the old black foreign cloak with the cockleshell badge, and he carried his helmet in the crook of his arm. He looked at her, eyebrow cocked.

Like a dark flame, she couldn't help thinking. He was as brave and noble as any Saxon. A sennight ago she wouldn't have said it, but now she knew he would meet Prince Henry's wrath honorably, just as her own father and brothers would have. Honor was their code. Down to thirteen-year-old Wulfstan, who had stepped out to meet three Norman knights alone. Simon de Bocage too knew his sworn duty.

Ingrith stared at him. Holy Mother of God, that was what was wrong with it!

She had not seen it before. She had lived her whole life thinking the things men believed in were right, and good. But honor and duty would doom them both. It rendered her speechless.

She could only stare at him, knowing she wanted him to live long so that she could love him. She didn't want him to die or be crippled as punishment for breaking his oath. Especially when she was the cause of it!

He said, "Don't look like that. I will plead your cause, I promise. More than my own."

He didn't understand.

*Wait*, she wanted to cry out. She wanted to tell him not to do this. To come with her and they would run away. To some far place where they would be happy. But she could not move.

He went to the saddled mare and took her reins and walked her into the street.

He did not look back.

# Chapter Twenty

*T*he cook fetched a basin and some warm water, and Ingrith washed her hair. She couldn't go down to the stews alone, no woman could, but she had to clean herself and dress.

To make her hair dry faster she combed it loose down below her elbows. When it was cleaned with soap, she knew it would shine like bright metal. But it was still straggling and wet when she fetched the bundle of her clothes.

The remaining dress was not new, it was somebody's court gown of copper-colored silk. It had a great gathered velvet skirt that would be hot to wear in August heat and she had never seen a bodice cut so low. In all, it was a gown far too fancy for a hunting camp, but it would suit; she'd been thinking all morning of how she wanted to look when she went to Prince Henry.

The crowd of urchins watched as she searched for her shoes. When she found the red slippers she saw they'd been wetted and when dried they'd warped so they looked like shoes for lame feet. She could hardly pull them on. She had to go behind the wagon and some flour barrels to change while the bread cook stood guard.

When she came out the cook held up the polished lid of a pan and Ingrith looked into it. A wavering image looked back with long, flowing gold hair.

"Ah, dear, what a marvel!" the woman exclaimed. "It's that lovely you are."

Yes, she supposed she was satisfied. She gave the bread woman two copper coins to find a knight who would take her to Prince Henry's tent.

While the woman was gone Ingrith rummaged in the clothes bundle and found the red scarf with the glitter. She had no circlet like the Norman ladies, but when she went to see the prince she wanted to look like a great Saxon thane's granddaughter.

She sat down on an empty flour barrel and twined the scarf into a band with the gold pieces turned out to show, put it on her head and looked in the pot-lid. It would do, she told herself. It was more than pretty. Almost as good as a fancy gold circlet.

The cook came back with a bald knight a little the worse for an afternoon spent in the taverns. When he saw Ingrith his eyes widened. He quickly adjusted his jacket, wiping his mouth with the back of his hand.

"Hosatus Mayel of Maubourguet, demoiselle." His south of France accent was gnarly. "So you want to go to Prince Henry, is it?" He fingered the coin the bread cook had given him, then handed it back to her. "I make you this service gladly, young beauty, without a price. If anything, it is the prince who will pay me."

They went out into the street. The day was waning, a hot wind blew. Some hunters had returned. Wagonloads of freshly killed deer stood under the trees with huntsmen and grooms already skinning and dressing them. Jongleurs and ropewalkers were setting up their stages by the taverns. Ingrith slowed to watch, thinking of Anorlyx the dwarf.

"Don't lallygag," the old knight told her. He took her arm. "I don't want to have to draw me sword on some sotted sprat who thinks to take you from me. Hosatus Mayel is known, young demoiselle, there's not many who think to challenge me. And those that does soon regrets it."

He guided Ingrith through horsemen and wagons, talking all the time. The velvet skirts were heavy, she walked holding them in both hands, and the warped shoes pinched. She worried over what she would say to Prince Henry. She lifted her chin under the stares, her drying hair blowing loose over the shoulders of the copper-colored dress.

They passed through the crowded alley. Houndsmen kenneling their dogs for the night stopped to watch. Knights came out from under the trees with drink in their hands. Even the benches of whores were silent as Ingrith and the old knight went by.

"Aye, stare your eyes blind," Mayel muttered. "Once the prince sees you, demoiselle, they'll mind their manners. But it's rare as snow in midsummer to see a young maid so fair as yourself."

Ingrith wanted to be beautiful. She wished she had fine jewels and a maid to follow her. She wanted to go to a prince of the conquerors of her people like a Saxon queen. If she was going to plead for Simon de Bocage, it was the only thing to do.

They turned at the tents that housed the king's

attendants and servants, down a country lane lined with the nobles' camps. A party galloped up, dirty and laughing, flung their reins to the grooms and went off toward the king's lodge. At the end of the lane several tents were clumped, one bearing the standard of one of the Clares, Robert of Meules. Beyond stood a gray and blue tent with knights around it, standing and talking.

"That's the prince," the old knight told Ingrith, pointing. He motioned to her to wait, then went up to the guards. He stood talking with them, gesturing. They lifted their heads to stare at her. A fine horse, still saddled, stood at the front of the tent, a young groom holding its reins and talking to it. Several men in hunting clothes went into the Clares' tent and came out again.

Ingrith wondered if Simon de Bocage was already inside. The longer she waited the less certain she was of what she was going to do. They could not punish him, when what had happened was all her doing.

It was true that she had only wanted to see Simon blamed—killed, even, if it came to that. He had been like any other Norman, to her mind.

Now she did not see how she could have been so blind. She alone had tempted him. And now, God help her, she loved him! It was her penance for what she'd done, Ingrith told herself, to go to Prince Henry and not only explain but to bargain. She had thought about it all day. She was trying to think of something that would be clever.

A tall, gray-haired man rode up, dismounted, and tossed the reins of his horse to the groom. He started toward the tent.

She had waited long enough; it was easy enough to fall in step behind the richly dressed noble. The guard knights saluted him. Mayel talked on, not noticing. She followed the Norman lord under the flap of the entrance.

As they stepped inside a voice called, "Ah, Robert, you must hear this. I have a knight sent to me by your Clare cousins in Chestershire to pledge something or other. And, God's face, bring me a gift that is no gift, he tells me, as he has sampled it on the way."

The inside was bright with candles though it was daylight. The outer room contained a table and some chairs.

Ingrith could not see the speaker. Simon de Bocage stood by the table, a rigid figure in black, his helmet held under his arm. He did not turn.

"A pledge, Henry. But not something or other." Robert of Meules stepped forward, shedding his hunting jacket. "Malmsbury and those who love you in Chestershire are more gracious than that. What is the gift?"

When he moved, Ingrith could see the prince seated behind the table, writing. She was surprised that he was not handsome. The old Conqueror's son was perhaps thirty, squat, broad in the shoulders like his brothers. His nose was beaked, and he wore his dark hair long and well oiled. His face was full of bad temper.

"I am the gift," Ingrith said. She stepped forward, head high, although inside she was suddenly shaking.

The prince jerked his head up. Robert of Meules

turned and stared. She did not dare look at Simon de Bocage.

"I am Ingrith Edmundsdaughter," she said. "Leofwine, King Edward's thane, was my grandsire."

There was a moment in which no one moved. She knew from their expressions how she looked to them. The swarthy prince's eyes went wide.

"Sweet Jesu," Robert of Meules muttered.

Prince Henry pushed back his chair and jumped up and came around the table. He stopped in front of her and looked her up and down.

"Yes," he murmured. His darting glance examined the glittering red band, the court dress, her breasts in the low neck of the gown. You could see it in him, Ingrith thought, that women were his great vice.

He began to grin, his eyes hot and dark. Slowly he took Ingrith's hand and lifted it to his lips. The prince was not tall; she overtopped him.

"Saxon, yes. Leofwine the thane." He did not let her hand go. "Old Leofwine conspired to put Waltheof on my father's throne. That was a long time ago." His eyes devoured her again. "Your name is not Saxon."

She blinked. One could believe this prince knew everything. "No. My grandmother was Norse."

"Ah." Still smiling, he looked at Simon de Bocage. "Do you know Geoffrey de Bocage's son, Robert?" he asked the other man. "He is a de Jobourg cousin, he was with my brother Robert at Antioch. They call him the Leopard. Every man in my camp will tell you of him."

Simon stared straight ahead. "Sire, I was the

Count of Flanders's man at Antioch. Not the duke's."

The prince acted as though he hadn't heard. He held Ingrith's hand and put his other at her waist and walked to the table. He turned her around.

"Look at her," Henry said in the same voice. "She is flawless, is she not? It is a magnificent gift, Robert. Should I be beguiled?"

Robert of Meules poured himself some wine from an ewer nearby. "She is lovely." His eyes were on Simon.

The prince gave a sharp bark of laughter. "A perfect Saxon piece. Have you ever before seen such eyes? Such breasts? Ah, Robert, 'tis plain, the reason why my gift did not reach me untouched!"

Holding her by the hand, the prince swung Ingrith around in a small circle. The great velvet skirt belled out. Apprehensive, she looked at him over her shoulder. Up close you could tell how angry he was.

"Henry," Robert of Meules said.

The prince pulled her to a stop before the table, no longer smiling.

"Prince Henry," Ingrith cried, "do not punish de Bocage, he is a true knight!" She considered dropping to her knees before him, but was afraid and confused. "Whatever Simon de Bocage has told you it is not true. I swear on the Holy Virgin he would have kept his vows but for me!"

At the noise a guard knight stuck his head in the tent. Impatient, the prince waved him out again.

Simon de Bocage broke in, harshly. "Sire, do not heed her. She is young, she sees things simply."

"Ah, but I like that." Henry gave him a glittering

look. "Women should be simple creatures, it is their great attraction."

Ingrith looked from one to the other. She was not sure if the prince was going to kill him.

"I will do whatever you want," she begged, "I will be your slave. Only forgive him, milord, what he has done!"

"Forgive." The prince went to the table and poured himself some wine from the same ewer. "You see what has happened, Robert," he said to the Clare. "This trusted knight de Bocage was sent to help his prince, but on the way he was overcome by passion's unholy fires. So the great Leopard put aside his knightly honor and ravished what was not his." His look surveyed Ingrith over the cup. "On the other hand, my enchanting gift now says she ravished *him*."

Robert of Meules tossed off the last of his wine. "A false knight is a grave matter, sire."

"Would that were the sum of my woes." Henry paced back to him. "But no, he has surrendered his sword, he is abjectly mine, de Bocage says, his life to do with what I will. He would gladly die to atone for his oath-breaking, as he wants to see her free of her"—he stopped and stared at him—"good fortune. God's face, Robert, I am hardly flattered."

Ingrith gasped. Simon de Bocage had said he would die for her. She could not believe it. He wouldn't even look at her. He stood as if carved out of stone, letting Prince Henry mock and berate him.

The prince walked to the table. "I did not hunt after noontime," he said, his back to them. "How did you fare, Robert?"

The Clare shrugged. "Two stags, both small. The

king did well, they are bringing his kill back in three wagons. Will you dine with us tonight?"

"Yes, we all will, by my brother's order." He turned back, eyes on Ingrith.

"I want to speak," she said. She twisted her hands. "Prince Henry, I swear on my father and grandsire, the noblest of their Saxon blood, that I boldly assailed Simon de Bocage when he was drunk and forced myself on him so that I would lose my maidenhead and not be worthy of you."

At the look on his face she faltered.

"Sweet Mother in heaven, I will do anything you say," Ingrith plunged on, "you have only to teach me how to please you, although Lord Malmsbury's bawd mistress has shown me many things which I will be glad to do. I beg you, I do not want my freedom now. I would be pleased to be your faithful whore. And even when I am old you may put me in the kitchens, and I will work there—"

"By the Cross!" It was a shout. The prince turned to the Clare, furious. "I tell myself they have not been sent to mock me, Robert. If I thought that I would kill them both."

The Clare wiped the smile from his face. "Oh, I doubt it, sire. The girl is certainly, ah, guileless."

The prince paced down the tent. "God is my judge, why did they think this would aid me? De Bocage, having sinned, would nobly die to gain the girl's freedom from punishment. My beauteous gift, from those who seek my success in Chestershire, nobly offers herself to save *him* from the same fate. Meanwhile, Robert, we go to dine with my brother tonight, just as nobly to withstand those peculiarities who fawn upon him. It is wondrous, is it not?"

The prince went behind the table and sat down. He rested his chin on his clasped hands.

"God's truth, I tell you such an excess of nobility must not go unpunished. De Bocage, when we return to London you will be rewarded for your betrayal. I will see you wed to your puissant trull."

Ingrith cried out. The prince did not look at her.

"You may regard this," he went on, "as not the best of marriages for a far-famed knight, but console yourself, they tell me whores make good enough wives. You chose, anyway, when first you tumbled her. Put her somewhere," he said, picking up one of the vellum sheets, "and come back. Nothing has changed. Robert Meules and I dine with the king, and you attend us. Tomorrow you will be with me in the hunt."

The Clare stepped to one side.

Simon had not moved. "Sire," he said. His face was like iron. "The girl fares ill with this. Grant me this boon, that you will be generous with her."

Henry's eyes narrowed. "She is going to have a far-famed hero to marry, is this not generous enough?"

He set his jaw. "No, milord, she does not want that. Free her. Send her back to her mother and sisters."

Prince Henry jumped up.

"Out!" The vile temper that ran in the old Conqueror's family burst forth. Henry's voice rose to a shriek. "I said get out!"

The Clare raised his hand warningly. Simon saw it and backed toward the door. He reached for Ingrith, and pulled her with him.

Robert of Meules stood aside to let them pass.

# Chapter Twenty-One

"You told Prince Henry you would die for me," Ingrith cried, "I heard you! Now you won't even go with me into the woods to lie with me."

She knew Simon wouldn't answer. He was counting out a stack of coins on the cook's wooden table.

King William had held a great feast with his nobles in the night, and the noise had kept everyone else awake. Ingrith had waited for Simon but he had been with Prince Henry and his friends the Clares, and she'd ended up sleeping on a blanket under the wagons with the fry cook.

He said, without looking up, "If we went into New Forest to couple we would get shot at. Stag season is a poor time for dalliance."

She stood thinking about it. At least he had answered her. But from his manner one wouldn't think Prince Henry had promised to see them wed.

Around them the cook wagons were idle. The women stood with their arms crossed over their chests, talking together. The packs of beggar children had gone off somewhere, even the whores and their stools were gone from the street.

It was said the king's hunt started without fail at dawn. But now it was late morning and King William was still in his lodge. The whole of Brockenhurst waited.

Simon reached over the table with the leather purse full of coins. "Here, take it. I must return to Prince Henry and Meules. They were with King William and Walter Tirel when I left."

Ingrith stared at the pouch. It was heavy, full of the coins from the saddle kit. "Why are you giving me more money? I still have the coins you gave me yestreen."

He leaned against the wagon's side, legs crossed, watching her. He was wearing the velvet shortcoat she had bought him in London. Freshly shaved and with his hair trimmed, he was burningly handsome.

"I want you to go to Wroxeter, to my mother's house there. You will need the money. I will find two knights here in the forest who can be trusted to take you, and you must pay them. And get a small wain. I don't want you riding up behind them."

She knew why he didn't want her riding a pillion behind strange knights. She still remembered the time he had dragged her down from the horse to take her against a tree. Thinking about it, her cheeks grew hot. "Why would I want to go to Wroxeter? Prince Henry said he would wed us in London."

"Will you hearken to me for once? You will go to Wroxeter and stay in the Belefroun house as I told you." He held out a packet tied with a leather string. "The beadle at St. Margaret's has the key, this is my letter to him to let you in. This one"—he put the other packet, wrapped in cloth, into her hand—"is for Judah Ha-Kohen the leech, in the Jewry in Wroxeter. It tells him to hold what he has of my property in your name for now."

Ingrith stared down at the packets, feeling a foreboding, like a chill, along her neck and arms. She whispered, "You are not going to wed me."

"Wed you? God's truth, it may well be that when Henry gets to London a marriage will be the last thing on his mind. Look at me." When she did he said in a different tone, "Can you promise me? I want to know that you will do as I have told you."

Promise him?

She stared at him with suddenly trembling lips. She wanted to throw herself into his arms and beg him to let her stay. She knew he was not angry with her, except perhaps that he had been told to marry her, but he was sending her away to Wroxeter. He was giving her money, a place to stay, as one did with a leman.

With a sinking heart she said, "You are going away, to Paris. You said that to Gilbert, that there are schools there, and you want to go to them."

"Sweet heaven, you hear everything, don't you?" He unfolded his arms and stepped away from the wagon. "It grows late. As soon as they can get the king in his saddle I go to hunt with Prince Henry."

"Don't go yet. Tell me—" She put her hand on his arm. Anything to keep him there a few moments more. "Tell me what the king dreamt of, to keep him from the hunt." The whole camp talked of it. It was not like William, the most avid of stag hunters, to be late.

He shrugged. "Some ill humor, dreams, he's had many since he was mortally sick some years ago." He carefully took her hand from his arm. "I know only what Prince Henry told us, that his brother woke last night and said he dreamt that leeches had tried to bleed him. And that when they did, a bright stream of his blood shot up into the sky, covering the sun and shutting out the light."

She sucked in her breath. "Holy Mother."

"Yes. He took it as a bad omen. The worst. The king would not go back to sleep, but had his friends routed out of their beds to come and do more drinking. Which they've done since dawn. When Prince Henry went to them this morning they were at a late and very drunken breakfast."

He moved to go and Ingrith knew she could not hold him any longer. Terror made her burst out, "Please do not put me away from you in Wroxeter!" She fell to her knees, skirts billowing against the dirt. She threw her arms around his legs and held him tightly. "I will gladly live in mortal sin with you," she wailed. "We do not have to wed!"

He muttered something under his breath, then reached down and lifted her to her feet.

For a long moment he gazed into her uptilted face with its smudge of tears. Then with a groan he pulled her to him and kissed her, his mouth rough, devouring. It was as though he too could not let her go.

When he pulled back he lifted a strand of her hair and gently kissed it. Then her hand, his lips warm against her fingers. Ingrith shut her eyes, tears glistening under lashes.

"Swear on the greatest oath you can think of," he said hoarsely.

"On the Blessed Virgin."

"That no matter what happens here, you will go to my mother's house in Wroxeter."

Ingrith opened her eyes. She wondered why he had said it that way, but he had already released her. He stepped back, turning to go.

She watched him walk away to the horses and untie his mare to use on the day's hunt. She wanted to follow him, trailing him the length of Brocken-hurst's alley.

Instead she leaned against the wagon, her hands to her mouth, choking back the sobs that fought to come out. Rivulets of tears dripped down over her knuckles.

"Now, girl, there's nothing to cry about." The fry cook came up carrying a wooden bowl of dough. "Sent you away, has he? I saw the purse he gave you, generous young knight that he is."

The cook jabbed the firebox with a long stick charred from being used as a poker. She threw a few sticks of fat wood on the embers and they blazed up. Groaning with the effort, she slid the kettle of cold mutton grease over the flames.

"You'd be surprised," she said, her voice cheerful, "at those like your knight what leaves their doxies with no more than a half-skin of wine and a piece of bread and no thought of where their next meal will be coming from."

Ingrith kept her head ducked so as not to let the woman see her tears. She went to gather her gowns and her cloak and pack them again in the bundle.

She paid one of the beggar children half a copper to watch over King Harold.

"I'll be back," she told the cook.

She started down Brockenhurst alley. A blowing of horns in the forest announced that the king and his party had gone off to hunt, even though it was well past noon. Riders came galloping through to catch the main party, houndsmen running behind with their packs of hunting dogs, six to a leash.

In the cooks' camp that morning all the talk had been that this was the last day of the king's hunt, that because of his dream the king no longer had any stomach to pursue the stags in New Forest, but would return to London on the morrow. Now rumor was becoming fact, for the roads were crowded with people streaming north. Across the way in the open-air taverns the acrobats and jongleurs were taking down their stages.

Ingrith stopped in the middle of the roadway. She was not exactly lost, but since she'd come to New Forest she, who'd been born to the woods, was not all that sure of her way. She was looking for the wagons that the sheriff of Hampshire had supplied to bring out the deer carcasses. Between two groups of horsemen a woman came riding up. A young girl in the gaudy, unmistakable clothes of a whore followed her on a jennet.

"You there, demoiselle," the woman called. "Be still a moment, let me talk to you."

Ingrith walked faster, holding her heavy skirts out of the dirt. She crossed into the path of some sutlers who were breaking camp, loading their stock of wine and meat pies onto their wains.

The madam rode her mare right through the sutlers. In spite of the noonday heat she was gorgeously dressed in a samite tunic, over it a fine satin tabard, and she wore a blue velvet cloak. Under rouge and white powder her face showed its wrinkles, but her body was still shapely.

Her sharp eyes took her in as she leaned from the saddle. "Now listen, girl, Clarys of London can do well for you. I wouldn't ask you to do no regular trade, not a girl what's as fine looking as you, and not when I can get you some nice arrangement with a noble gentleman. An earl's not out of the question, that's how high you can go. And bless you, I won't pair you with none that's evil or strange in their habits." When Ingrith turned and looked at her she went on, "Come, there's plenty what noticed you here, that you was supposed to go to Prince Henry."

The whole of Brockenhurst knew, Ingrith thought. Even the doxies. She turned her back and walked rapidly on.

"Fifty percent," the madam was saying as the horse kept up with her. "And you don't have to give me a yea or a nay this moment. But if I was you I wouldn't wait too long. You don't want somebody's lackey to take by force what you'd be better off selling, now do you?"

That was a thought. Ingrith touched the leather purse on its strings deep in the velvet skirt. She'd been told that many of the wagons for hauling the killed deer were never used, that some were always sent back to the villages. She was going to pay one of the drivers to take her out of this accursed place.

"Listen, I'm talking to you." The madam looked down at her. "That knight, the one they call the Leopard, he's not for you, girl, that sort never is.

And he's evil-marked, like those they say are his people.'' When Ingrith shot her a startled glance she went on, "Girl, mark my words, if anything's to happen they'll blame *him*."

She stopped short, not sure what she'd heard.

The other woman reined in her horse. They were right in front of the whores' gallery, but there were only a few women sitting in the hot sun.

"Well, what will it be?" the whore mistress said. "You come to London, and I'll set you up in fine trade and we'll make our fortunes. Stay here, and you'll be rough-tumbled by a pack of bootlickers, you can take my word on it."

Ingrith took hold of her bridle. "You must tell me what you mean. What's to happen."

"What's to happen?" The madam pulled the bridle out of her hand. "Girl, if I knew, would I say it?" She turned the palfrey around, giving up. "They made sport of it, didn't they, the reason you're here? That the Leopard sampled a bit before he got you to the prince? Now that that's known," she flung over her shoulder as she rode off, "you'll be a fool if you stay."

Ingrith watched her go. She touched her hand to her lips. Simon de Bocage was sending her away, not wanting her. But he had kissed her. It seemed as though she could still feel it, warm and burning, against her mouth.

She stood in the middle of Brockenhurst alley, jostled by hurrying bodies. Lackeys, traders, villeins, soldiers, whores, and mummers flowed through Brockenhurst and into the road toward London. She needed to get back the other way, to the fry cooks' wagons. She began to push against the crowd. Immediately two knights seized her, offering her money. She kicked out at them and fought them off, her heavy skirts dragging.

Simon had said farewell to her with that kiss. Go to Wroxeter, he'd told her. Not to put her aside but because he wanted her to be safe in his house. Dear Mother of God, what did he expect to happen? Whatever it was, she had to go to him!

At the cooks' wagons, trade was brisk, with crowds wanting fried bread for the journey. The cook over her steaming kettle didn't have time for her. Ingrith hurried past.

Simon had taken the Saracen mare to the king's hunt. That left the huge gray mountain of a destrier. It stood with its nose in a wooden bucket filled with oats, just as she had left it.

Her throat filled with terror. It was not only a horse, but a stallion trained to battle, to fight. She bent and took the bucket away and hung it on its nail inside the wagon. The destrier stuck its massive head out to her, its ears forward.

She knew she should speak, it was what its master always did. But the words faltered. "Nice horse," Ingrith whispered.

She felt stupid speaking to the stallion as though it could understand. She found the bridle. Slowly, she walked to the destrier's head and stood on tiptoe to reach to put it over its ears. It stood still, watching her. The bit would not go into its mouth, it wouldn't let it.

"Simon de Bocage, your master." Blessed Mother, if anyone saw her they would think her mad, talking to a horse. "Simon de Bocage is in the

New Forest with the king," she pleaded. "I must go to him there!"

In the distance horns were blowing. The beggar children raced screaming through the crowd in the alleys. She could hardly hear her own voice.

The big horse stood with its great yellow teeth clamped together, ears cocked forward. Ingrith stared at it, wondering what she would do if she could ever get it into the forest. Norman nobles hunted the deer from stands where their lackeys carried tables to set up under the trees. With ewers of wine and trays of food, they waited for the beaters, serfs brought from Normandy, to drive the deer past. It would take a toilsome search even on horseback to find Simon de Bocage with the prince.

She stared at the big horse. Time was passing. When the sun went down the hunt would be over. How would she find him?

She led the horse by the reins over to the flour barrels, the bit still dangling. The destrier pulled on the lead, playfully. She tried again to slide the bit between its teeth. The stallion opened its lips, rolled the metal piece back on its tongue and held it there for a long moment. Then it began to chew the metal between its back teeth with a loud crunching.

"Mother of God!" Without thinking, she seized one of its ears and pulled its head down. Surprised, the horse opened its mouth and stuck out its tongue. Quickly she grabbed the metal bit before it could spit it out and shoved it back in its jaws. The bit sank out of sight. The destrier blew air out, noisily, through its nostrils.

Ingrith sat down on the wagon wheel, breathless.

She was sweating, streams of wet ran between her shoulder blades. It was done, though. Now all she had to do was mount.

The stallion mouthed the front of her gown. Impatient, she pushed it away. She looked around before climbing the flour barrels but there was no one to help her. The cooks had wandered off although their fires were still going. Through the trees she saw a wedge of horsemen coming down at a gallop, scattering the crowd. One of them jumped his horse over a wagon. Someone screamed. The nobles raced away, shouting something, toward the northern road.

Bracing her hand against the wagon, she scrambled up on the barrel and pulled the destrier to her by its reins. As soon as she tried to put her foot over its back it began to walk away. She hauled it back. She had seen Simon spur it, but she didn't know anything to do to make it obey.

"Go to Simon de Bocage, your master," she cried.

It turned its huge head to look at her.

Trembling, she leaned out and slid her knee along its back. It stood still. She thought of its yellow teeth. The mare used to try to bite her.

She hiked herself onto the destrier's back. The horse stood motionless. It was truly a mountain of an animal, twice as tall, twice as heavy as the cooks' mules tethered around them.

She leaned forward, kicking it in its massive sides with her heels to get it to walk. It just stood there. She pulled on the reins, trying to turn its head.

"Walk," she commanded. "Go to Simon de Bocage!" She was quaking with the effort, and the whole of New Forest was still ahead of them.

Ducking under the trees, a knight cantered a big roan horse among the wagons. The red horse wheeled, then trotted back. The knight was looking for something. Seeing Ingrith, he reined in sharply.

"Sweet Lady of Mercy," he shouted, "it's you! I had thought not to find you, but I heard someone crying the name of Simon de Bocage."

"Gilbert," she breathed. It was Gilbert de Jobourg as she'd never thought to see him, without his helmet, covered with dirt, and with more than one day's growth of beard. He looked as though he had slept in the saddle.

He trotted the big horse past the wagons to peer at her. "Girl, do you know me? It is I, Gilbert de Jobourg of Morlaix. I have been seeking my cousin Simon."

She could have thrown herself at him, she was so glad to see him. There was a burst of noise beyond them, horns being blown, people scattering. The cooks came running back to their wagons.

"He is in the forest," Ingrith shouted. "He hunts with the king and Prince Henry."

Gilbert did not dismount, he sat staring. "What are you doing on a horse?" Then, before she could answer he cried, "God help us, we must find him. Have you heard nothing back here? Someone has just killed the king!"

# Chapter Twenty-Two

Gilbert took Ingrith's reins and pulled the destrier down a small path into the woods. From behind the Clares' tents they could hear the frenzy of the camps breaking up. Now and again a horseman would plunge out of the trees and through the cooks' camp and onto the Brockenhurst road. It was as though the forest were spewing the king's companions like a volley of loosened arrows.

"Who has killed the king?" Ingrith cried. She still could not believe it. "Where is he? What will happen to us now?"

"I don't know." Gilbert stared at her. "Would to God that I did."

Under the trees the dappled sunlight was warm on their shoulders. Horns blew throughout New Forest in frantic summons. There were shouts, hounds baying, fainter cries.

Gilbert said, "We have found out too late, my father and I, that they planned to blame Simon, saying that he is a Jew." He gave her an agonized look. "God send them to eternal damnation, these betrayers will make him guilty, and all the Jews!"

She didn't understand what he was shouting. "Sir Gilbert, there are no Jews here. Certainly none in New—"

"Simon is here." He reined in his restless mount so savagely the stallion reared. "Have you not heard their reasoning with which they so sweetly snared us, Malmsbury and Hatford and the accursed Clares, that my cousin Simon is a Jew through his mother's line? Think of it, girl." He leaned forward and shook his fist. "The throne of England can be seized without a debt to pay! Now that the king is dead they will drive the Jews out, calling it conspiracy, and murder, and high treason. They will pay them nothing, they will gut them, and hang them!"

She gasped. "They will hang Simon?"

"Nay." He glowered at her. "If they are clever the Clares will kill him here, in New Forest. Then there will be no witnesses to say him innocent."

"Holy Mother." Ingrith put her hand to her throat, thinking: If they have not already done it. Gilbert did not have to say it; it was on his face. "Where is the king? You do not know if they have really killed him."

"He is dead, believe it. Do you not see how they are running now, those great ones who fawned on him?" He suddenly put his hand before his eyes. "Ah, Christ, my father sent me to Simon, whose— life—we hold dear. I must go and help him."

Ingrith was thinking of the Jews in London and how afraid they had been. Not knowing, Simon had said, what they feared. A plot to kill the king. And Gilbert of Morlaix was part of it.

"My father lent himself to this," Gilbert went on, "as did all of us, to our everlasting grief. For we have, all unwitting, betrayed a good man. Do you understand this, girl?"

She was understanding all too well. There were more in this than just Gilbert and his father and the plotters around Malmsbury. She remembered the friar and the friends of Duke Robert.

She reached out and touched his arm. "Sir Gilbert, do not stay in New Forest. If you are found so far from Morlaix they will say you have been a part. And your family will suffer greatly."

"Girl, that is damned good thinking." He stared at her, his ruddy face slack. "But as God is my judge, I cannot leave. I must help Simon for what we have done to him."

"I will search for Simon de Bocage." She saw the look on his face. "Sir Gilbert, I have lived a serf's life, I am more woodswise by far than you. And you cannot be here to be caught."

He hesitated. "I will find him," she promised. "I have only to learn how to make this horse go where I would take it."

A small wind had come up and they could smell the burning. Beyond, the cooks' camp was already deserted; the mules were hauling the last of the wagons into a great tangled melee in the alley. The king really is dead, Ingrith thought. It was as though the world had come to an end. She still could not quite believe it.

Gilbert made up his mind. "You are a true Saxon woodenhead, girl, fearless to the core like the rest of your people. But you are right. If I am found here in New Forest there will be unending vengeance on me and mine. Now, as for Simon's horse—"

He reached up into the tree and broke off a small branch. He stripped the leaves from it on all but the end, and handed it to her.

"I know Goliath. He is a brute, but all he asks is a switch on his rump and he will serve you well. Here, let me give you this." He rummaged under his mail and brought out a purse. "Don't go alone into the forest. Hire some of the English to help you, if the villeins have not fled. Christ knows there are no Normans left in it. From what I see they are trampling the trees to get out."

Ingrith took the purse, heavy, full of coins. She knew Gilbert only wanted to aid her but at this rate she was getting rich.

"Are you sure you will fare well enough?" He avoided her eyes by looking away into the woods. "You are a damned fine girl. It is a pity Simon has no way with women. But every man is a fool. Think on it."

He kicked his big red horse forward. Then he stopped the destrier at the edge of the clearing and turned around in the saddle.

"Give me your word you will hire the English to do the searching," he called back.

Ingrith waved to reassure him. Gilbert finally rode off.

The switch worked well. At one tap Goliath lunged forward, nearly unseating her. They charged through the underbrush, flushing birds, tearing leaves from bushes and small trees. At last, after the destrier was lathered and tired, she was able to turn him. With the sun on her left, in the west, they began to make narrowing circles, searching through the deep woods of New Forest.

It took all of her balance to keep from slipping from the horse's huge back, riding as she was without a saddle. But the destrier was docile enough, allowed her clumsy jerking on the reins without temper, and seemed to understand when she cried Simon's name. Ingrith told herself she could not stay terrified forever; the search to find Simon was enough.

It was late afternoon, the air unnaturally still. Following a stream, Ingrith came upon a hunting stand with an overturned table, its linen cover thrown against the grass. There was only one silver cup, but some noble's red linen jacket was still hanging on a limb of a beech tree.

Past the deer hunters' stand the woods grew deeper, thick with climbing green vines that reached into the tops of the trees. There was no clear path, and the destrier, tossing his head, did not like pushing through the overgrowth. Ingrith struggled to keep the big horse turned toward the south. Once she glimpsed a fire but the forest was green, and it did not spread.

The woods opened on a wide meadow filled with tall grass, deer country. The sun, deep gold in the west, blazed on the glistening marsh. The air was full of flies.

Ingrith pulled Goliath to a stop. It was as though no one were left in New Forest. Even in the hot sun her skin felt chill.

She prayed that Simon de Bocage was still alive.

* * *

At the edge of the meadow the mallow wort had knitted together in a thick yellow bloom. Against it the man had flung himself, his pale gold hair trailing off into the carpet of flowers. His silk short coat had gold buttons, ruby-centered, and he wore a gold chain about his neck.

"He were standing there," the carter said, pointing. "And the arrow come true and hit him through the heart. Then the king, he pull arrow out, stout man that he was, and fell." He pointed to the ground. "And 'er kept pumping, as heart will do even when sore pierced, letting the blood out. And the blood spread n'ere and n'ere, a great lake of it. He had a lot of blood, King William."

Yes, a lot of blood. Simon looked down at his feet. He was standing in the shining black puddle. He stepped back.

Before Prince Henry had flung himself on his horse to leave New Forest, Simon had been told to find the king's body, and the others of the king's company in the care of it. But there had been no others. He had not expected to come upon the king's deer stand deserted, the king still lying there in his blood.

"None have come out of Brockenhurst for his body?" he asked. "Not even Eudo, the king's steward?"

The carter shook his head. He was a husky yeoman with drooping moustaches in the old Saxon style, but he spoke good Norman French. "Nay, all gone. Leaving him here."

The Englishman had not been there at the death, but had been told the story from lackeys who had taken to their heels, streaming along the forest road looking for horses to take them back to London.

And no better than their masters, Simon thought. It was worse to think of England's highest nobles, even churchmen, deserting their king. He bent down to look at the body.

William Rufus had been a coarse and blasphemous ruler. But there were many, especially knights who had fought with him, who praised him, liking him for his chivalry and generosity. Now he had died unshriven in New Forest. His fate at best? Purgatory. At worst, hell, according to the mother church. Strangely, Simon found he did not believe it.

The features that had given William his nickname, Rufus, were not so flushed in death. Pale-fringed blue eyes regarded the sky emptily. Except for the arrow's hole in his chest and the gouts of blood that covered him, he still looked a hale, hearty man. King William had been forty.

At that moment, Simon was thinking, Prince Henry was racing for Winchester with the one man, King William's treasurer, William of Bretuil—a Clare—who had the key to England's treasury. *I will be crowned in three days*, the prince had said before he galloped away.

"The king, and what they say was the lord of Pois," the carter was saying, "was shooting at a stag coming there." Again he pointed, this time to the meadow. "His men said the king liked the Frenchman as he was a fine shot."

Simon said, "Walter Tirel." He looked around seeing the ground was well trampled. Many had come to look, then gone away. "Tirel has hunted with the king often this summer."

The carter looked at him out of the corner of his eye. "Aye, and when the king took the arrow through his heart, this Walter ran to his horse and mounted it and never looked back. Gone away, he was, before the rest knew what had happened."

Simon studied the dead man. Prince Henry had sent him to the hunting stand knowing well what he would find—a body of a dead king with no one to claim it. It had been the same at the old king's death: all his magnates and bishops gone off to leave the old Conqueror on his deathbed to be robbed by his servants. Prince Henry, he remembered, had not been there, either.

An eerie feeling crawled the length of Simon's spine. He could have taken more than one of the Clares' household knights with him into the forest to find the king's body, but they had sent him alone. He tried to shake off the knowledge of what that meant.

"We need some stout men to move him." They might as well begin, the sun was growing lower in the sky. "I have just come from Prince Henry, who wishes to see his brother well buried."

When the carter didn't answer Simon turned to look at him. The Englishman was staring, slack-jawed, out into the marsh.

Simon got to his feet. He lifted his hand and stood shading his eyes.

Whatever it was, looking west into the sun made it blurred, surrounded by light. But he would swear, dazzled even as the Englishman for a moment, that some faerie vision had appeared.

It seemed to be, Simon told himself, disbelieving, a phantom queen, her flowing hair loose and shining, riding a gray specter of a charger through the high marsh grass. The same feeling returned to creep up his back and raise the hair on his head.

The next moment he knew.

"Sweet Jesu!" He started into the meadow. "Have a care with Goliath," he shouted, "or he will sink in this mire and it will be the devil pulling him out."

Ingrith Edmundsdaughter splashed toward him on the big horse. He could not believe this either, that she was riding his charger.

The destrier approached the edge of the marsh at a splattering gallop and skidded up before them. Simon stepped forward but she had already launched herself at him. She half slid, half fell down the destrier's barrel, and hit him full in the body with her own.

She wrapped her arms around him, breathless. "You must leave here!" Her eyes found the dead king and she quickly looked away. "They think you a Jew, Malmsbury and the others! They will say you killed the king. Gilbert came to tell you but he couldn't find you."

He held her away from him, looking down into her beautiful, anxious face. Then Simon suddenly threw back his dark head and laughed.

She gripped his arms. "Holy Mother, what is the matter with you?"

"So that is the plot," he shouted. He grabbed her and swung her around. "Sweet Blessed Mary, after all this to finally know it!"

"Stop," she cried. "Stop laughing. Are you mad? We must run from here!"

"So Henry and the Clares will drive them out, poor old Ha-Kohen and the rest of the Jews, so as not to pay them the money the king has borrowed?" He gave her a crooked smile. "Because they will say I, Simon the Jew, am the king killer? God's wounds, but that is a scheme of the noblest order. They should be exceeding proud of it!"

He put his hands under her elbows and moved her to one side. "Where the devil is the Englishman, the carter? I need men to take the body down to the road where a wain can reach us."

"I would kill them for this!" Ingrith cried.

"Don't be an innocent. Duke Robert's men and your precious friar would have served us the same, had they caught us."

"They were Duke Robert of Normandy's men? Mother of God." She followed him. "Come away," she pleaded. "Oh, do you not understand? They want it to seem you have murdered the king!"

"I am told it was Walter Tirel." He smiled again. "Since Tirel has fled, all will be certain of it."

Her eyes were wide. "You know who killed the king?"

"Someone does." He strode back to the body. "Where are the damned English? They are somewhere about, are they not? I can hear their loutish breathing."

She looked at him, doubtful. "They are only in the woods, watching. The English have nothing to do with this."

"Call them." He was impatient. "We need a wain. I am going to take King William to Winchester and lay him at Henry's feet." Even as he spoke he knew by the time they got to Winchester Prince Henry would be in London. *In three days I will be crowned*. It was the prince, Simon told himself; he could not believe the Clares alone had done it.

"We will find some bishop or other to bury him," he told her. She was still standing there staring at him. "Will you do as I tell you? Call out the English. They will come for you."

"The Normans will hang you," she whispered, "for high treason. Gilbert said so."

"Sweeting, only a guilty man would run. As Tirel did. No, God rot them, I will bring King William out of New Forest and the devil with them! And by the Cross, I'll not let them cheat the Jews. If for nothing else but that they are my mother's people."

She looked at him for a long moment. He burned with a dark flame, triumphant. And she knew he was right.

Ingrith turned then, lifting her dragging skirts in her hands as she walked about the clearing calling out in English for those who heard her to come out. After a while the carter came briskly back up the path. Then two ragged villeins stepped out of the trees.

Simon stood watching them, hands hooked in his belt. "Come, I will pay you," he shouted.

A man and a woman, charcoal burners as black and knobby as their sticks, came slowly across the meadow. There were doubtless more in the woods around them, but they did not show themselves.

There was nothing in which to wrap the king's body and it continued to bleed. The villeins would not look at it, taking the flow as an evil sign. Simon took the saddle blanket from the mare and between them he and the carter hoisted the body on the horse. The Englishman led the mare, with the charcoal burners on each side holding to the king so that he should not slide off. A handful of others materialized as they went along the road, coming out of the woods and the clearings.

Two miles away they found the carter's half-grown boy holding the mules' heads. When the king was lifted into the cart the blanket fell away. He had become stiff; William Rufus now held up his arms, bent at the elbows, blue eyes staring into the sky as if pleading for mercy. After one terrified look, the two villeins ran away.

Simon cursed them, fervently. The carter got into his seat and whipped up his mules and the wagon headed down the forest road. He boosted Ingrith onto the destrier, then got up behind her. It was the first time she had ridden before him. She leaned back against him with a sigh. "When the old Conqueror died, all ran away from him, too."

"Yes, I have heard of it." He pressed his face against her neck. She smelled of the heat, and of flowers.

The birds had begun to sing now that it was twilight. The woods were still full of a faint smell of burning. Along the road they began to pass things dropped or thrown away in the royal hunt's rush to leave New Forest: a cape, a quiver of arrows, even a shoe. The wagon rolled slowly, the destrier and the mare ambling at a walk.

"Where are we going?" Ingrith wanted to know.

It was a good question. Simon was thinking: Here you have us, the Clares' whilom Jew as the Clares see it, and Prince Henry's would-be harlot. Taking a dead king to be buried. The irony of it was plain.

*The devil with it, I am the hero of Antioch*, he told himself. *And she is the most beautiful woman in England*. King William, for all his wicked life, could find no better.

"To Wroxeter," he told her.

She swiveled to look at him, great azure eyes close to his. "To Wroxeter? To live there? Will you become a Jew?"

He tightened his arms around her. "I will live there with you. As for the other, it bears thinking about."

He heard her laugh.

On the edge of Brockenhurst village they began to hear a noise like a huge murmuring. Farther on they saw crowds pillaging what had been left behind. Looters poured out the door of the king's lodge, their arms full. There were no men-at-arms or knights to keep order, the magnates of England and Normandy had fled. The great silken tent of the Clares lay collapsed and untended in its field. In front of it a handful of servants stood about, talking. The cooking camp was a shambles of refuse, a wagon wheel, a few empty flour barrels. And a shape like a large rat hopping about.

"King Harold!" It was a screech. The carter and his boy turned around, alarmed. "King Harold! Ah, Holy Mother, those brats have not eaten him, after all!"

Before he could seize her she had scrambled over the destrier's withers and to the ground. She landed on her hands and knees, a copper-colored bundle in the court gown. Then she was up and running after the black and white ball that hopped madly ahead of her. She grabbed it, staggering headlong, almost falling, and caught it and held it up to her face.

Simon reined in the warhorse. Ahead, the wain with the blanket-covered body of King William was attracting a crowd. The little charcoal burners on either side were holding their own, but the carter's mules had been pulled to a halt and the Englishman needed him.

Simon stood in the stirrups and called to Ingrith to come.

She whirled, holding the rabbit in her arms. It was dusk, gold light with motes of dust glittered around her.

He stood transfixed. This was the moment, now, before the storm broke, before Prince Henry seized his throne. The moment of calm while they were yet poised on the edge of time, and what was to be.

He wondered if she knew how gloriously beautiful she was. How much she lightened his soul.

How much he loved her.

He held out his arms, and she ran to him.

# Epilogue

When the bell to the outer door rang Ingrith went to answer it, leaving the apprentices in the counting room to finish their work.

A strong summer wind blew in the street of the wool factors. When she pulled the door open a gust took it and she had to hold it with both hands. The three men standing on the doorstep were red with the heat and thirsty-looking.

"Ah, Judah Ha-Kohen." She shifted her youngest, Aethelred, on her hip as she stepped to one side to let him in. "Come in, it is very good to see you looking so well."

"Lady." He was an old friend; he lifted her hand to kiss it. "Your beauty is astounding, as always." She was half a head taller, he had to look up when he spoke. But the admiration in his eyes was genuine.

She smiled. She wanted to remember to ask him about his new grandchildren, Hagit's and his other daughter's, she couldn't remember the girl's name. Hagit had married well, a handsome young banker from Köln. Over her shoulder Ingrith called for one of the boys in the counting room to bring a pitcher of wine.

Behind Judah were two men wearing the wide-brimmed headcovering with the raised cone in the center that was coming to be known as the Jewish hat. Both had full, curling beards and dark eyes, squat, middle-aged men with tentative smiles.

Well, there was no need to be tentative in the house of Simon de Bocage. Although she knew how much they worried, and with good reason. But they could not dispute they now had a good friend in King Henry.

The boy came into the hall with the wine and a tray of cups. Ethelberga toddled out of the counting room behind him.

Ingrith took her daughter's hand. "Come, gentlemen. Let me give you refreshment." She pulled Aethelred's fist out of her hair and steered Ethelberga toward the new parlor in the back of the house. "Ha-Kohen, I am glad to see you because I wish to give you a new tallying for your son-in-law's Wroxeter account. His figures for the wool assays do not match mine."

She heard the men behind her talking in their Hebrew tongue. "You know I do not cipher," she went on, "I keep my accounts in my head. But for three times, now, it has been Elias ben Ezra's errors, not mine, for all that he says that machine of his cannot make mistakes."

Judah Ha-Kohen turned to look at the others. "My lady, you are always right. It is merely difficult for my son-in-law to acknowledge it. I will tell Elias you have corrected his accounts again."

One of the men said something and he smiled. "I apologize, dear lady, but I am reminded by my companions that it is your learned lord we come to see. Here are Samuel Usque from York, and the very esteemed rabbi, Sabah Noredin Levi, a great scholar. We would consult with your lord about a letter."

Ingrith nodded. She led them past the parlor to the back door and motioned for them to be careful on the step down.

The area by the kitchen was used for storage. Now it was full of boys sorting wool bales. Her oldest child, Harold Magnus, sat on a barrel keeping the tally sticks.

"We need, honored lady," the physician from York was saying behind her, "a translation of some letters which were sent us from some merchants in Odense, in the Emperor's domain. Rabbi Sabah Levi has heard that your venerated husband, the scholar Sir Simon, knows the Danish tongue."

Ethelberga stumbled on her fat legs and sat down on the kitchen path. Judah Ha-Kohen bent and picked her up and carried her a few steps, ruffling her silky black curls, before he put her back on her feet again.

"Yes," Ingrith said, "my husband studies Danish. He says it is very like Swedish. Or Finnish. I forget."

"Mother," her son Magnus called, "are you going up to see Father in the tower?" He flashed his handsome white-toothed smile at them. "Oh, please, may I come?"

She shook her head. "Finish what you are doing. You know your father will want to see how well you have kept the arithmetic."

They saw him make a face. Magnus preferred to study the knightly mastery of arms. To which his mother, if not his father, was unalterably opposed.

Judah Ha-Kohen beamed at them. "Lady, such beautiful children," he murmured. "They grow more handsome each time I see them. Your boy is the image of his father." He hesitated. "Also, if I may be so bold to say so, his grandmother, Sophia, of revered memory."

Behind them the rabbi and the cousin crowded up to see tall, broad-shouldered Magnus. "You should pardon my saying it," Ha-Kohen went on, "but your children don't look Saxon." He looked around, lowering his voice. "Is it true that with your boy children, your lord Simon de Bocage has called rabbi ben Josef to—"

Magnus jumped down from the barrel.

"Everyone asks that," he said cheerfully. "I don't mind showing them. To be tolerant is to demonstrate the brotherhood of man." His hands worked at the belt of his hose. "Actually—"

Ingrith quickly stepped to him. She put her hands over his. "You have been told what is yours is yours," she said, "and not the business of others to know." She brushed his dark curls back lovingly. "Pray, who told you to say that?"

"Father." He grinned. "It sounds very grand, doesn't it?"

He went back to his seat and picked up his tally stick. Ingrith led the Jews down the path through the kitchen gardens to the new stone tower at the edge of the river. Looking up, the rabbi suggested they wait outside.

"No," she told them. "It will not make any difference." Simon had been working on the transcription of Saxon and Norse law from English shire courts all summer for King Henry. It was never-ending. But the king, who was revising the English coda, was both pleased and insatiable. "He won't stop unless we come up."

She shifted Aethelred to her shoulder. They went through the tower's ground-floor room that was used as the library. The new clerk, a Cistercian monk from Normandy, jumped up from his table as she entered, but Ingrith motioned him back down again.

The stairs were narrow. Behind Ingrith, Judah Ha-Kohen picked up Ethelberga to carry her. The tower room was always cluttered, with things blocking the door. When she pushed on it and it didn't give Ingrith realized one of her other sons was seated on the floor behind it. She could just see him when she put her eyes to the crack. He had his father's sword dragged across his lap.

She handed the baby to the rabbi.

"Samuel?" She slowly pushed the door in. Her five-year-old scrambled away, his shock of gold-colored hair falling in his eyes. "Simon, I wish we could put this thing up." The two-handed weapon was so heavy she could hardly lift it. The sword and the old shield were left out for the Crusaders, both old and new, who came to see the famed Leopard of Antioch. "Especially if you are going to let Samuel play up here with you."

He looked up then. His dark eyes went to her with the sensuous, quizzical look that always caught her breath. He gave her Magnus's same crooked smile. Then he greeted the men who had just crowded in the door after her. He did not get up, the vellum sheets of King Henry's translations covered the table, the ink freshly sanded.

Her husband held out his hands and took Aethelred, settling the baby in his lap. Ingrith went to stand behind him as the Jews explained their problem with the Danish letters. They were speaking Hebrew, she didn't understand a word.

She ran her fingers softly in her husband's dark, curling hair. There was, she saw, a bit of gray in it. For the first time she realized all the knights who came to see him, the old Crusader comrades, were not getting younger. Even though some of them talked of going back to Jerusalem, to war with the Turks and the Saracens.

The featherlike stirring in her belly distracted her for a moment. Judah Ha-Kohen was saying something in English about the Jews in Odense. Not a new community, but growing very rich.

The baby's dark head and her husband's, the same color, were close together. Aethelred was teething. He chewed happily on his father's wrist, a line of drool dropping down to the sanded parchment. The last two after Samuel had been dark, Ingrith was thinking. It was time for another baby who looked like her.

She pulled her husband's head back to rest against her stomach. Interrupted, he looked up at her. Aethelred stood up in his lap, hands in his father's hands, bouncing from the knees.

*I adore you*, Simon mouthed, upside down.

She bent and dropped a kiss on his forehead.

Beyond his work table the tower window opened out on the river. She could see her flower gardens, the dock where the boys had their punt. She knew he watched the boys boating, sometimes, when he was working. Rolf, the new joiner, was making more rabbit hutches. She had always liked keeping her rabbits. Now the hair had been found to make a very fine yarn, an experiment from Flanders, but said originally to be from the east. From someplace called India.

Ingrith straightened up, putting her hand to her back. She hadn't picked out a name for the new baby yet and she supposed she should. She counted out the children's names in her mind beginning with her oldest, Harold Magnus, for the last Saxon king of England. Then Aelgifu, Edgar, Wynflaed, Ethelberga, and Aethelred. And, of course, her golden one, Samuel.

Yes, she thought, it was time for another fair one. A girl. She rested her hand on her husband's shoulder and with the tip of her finger stroked his cheek. Even though he was talking, she felt him smile.

If it was a fair little girl, it was time for another Jewish name. It pleased her to do it that way.

She liked, Ingrith told herself, Rachel.

# Author's Note

*C*ommon folk carried King William's body in a cart to Winchester for burial. Walter Tirel fled to Normandy, lived to go on the next Crusade, and maintained his innocence to the end. King Henry I neither rewarded him nor sought revenge for his brother's death.

Duke Robert's friends in England endeavored to maintain the status quo until the Conqueror's oldest son could regain Normandy. So they would have pursued what they thought was an assassin intent on putting Prince Henry on the throne. As it was, Henry captured and imprisoned his brother some years later, gaining both Normandy and England for himself.

I have taken Orderic Vitalis's account of the incident with the king's shoes, and adapted freely Eadmer's tale of the Jewish merchant who tried to keep his son from becoming a Christian. A case heard before King William Rufus himself, not Ranulph Flambard, but with the same outcome: the merchant was cheated out of his fee, without satisfaction.

Prince Henry crowned himself king of England in three days, as he promised, and married Eadgith, the last of the Saxon kings' line, taking her out of a nunnery to do so. He continued his brother's good relationship with Jewish moneylenders.

Many historians now believe the assassination of King William Rufus was engineered by the wealthy family known as the Clares, Prince Henry's ardent friends.

I have taken the liberty of making Sophia's and Alwyn's sons some five years older than they would have been in 1100.

HERE IS AN EXCERPT FROM *HEAT OF A SAVAGE MOON*—A PASSIONATE NEW HISTORICAL ROMANCE BY JANE BONANDER, COMING IN JULY FROM ST. MARTIN'S PAPERBACKS:

Jason was bone-tired. Two full days at the vineyard and another at the reservation weren't usually enough to tire him out, but two cases of croup, three deliveries and a false labor had kept him up two nights in a row. Grinning wryly, the doctor wondered what had happened nine months ago that had led to the rash of births this past week.

Leaving the smithy, he dragged himself across the quiet street to his office. The sun was just staining the eastern sky, throwing soft shadows against the sides of the buildings. Opening his office door, he stepped silently into the room. *What the hell—*

He stopped short, his heart meeting his throat. Earl Tully was asleep on the bed, his left leg outside the bedding, resting on a pillow. Stepping closer, he saw the bandage around the marshal's calf. Spots of blood colored the surface, seeping into wide reddish-pink circles against the white cloth.

Jason's heart all but stopped when he glanced at the big easy chair by the stove. Curled up, sound asleep with her feet tucked under her and her head resting on the arm of the chair, was Rachel Weber.

He stepped closer and stared down at her. The familiar memory, old yet still irritatingly painful, finally lunged to the surface of his mind.

*Regina.*

The kerosene lamp flickered on the table beside Rachel, flinging its quivering light over her as she slept. Her hair, the rich, thick color of cognac, shimmered with red, brown and gold streams of light. *Regina.*

He couldn't believe the emotions that battered his insides. Years ago he'd purged himself of all feelings for the pretty, shallow woman for whom he'd almost changed his life. Now, suddenly, all of the feelings flooded back to him.

He studied Rachel. She still looked young. Too young to be involved with an unprincipled man like Weber. And damn, she was a frail, pretty creature, in a delicate, porcelain kind of way—if you liked the type. He'd decided long ago, after Regina broke their engagement, that he didn't.

Rachel's long, dusky lashes lay on her cheeks, the curved ends feathering lightly along the rim of her eyelid, so thick, they bunched up in the outer corners of her eyes. Her face had a child's roundness to it, and suddenly she swallowed, pulling her mouth tight, causing dimples to delve deeply into the sweet pinkness of her cheeks.

His gaze roamed over the rest of her. Full, round breasts pressed against a white batiste blouse that had some sort of frilly design and a high, hand-embroidered neck.

Bringing his gaze back to her face, he was momentarily startled to discover she'd awakened and was looking at him. Big, blue-gray eyes held his.

"What happened to Tully?"

She visibly cringed at the sound of his voice. He hadn't meant for it to come out quite so harsh.

"Oh, I'm ... so ... so sorry," she stuttered, struggling to unfurl herself in the chair. "He ... he was shot, and I'm afraid it's my—"

"Shot?" He couldn't ignore the husky, sleepy tone of her voice. "How did it happen?"

She slipped her feet out from under her blue skirt, pushed back her hair and rose from the chair. She was taller than he remembered. Her chest was high and full against her blouse, and her waist was tiny before her skirt flared gently out over her hips. And her hair ... the brandied mass smoldered like kindling in the light. He shook his head, emptying it of poetry.

"We were standing outside the church," she began, nervously smoothing down her skirt. "Everyone else had ... had gone, and he was going to walk me back to Ivy's." She brought her small hand to her chest, unconsciously displaying the finger that held her thin gold wedding band. "He ... he shoved me to the ground and we heard a gun shot. He was hit in the leg."

Her no-nonsense recitation surprised him. The flat, Yankee twang annoyed him. Even though he'd spoken to her before, he'd somehow expected to hear the sweet confection of a Georgia drawl—like Regina's. He'd also expected her to start to cry, like she had the first time he'd seen her.

"Did you see anyone?"

She looked at him and frowned, then averted her

eyes when she found him watching her. "No, I'm sorry, no."

"Was there much bleeding?"

"Um...no. Not too much." She blinked nervously, then swallowed, unconsciously revealing those damned dimples.

He glanced at the marshal, then turned to leave. "How long has he been asleep?"

"Not long," she answered, looking at the pendulum clock that hung on the wall. "Maybe an hour. I'm sorry, but it took a little time to make him comfortable," she added, timidly following Jason into the larger room.

"Dammit, can't you say anything without apologizing for it?" He slammed the glass door on the cabinet so hard, he was surprised it didn't crack.

She jumped, then stared at him, her big light eyes filled with confusion. "I...I'm sorry, I don't know what you mean."

"Never mind," he muttered, picking up a wad of bandages. God, but she really was a mousy thing. He still couldn't imagine how she and Weber had ever gotten together. She had all the earmarks of a frightened virgin. He hadn't figured her out.

"May...may I go now?"

He turned and stared at her. She looked like she didn't have a friend in the world. Her small shoulders sagged and her head was tilted to the side as she looked up at him, those big, light eyes seeming to beg for—something. His carefully armored heart cracked ever so slightly. "Are you leaving Pine Valley soon?"

She looked at her toes. "I...I can't leave just yet. I'm still waiting for...for the voucher."

Oh, yes. He remembered. That possibly non-existent pay voucher from the government. He hadn't known Weber any better than he'd had to, but he knew the man had probably died without a cent to his name. He wondered what the mousy widow was living on in the meantime.

"Do you still need a job?" He could have bitten his tongue. He wanted her tiptoeing around his office about as much as he wanted a broken nose.

Her head jerked up, her glance taking in the room. Then she stared at him, innocently batting those big, vulnerable eyes. "Here?"

He nodded, swallowing his exasperation. "Here." He could see a mixture of excitement and fear flutter over her features.

"I . . . yes, I could use the job. . . ."

*HEAT OF A SAVAGE MOON* BY JANE BONANDER—COMING SOON FROM ST. MARTIN'S PAPERBACKS!

She was a pawn in one man's quest for power.
A man who stole her legacy and ignited
a passion deep within her...

# BLOOD RED ROSES

## KATHERINE DEAUXVILLE

"A DAZZLING DEBUT...
A love story to make a medieval
romance reader's heart beat faster!"
—ROMANTIC TIMES

Heading for a new life in California across
the untracked mountains of the West,
beautiful Anna Jensen is kidnapped by a
brazen and savagely handsome Indian who
calls himself "Bear." The half-breed son of a
wealthy rancher, he is a dangerous man with
a dangerous mission. Though he and Anna
are born enemies, they find that together
they will awaken a reckless desire that can
never be denied...

# SECRETS OF A
# MIDNIGHT MOON
## Jane Bonander

### IN THE BESTSELLING TRADITION OF
### BRENDA JOYCE

# The historical romances of
# JEANNE WILLIAMS
## from St. Martin's Paperbacks